Gondor Kane

Best
ReGARd
Gond
Une

Gondor Kane

Legal ARROGANCE

with
Vivian Harris

Published by
PLAYA BLANCO PUBLISHING

Canadian Cataloguing in Publication Data

Kane, Gondor, 1946-
  Legal arrogance

ISBN 0-9683660-0-7

  I. Harris, Vivian, 1957- II. Title.

PS8571.A429L44 1998   C813'.54   C98-900533-X
PR9199.3.K36L44 1998

Printed and bound in Canada.

Archaeology of a Murder

archaeology:

1) systematic description or study of antiquities

2) the scientific study of the remains and monuments of the prehistoric period. Archaeology displays old structures and buried relics of the remote past.

Chapter One

She had been shot by a single bullet at close range through the back of her head, behind the right ear. Death had been instantaneous. The bullet had made an exit wound through her hair beside her left eye, and was likely embedded in some gyproc in the wall. We'd look for it, but we might not find it. The back of her head was a mess. Yuk everywhere. She was semi-nude, wearing only a short-sleeved, low-neckline cowboy shirt that barely covered her breasts.

I always take notes: mental notes, notepad notes, recording my own intuitive messages to myself. I hear things: peripheral stuff, like the bad jokes that McInnis and Sheedy tell each other when they have to cut duty at an ugly crime scene like this one.

"Real knockout, hey McInnis? Waste of a bullet."

"Yeah, where was I when this beauty needed the shining armour? What a gorgeous gal!"

"Alright, you guys, knock it off," I bellowed, "if you spent as much time checking the details around here as you spend bullshitting, we'd have this case solved already."

"Sorry, Holt," muttered McInnis, "just got a bit carried away, I guess. Tough scene." He shook his head sorrowfully, perhaps because he didn't have enough armour to go around to protect and serve all the women he would have liked.

"Yeah, boss... you get overwhelmed with it. Stinks," remarked Jim Sheedy. He's a sensitive guy and has an endearing tendency to support the under-dog. By contrast, Rod McInnis likes to play tough-guy games, the kind that are sometimes challenging. The mental gymnastics around these men can be interest-ing, especially when you're the leading lady detective on a homicide case. They go to some trouble to figure out your next move, and McInnis always tries to bait me.

I decided to help them get back in line.

"Did either of you find a murder weapon?"

All business now, McInnis remarked, "Nope, we're probably looking for a .22. Anything much big-ger would have made a terrible mess, instead of just the little mess we have here. Good thing they didn't hit her pretty little chest. What a babe," he remarked again. "Why, if I had met her only a week ago..." he clucked softly to himself.

I ignored him. Partly because I knew he was try-ing to goad me on, and partly because I had a long day ahead of me and I didn't have time for shenani-gans right then. My timing was always better than McInnis' anyway. I'd get him later.

"Did either one of you spot any signs of a force-able entry? Looks to me like she might have been expecting a little private party that went bad on her."

"I think you're right, Sam," agreed Sheedy. "She must have been down at the Stampede grounds. There's a candy floss cone in the garbage and a half-eaten candy apple in the kitchen." He flipped through some notes he'd recorded, in between joking with McInnis.

"I found her I.D. Name's Ali York. Single, thirty years old. I got a chance to talk to her neighbours. Except for an old lady next door by the name of Schultz, who brought her some banana bread every now and again, nobody knows her real well." He looked up at me expectantly.

I nodded. "Go on."

"Mrs. Schultz says that the victim was a paralegal at a law firm here in town."

"Where?" I always play close attention when the law has some potential to get messy. Lawyers are too smooth for me. Good liars. Make their living at it. And, if I recall correctly, better at paperwork than...

I coughed, interrupting my thoughts and Sheedy's concentration. – Enough, Samantha Holt –, I chided myself. – You're as bad as McInnis.

Sheedy droned on. I blinked my eyes a few times to remind myself that he had done his homework. I owed him some attention. "A firm by the name of James."

"I'll check them out." I had no idea why I wanted to check out some lawyer, except maybe to watch his reaction when I told him that his latest exploit was dead. All part of the game. Ali York had been a lovely young woman. Her role at the law firm had likely been a double-twister.

"Oh, yeah, and Mrs. Schultz," interjected Sheedy, "she offered me some banana bread too. Seems that she remembers seeing an older lady and a younger man here at some point in the recent past. She's not sure if they were together or not, but she observed them on several different occasions. She might be able to give us a description of the individuals if the police artist helps her out."

"Good, very good. We'll have some sort of composite drawing prepared from her recollection, shall we?"

"Yup, you bet, Sam." Sheedy is always attentive enough and thorough, if you concentrate on pulling him away from McInnis.

We were interrupted by a bombardment of detectives who were preparing to set up more detailed investigation activities. No one found any obvious clues, but no one was looking for the real Ali York, either.

That's one thing I always do. Look for the dead. Oh sure, I knew she was lying on the floor looking ghastly, but she had left behind some of her spirit, too. Bits and pieces, collectibles, particles of who she is. Note the present tense. Is. Not was. No one gets murdered and just checks out. They continue to control their life from wherever it is they go, overseeing it until they're satisfied that the people who are left behind have been settled nicely.

I never talked about my theory in police school.

Ali York was no exception to that theory. I liked to engage Sheedy and McInnis in my musings. They often thought I was out of my mind, but they humoured me.

I decided to try Sheedy's impressions first. "Sheedy, what do you make of that quilt on her bed?"

He stepped closer to examine it. "Looks homemade, Sam. It's been stitched carefully to arrange the scraps in a pinwheel design. Maybe it's her first try. Some of the pinwheels are a bit crooked." He lifted a corner gently to examine the handiwork. "Look, you can see where the colours clash here and there, and close to the edges. It's faded, probably been washed lots of times. She worked hard on it."

He stopped again, waiting for my feedback. I smiled at him. Sheedy was an astute observer, and we were already making assumptions about the persona of Ali York, based on her stitching performance.

McInnis croaked, something like a laugh. "So, when did you take up quilting, Mr. Suzie Homemaker? And what is this, anyway? A murder investigation or a quilting class?"

"My mom taught me a little about quilting, jackass," retorted a testy Sheedy, "and it would be more like a murder investigation if you'd stop talking and do your job."

McInnis ignored him, having received the reaction he expected. He looked at me quizzically. "What does her quilt have to do with the investigation anyway, Sam?"

"Maybe nothing. Except if Sheedy's assumption is right and the quilt was her doing, she was a perfectionist, perhaps in need of some warm memories to nest in." They both stared at me as though I had two heads.

"If you look around at her belongings," I went on, "the things she surrounded herself with, maybe some clue will fit the puzzle later on. Remember details, guys." I doubted that the explanation would help either one of these yo-yo's, but I kept hoping that Sheedy and McInnis could be different observers and perhaps different kinds of cops under my tutelage.

I glanced over at the windowsill, and they followed my eyes. A strong afternoon sunlight flooded through the bedroom, washing the colours of some multicoloured bottles that adorned the ledge. I use the word 'adorn', because the bottles seemed to have been placed carefully, with some thought to colour and size. A hand-lotion bottle that was shaped like an hourglass stood in the centre of the arrangement, kind of like the tall kid at the back of the classroom picture.

"For instance. Why do you suppose that Ali York would have gone to such trouble to display bottles that normally belong in the bathroom?"

"Cause she needed expensive help," joked McInnis.

He was probably right. But there was more.

"Yeah, so that could be part of it," I remarked, "but look a bit further. All this glass seems to be arranged for focus and effect. Do you get the impression that this is more like an archaeology site, guys?"

"Oh, come on, Sam. We're investigating a murder. It's that simple," barked McInnis.

Sheedy interrupted McInnis' tirade. "You mean like finding goddess figurines that archaeologists find at digs?"

I nodded. "Yeah, Sheedy. Just like that. She's got cough syrup in an amber glass, mosquito-repellent in a red glass, nail-polish remover in a blue glass bottle... it all has to mean something. Notice the little bright-coloured miniature bottles in the sill corners."

McInnis coughed. "I say the woman was weird. Cute, but weird," he pronounced. "I'm glad I didn't meet her in some bar."

"That's my point, McInnis. Discard the evidence if you like, but this woman was different: worth investigating. Even if she was weird. Everything you see in this room, not just her physical body, are the remains of Ali York."

They said nothing, resuming their duties for dusting prints. I decided to check Ali's medicine cabinet for traces of her behaviour. I found bandaids and some antiseptic ointment. No lipstick, powder, smelly stuff, birth control pills, nothing. And yet, what about that windowsill? The woman was an oddity indeed. She aroused my curiosity.

Sheedy picked up a half-filled coffee mug, pouring its contents into a tube for later analysis.

I watched him absently while I thought about Ali. I asked her - woman to woman. Who are you?

I had forgotten to check the night table. A bottle of pills sat there and a small book, the kind that you could pick up in a craft shop. No one had noticed it yet. Amazing how detectives could look for hair under fingernails, teeth marks, anything, but ignore the more obvious material artifact of a book.

The date on the pill bottle read July 4. Forty-eight hours ago. The label read 'Desyrel' 100 mg. 'Take two tablets twice a day. Product may cause drowsiness. Do not consume alcohol with medication.' The pharmacist had filled the prescription with thirty tablets. I counted them up. Twenty-two remained. Ali appeared to have taken her medication religiously. So this stuff was potent. Tranquilizers? I would look that up later.

I drew out a plastic evidence bag and a pair of dissection gloves from my purse. Slipping them on, I dropped the pill bottle into the bag. I picked up the book, flipping through it to see what kind of reading taste Ms. York indulged.

It wasn't a reading book at all, but a diary.

Well, well. Oh, I know I should have had it dusted for prints, but my little voice said no. It wouldn't be worth the dust. I decided to slip the book into my purse, planning to read it at my leisure. I thought it might be more than just a piece of loose evidence.

I popped the plastic bag into a satchel I'd brought with me. I'd seen all I needed to see of Ali's life. For now. Before I left the scene, I pulled the quilt over the lower half of her body. The other detectives would complain. Some would even say 'Sam Holt was here', but I didn't care. As long as I was on the scene, there would be some dignity in her death.

"Let's get out of here, guys, I've seen all we need to see for now."

Chapter Two

Somedays I don't know why I care so much. It doesn't pay to care. Another senseless murder of someone who seemed to have so much to live for. Ali York was gorgeous. She seemed to have a good job. Maybe she had some problems, but who doesn't?

I had real difficulties with ugly scenes like this. The worst of it was that the crime could very well go unsolved. All those statistics - man-hours, (God, I hate that term) and you didn't necessarily get anywhere on a murder investigation.

Man-hours. I've heard that term ever since cop school. I disliked the term, but I never had second thoughts about becoming a police officer. Even the jokes weren't so hard to take when you knew your pals just threw them at you to test your reaction. It was another kind of exam; one they wouldn't have given to each other.

What no one knew, not even myself, until I really had to function as a woman in a man's world, is that my two older raunchy brothers had taught me well. Not for me was the world of dolls, dresses and makeup. We grew up close to Nose Hill in northwest Calgary in the mid-sixties, when men were men, women were ignored, and the range cattle were nervous. Any girl who couldn't snare a gopher and walk five miles with cactus prickles poking painfully in her feet was not destined for survival. My earliest memories included hunting mule deer and pheasant on what is now Crowchild Trail in northwest Calgary. The smell of the deer and moulding leaves form part of my memories and psyche. The actions of my past merge with the challenges of my present.

I have been conditioned.

Police school was a picnic by comparison. I lived an independent life, and considered myself an able woman. To me, it was all a matter of acting on my abilities, and making sure that everyone else realized what I was worth. The unfortunate twist to it all is that I always figure I have something to prove to men and to myself. That competitive factor always erodes relationships for me. Police school seemed a natural place to pit myself against the opposite sex. I could climb higher, run faster, shoot straighter, and go farther than any man I knew. If I didn't know how to do something, I learned - and eventually did it better than my male peers.

In my last year of police school, we did a wilderness survival weekend just for fun. Some of the guys had no idea how to live through that weekend. I did. 'No booze, guys, just your Swiss army knife,' I said. 'Get in touch with your dark side.' The coyotes howled at night. Some of the guys had never heard that sound. Talk about spooked. I snared some bush rabbits with some picture wire I had brought in for the trip, and ended up feeding the guys.

I walked into the bush on Friday night one Samantha Holt. By Monday morning, the guys were calling me Sam. I figured I'd won a great coup. Survival training in cop school meant a lot of different things. For the guys who now called me Sam, it meant that they had learned how to snare rabbits. For me, I stopped trying to compete and learned how to follow my gut feelings.

The man I was seeing at the time was in law school, and his cronies were putting the pressure on him to find a suitable wife. Most of the women they dated were going for an English or Home Economics degree. I was going to be a cop. It was a bad deal in the long term for him, and he wasn't prepared to come along.

I always knew that becoming a cop was right for me. I could read people. No, actually smell them, from ninety paces. For lack of another description, call it women's intuition. It was the same kind of knowledge that came into my head when I went hunting or looking for rabbit tracks, or staying still in the forest for hours while the birds chirped on willow branches only inches away.

As a detective, I was also a hunter. Cree hunters believe that the animal gives itself to them if they respect the spirit of the creature. I believed that, too. It wasn't a relationship based on power differential, or one in which the creature was smarter. It was all about knowing that the bear is proud, the deer skittish, and the beaver a stubborn rodent. It was a matter of listening to the wind; of knowing the terrain and following the tracks.

For a lot of women, it wasn't that simple. Ali, for one.

I had these reflections in my car as I travelled home in the Stampede City of Calgary. Stampede week traffic meant that you might encounter a horse along the street, or some easterner pretending to be a cowboy. It was relaxing to drive home thinking about my day, and replaying where I'd been.

The world and my career moved on. I learned to accept the fact that most men aren't prepared to hang around and share me with my odd hours. I am known in the force for being a thorough nut on a case; unorthodox, relentless and exceptionally irritating. I'm not popular with everyone and there are many who think I'm incompetent. Be that as it may, I've fallen in love with my job, and over the years, I selected companionable men who could handle second place. My thoughts brought me to Ali, the dead woman. What did she think about men? What kind of relationships had she cultivated?

My musing stopped as I arrived home to my little haven in Hillhurst-Sunnyside. It was a tiny duplex shaded by a blue Spruce, with a vast kaleidoscope of flowers at the back. I let myself in, then meandered outside to my papasan chair on the back porch, where I flopped down, exhausted. The sun was gloriously hot on my body. I loved to watch my perennials stretch and compete for a place in that sun. Plants never talk back and they never get murdered enough to spill blood. Today, I was just content to watch them live.

And I was content to be alone. The attention of men had become almost unessential for me, but what about Ali? What was she all about? She was cute. She was too gorgeous for her own good. Women like that needed all the brains they could get or their bodies were exploited.

What could have been going through her mind before she died?

I heard the front door open abruptly and slam.

"Honey, I'm home!" It was Richard. Six foot one, blonde, lean, drop-dead gorgeous, and gay. I delight in having him around because he's a good cook, a great listener, keeps the place tidy, and he serves me a great scotch and water.

"Hey, did you hear me, lady'n blu?" He also amuses me.

"Sure babe, I'm out here!"

He noticed my stockinged feet on our patio table, but said nothing. I knew he was holding his tongue, biting it actually, to keep from nagging at my bad habits. "Ugly day, huh?", he questioned knowingly.

"Yeah, messy murder. Could use your help on this one. The victim was taking some sort of drug." Richard is a psychiatric nurse, both professionally and here at home.

"Oooh, that's just what I need after my last shift."

"Sorry, Richard, I'm wrapped up in my own stuff. Tell me about yours."

"Well, we had no suicides at least. Had a Jane Doe who got dragged in by four of your boys. Finally had to strap her down and put her out. But hey, it's all part of life's rich tapestry, right?"

"Yeah, but see if you can figure this one out. 'Desyrel' - 100 mgs. Mean anything to you?"

He sat down in a lawn chair across from me.

"Sure, it's one of the newer, less used antidepressants. Tends to have more manageable side effects than the older types." He sat down beside me, ready to hear it all.

"Interesting", I muttered. "This woman was murdered, there was no gun beside her, but I'm curious.

Is there any way that someone could get so spaced out that suicide would be a probability - I mean from side effects?"

"Anybody who's a newcomer to antidepressants will be at risk for all kinds of garbage. Not to mention a little known fact: if someone overdoses on A.D.'s, they're toast. An overdose on barbiturates we can save, but not if they're on antidepressants. Besides, even if you had found a gun, I still would have doubted suicide. Men commit violent suicides, often choosing to shoot themselves. Women prefer to go to sleep. Can I refresh myself with some spring water now, or do I wait for the next twenty questions?"

I got up to pace and think, circling around behind Richard. "Oh, Richard," I sighed, rubbing the back of his neck, "I'm sorry, let me get both of us something springy. This problem is going to bother me all night. Death was a matter of a messy gunshot wound. She took her pills as prescribed."

"Well relax, sweetie," he crooned, patting my arm, "I'll make us up a fine Greek salad with an even finer aperitif, we can shoot some backgammon, you can take a hot bubble bath..."

The snap of my fingers came too close to his nose.

He started. "Okay, okay, we'll make it a spinach salad and you can drink water!"

"No, no, never mind dinner." I paused, thinking of the diary in my purse.

He raised himself leisurely from the lawn chair before I could startle him again, sauntering inside to flick on the television.

It droned comfortingly, but at the six o'clock news, Ali was all over the screen. I watched from the cradle of my chair.

"Shit."

"What, babe?" Richard caught my expletive.

"Nothing, Richard, the news just unsettles me a bit." A bit. Sure, sure, I couldn't even arrive at step one in a murder investigation, and the press think they have it solved already.

The news report covered a lot of air time, and I just knew that tomorrow would be a disgusting day. I tried to close my eyes for a moment, concentrating on Ali, conjuring her in my mind.

I decided to check with Sheedy or McInnis to see if any developments had come up that I should know about before tomorrow. I picked up my cell phone, and rang Sheedy first. He answered breathlessly.

"Sheedy, did you find anything new on York?"

"No, Sam, but I'm glad you called. I was just going to call you."

"What, what, did you find?" I pried.

"Nothin', but we got another phone call. Another young woman murdered."

Oh great.

I got the address.

"I'll meet you there as soon as I can."

I hung up, my hand still holding the phone like a lifeline. Richard peeked at me from around the wall.

"I'll hold supper for you, Sam."

Some men fit into my life just perfectly. Sheedy, McInnis, and Richard.

Chapter Three

McInnis got the door for me. I had to step over the body that was just inside. She was fully clothed, quite different from how Ali had been found. Nice-looking young woman, shot the same way as Ali, through the head. Same yuk everywhere. Probably the same assailant.

"Okay, guys, what do we know?"

"Her name's Maureen Rogers," announced Sheedy. "There's no gun lying around and no forceable entry into the apartment. She has her clothes on, so we don't suspect sexual assault."

"Have pathology check anyway. There was no apparent sexual assault with York, either. I don't get it. Was York's state of undress done to throw us off track? I'm trying to visualize the murderer. He's faceless, but I figure he had a special relationship with Ali, judging from the discrepancy in their state of undress. What are the differences here? Did the murderer have no sexual interest in these women? What does that mean?" I was thinking out loud, babbling, but McInnis and Sheedy mumbled some kind of puzzlement that was equal to my own.

"Anything about this one that reminds you of

the York murder? Besides receiving a similar gunshot wound, I mean."

McInnis grinned stupidly, finally admitting: "Nice looking young women. Seems like they both could have used a protector."

"Thank you for sharing that with us, McInnis," I added sarcastically, "Of course, that's the first thing I thought of myself. Let's start sniffing around, then."

I got up to check the bathroom. They followed. "We're looking for drugs, alcohol, pills, suicide notes... you know!" There were no pills, only some over-the-counter painkillers, toothpaste, bandaids. Nothing interesting.

Rogers' apartment was antiseptic compared to Ali's place. No weird decorations, just a few bland prints on the wall. I couldn't get a picture of her personality.

McInnis remarked on the differences.

"This babe didn't leave many clues about personal business. Not like the other one."

"You're coming along, McInnis, you're coming along."

Sheedy dragged out his notebook. "I checked with the neighbours on Rogers' employment record. The lady who phoned us, a Miss Nymand, says that she and Rogers were planning a quiet evening of popcorn and videos. When the victim failed to respond to the doorbell, the apartment manager was called. No one heard a thing. Miss Nymand confirms that Ms. Rogers was also some kind of paralegal type. I thought I would check into whether or not she knew York."

"Sheedy, I could kiss you!" I exclaimed.

"Hey, I interviewed some neighbours around

here too," McInnis announced petulantly.

"Great, McInnis, just find me the murderer next, would you?"

I didn't have the energy to stay and do my usual 'mental note' thing. Besides, as McInnis pointed out, there was less of Maureen Rogers to follow. She was almost like... an afterthought. What was twigging my sensibilities about these murders? Richard's comments? Perhaps. But it was more like... something just didn't smell right.

We left Rogers' apartment when the forensic teams showed up to do their stuff.

It was only a matter of time before Ali, maybe even Maureen, would leave tracks that I could follow.

* * *

I was concentrating on some paper work the following morning when the phone rang. It was a woman by the name of Leslie Reynolds, who asked to speak to the investigating detective on the York case.

I identified myself as such, and didn't bother asking her how she had come to learn of Ali York's murder. The news had hit this morning's paper, never mind last night's TV media carnival.

"Could you stop by my office, Detective Holt? I'm... so upset about Ali. I was her therapist, you see."

"I'd be very happy to, Ms. Reynolds. Sometime this afternoon?" She agreed.

Leslie Reynolds seemed relieved to see me later that day, although I couldn't fathom why. Maybe Ali was on her mind, too.

"Detective Holt, I'm so glad you responded so quickly to my call."

Leslie was a tall, well-proportioned woman. She

wore a long flowery skirt and a lovely knit sweater, which accentuated her beautiful proportions. Her hair was long, black, and flowing. I had all I could do to avoid stroking its smooth, hypnotic texture. She noticed my admiration and smiled. "I don't look like any therapist you expected to see, do I?"

I flushed a little at her insight, and returned the smile, shaking my head. "No, although I can see why people would be comfortable in your presence, you're... warm."

She offered me a chair, seating herself in front of me. I watched her cross her legs slowly and elegantly, clasping her hands as though she meant business now.

"My clients think so too. I practice feminist therapy, Ms. Holt. My practice involves facilitating the efforts of women to seek personal empowerment in their lives. I deal with a great many issues, family concerns, drug and alcohol abuse, and ... incest." She paused and stared at me. I wondered if I was supposed to know something significant, which I could not comprehend. Leslie seemed satisfied with my puzzled silence, and went on.

"I must confess, I am not certain why I called you, except that... I felt I had to. And here you are."

The warmth on her face drew me into conversation. I felt relaxed with her almost instantly. Her clients must have felt the same way. I surmised that she had much she wished to tell me.

I decided to take a chance on her. "Ms. Reynolds, is there anything you can tell me about Ali York's treatment? Can you help me at all?"

Her face darkened and almost crumbled. I could

see that she was fighting her emotions, trying to understand how Ali's tragedy could have happened. Why the terrible waste?

"Ms. York... Ali... had been in therapy with me for some time. She seemed reluctant to share the most intimate details of her life, but I was finally compelled to ask her if she believed she had ever been the victim of incest. Apparently I touched the right nerve. Over the last year, we had been engaged actively with the healing process. She had come far, to the point of actually confronting her molesters and instigating proceedings. It was part of her new sense of personal freedom. A major tool of that healing was a diary that she kept."

I started.

Leslie noticed.

"I believe I found the diary in Ms. York's apartment," I admitted.

She nodded. "Ali read from it sometimes in therapy. It was a disturbing account of her pain, but nonetheless revealing, in that her distress was relieved as she began to take action. We had made a pact that she would read her latest entries to me. We would then explore her feelings and statements." Leslie's face clouded again. "Oh, she would have had an appointment with me today." The sudden reminder caused Leslie's lovely features to crumble again.

I reached over to pat her hand. She received my touch easily enough, but shook her head. "I can't understand it. Ali was coming along so well, getting ready for her confrontation." Leslie looked at me imploringly and shook her head, ever so puzzled and clearly upset.

"Leslie," I felt comfortable enough with her to use her first name. She had succeeded in placing me in that space of mind, "have you any reason to believe that Ali might have purposefully put herself in some danger?"

Her beautiful black eyes bored into me. "That I don't believe, Detective Holt. She had been on antidepressants, although we had talked about the possibility of her stopping this treatment because she was so pleased with her life."

"Why do you think she was pleased?"

"She had acquired a new job with a lawyer by the name of Mr. James. I sensed that she was drawn to him, although this attraction might have been the direct result of coping with an incestuous power differential. I had hoped it was not."

The lawyer-thing again. I just simply would have to go and see this James guy.

"The odd thing about the diary," continued Leslie, "was that Ali thought she should make use of it someday. She believed that she might give it to the right person, someone who could make sense of it all. I know that sounds absurd, Detective Holt, like a ghoulish message from beyond the grave, but I thought you should know. If you have the diary in your possession, it's almost as though Ali chose you to complete her process of healing."

"Nothing can bring her back, Leslie."

"I know that, of course. But Ali needs to set things right. Even now. I feel badly that I could not help her finish that project."

"Leslie, guilt never helped anyone, and it won't help Ali now. If what she wrote will help us find her murderer, you may be sure that I'll use it."

She nodded. "I believe, Ms. Holt," aha, the first time she forgot my title. We'd made some progress. "I believe that Ali wanted you to have the book. The ceremony, if that's what you want to call it, is complete."

I had Ali's tracks. If I stood very still, I might hear her voice.

Chapter Four

I eased into my sofa to read Ali's diary. Richard was out, the place was mine. The atmosphere was set for Ali. I could check her story without interruption.

The diary was covered with a classic paisley fabric pattern, a bit tattered around the edges, but it reminded me of the art work in her bed quilt. The first entry was about twenty years ago, May 12, 1974. I calculated briefly. She would have been about ten. The script was large and shakily child-like:

Why won't he leave me alone and why don't mommy and daddy stop him from doing those nasty things to me. I hate what he's doing and I hate myself because of them. He said if I ever tell anyone he'll hurt me and my sister so badly that I'll be sorry I ever spoke. I believe him and I know he would hurt everyone if I try to do anything to stop him. My brother Luke is very bad and doesn't care about anything or anyone. I'm scared for my sister and me as well as mommy so I must try not to make my brother any madder than he already is. Thanks for listening, Miss Diary.

I set the book over my lap before I could go on to the next entry. I shook my head in disgust, almost sick to my stomach, but decided to persevere:

September 10, 1974: I've been able to stay away from Luke this summer. Went to grandma's house for a few weeks and read books. She teaches me how to quilt, too. Grandma doesn't like Luke, I can tell. She would rather have me there alone but she doesn't mind having Tanya around either. Tanya is my older sister and treats me like a baby because I'm ten, but soon I'll be eleven. I don't mind her, but she always pretends about things, like saying that Luke isn't really so bad. I can see her trying to defend me sometimes in front of mommy and daddy and if Luke tries to get mean and Tanya happens to be around, she won't let him touch me. I think she likes me but she won't share nothing with me, nothing about girls and boys or growing up. Sometimes I wish she would be my friend, but she won't. I feel so alone.

October 1: Daddy and Luke are the same. Luke knows that he can do whatever he likes because he is the boy and Daddy is in charge. Daddy says that I'm his special girl. I must always try to please Daddy, then Luke won't get me. Daddy promised. Tanya spends a lot of time with Daddy too. I can hear her cry when Daddy visits her.

I sighed again. I was reading about incest, and the special way that a little girl talks about her private horror. How much baggage could that little girl be expected to carry? And for how long? All I got from this exercise was more questions, but I had made up my mind that I would try to interview Ali's disgusting family as well as her employer, James. Her words called me again:

> I talk to Tanya about Luke, but she doesn't really listen. She tells me to keep quiet and not to tell everybody how weak and silly I am. Tanya says not to cause any trouble. Daddy would be horrible if I did. I am so hurt, Diary, you are the only one I can talk to. It's almost as though she likes Luke better than me now. I am so scared of the nighttime, because Daddy comes into my bed and does these awful things… I feel so sick inside.

I paused here. How did anyone escape the pain of this living hell? These were questions I could not answer. Ali had survived. From what Leslie Reynolds had said, I knew that Ali had not lived, in her final months anyway, as a victim. I read on:

> Diary, I like to play with my bottles now.

I pulled up my slouch at attention. The bottles! Where did they fit?

> I name my bottles, and play with them just like some kids play with dolls. But the bottles are more fun, because they don't look like plastic babies. They rescue each other. George is my hero-bottle.

A fantasy world! With rules laid down by Ali herself. A dangerously fantastic re-creation of her own life! She had saved those bottles I saw on the shelf. Perhaps as she looked at them, their presence reminded her that she didn't have to return to that place ever again.

I checked the dates to her entries. From the first 'bottle entry' to the next entry was a time span of nearly a year.

March 13, 1977: I feel kind of goofy, Diary, telling you about my bottles, but when I look at them really hard, I can see the smiles on their labels, just like real-people faces, only real people don't smile.

April 27: I have not written so much to you in a while. Mom got so mad at me for spilling stuff out of my bottles. I must stop this. I must be as grownup as possible.

The poor kid was clearly losing it. I was sick with the knowledge that her mind was bending around reality. She was articulating her pain through metaphors. Her diary entries were irregular as well, with long gaps of time undoubtedly marking the misery of her life.

The next entry was the beginning of the school year in 1978.

September 12: I think I will like school this year. I have some new girlfriends who seem to like me. I don't know why. Some of the boys like me too, they say I am pretty, but I don't really believe that. Anyhow I am going to the school shag with one guy. His name is Billy Corgan.

It seemed to me that Ali had begun to put layers of life on top of her suffering. The layers would be spongy enough to absorb the worst of the ugliness, numbing her pain. The problem was that the layers would probably compromise her happiness as well.

November 20: My teachers are really great. I actually like Junior high school, because they tell me that I am bright and perceptive. I had to look that up. It means that I am wise and keen and sharp, and that I know things that others do not see right away. I guess that's right about me, but I never thought of it before.

I'm glad I have some good things about me. I only have two things I don't like to do. I don't like to change my clothes in front of the other girls, because I don't like anyone to see my body. I don't like to look at it myself. I don't want to play on any intra-mural sport teams. Miss Willis, my gym teacher, said that I should feel comfortable enough with the other kids to play on some teams. I told her I would rather not because I wouldn't like to make any mistakes and have the others make fun of me. She said that I was too smart to make mistakes but if I made just one every now and then, it would be okay. I never thought of that. I decided to trust Miss Willis, just a little bit.

November 23: Luke started to call me ugly names today. I can name them, because they don't belong to me. Slut, whore, cock-tease… he can call me anything he wants, I won't hear it. I told him I would get even with him one day and if he ever touched me again I would kill him. He said he was soooo scared. I said I didn't care whether he was scared or not, he could spend the rest of his life wondering whether today was the day I would tell the police about him. He was so hateful, I could see it come out of his eyes. Then he threatened to kill me. I really am not scared of him. Bad people must be punished, and Luke is one of those people. I gave up long ago talking to Mom. She seems scared of Dad.

There was no natural movement in this family; they circled in a cesspool. I was loathe to interview them now that I knew the family secret.

As for Ali, well, I understood her somewhat. I had my share of unfortunate school memories. Junior high school was a bad time to get used to puberty, let alone fill the empty sockets of your personal agony. It seemed, however, that Ali was beginning to find her way around with a little help from her friends. I read on:

December 18: Billy Corgan invited me to a Christmas dance. I thought it was really nice of him. He's little and scrawny, but tough. I've seen him with some of the bigger boys who teased him at the beginning of the year. He got into a few fights and they don't bug him much anymore. He's kind of sneaky sometimes, like the time he pulled the fire drill bell. I know he cheated on Mr. Podlarski's science test, too.

December 21: Christmas Dance. Luke hasn't bothered me much for a long time. He was there at the dance tonight, and started poking at me, but Billy cuffed him. Oh, Diary, you should have seen the look of surprise on Luke's face. Billy is really my Georgie bottle, if you know what I mean! Life is looking better.

February 7: I read a poster caption today that said something about being happy. I thought about that a minute, and suddenly I realized that I wasn't happy. I don't even know what it means. I think I have been sometimes, like at the dance with Billy, when I could have said I was happy, but I'm not so sure. I just like to sit with books and read. They never hurt me.

I had read enough for now. Ali was a woman whose childhood had been stolen; a woman who had grown up too soon. I didn't know the woman, but for the child, I felt the most acute kind of pain.

Chapter Five

Theodore H. James figured that there was little wonder that most heart attacks, especially fatal ones, occurred on Monday mornings, after a quiet weekend. A body could not quite establish sync with the rigorous, hectic pace that was required to function first thing Monday morning. James was the kind of guy who evaluated these nuances of existence; the sort of man who cared for himself and the forces at work in his body. His attention to those details, he believed, made for a prime work of art. Theodore H. James was the best kind of art; a rare work indeed.

On this early July morning he slowed his pace for a few minutes, gazing down to the crowded Calgary street. It wasn't that hot outside. Stampede Week in Calgary wasn't always hot, but the crazed pace of partying often caused a great sweat for everyone, including James. This Monday morning, his staff ran around like mad dogs after their tails. Clients were arriving without scheduled appointments and whining: "Oh, Mr. James, could you spare just a few minutes of your time?" the phone pealed through the walls as though he were the only lawyer in the city and now, oh what now???

"A Sam Holt to see you, Mr. James," interrupted his receptionist, "wants to ask you some questions about Ali York's demise." His heart would not hold up. He could feel the mouse slowing down in the wheel as his thoughts turned to Ali.

"Send him in, Rene. Let's get this over and done with."

"He is a She, sir." One corner of Rene's mouth lifted a bit at the idea that she could correct His Oneness. "Cocky bitch," he thought. His life was full of them. "Very well, then, send HER in, please…"

"Mr. James will see you now, Ms. Holt," rang Rene's melodic announcement. Theodore H. James had some urgent work to be done, and letters that required immediate dictation and delivery. He had to formulate his thoughts and do some research before he could forward one of the letters and quite simply, he didn't have enough time to fart, let alone summon the energy to talk to some butchy police broad.

He sighed, then glanced up to catch her scrutinizing him from the doorway.

"Mr. James, I'm so glad you could take the time to see me. I realize I must be interrupting a hectic operation." He tried to keep the irritation out of his demeanour. She smiled then, disarming him. No butchy broad was this woman. He could see that she was muscular, though, with short dark hair and tasteful librarian glasses. All business, and yet, just a hint, he thought, of something worth taming. His evaluation was a bit slow this time; he realized that he had overdone his usual appraising glance.

Holt examined the bar in his office. He followed her gaze.

"May I offer you a refreshment, Ms. Holt? And

please call me TJ. All my friends and acquaintances do."

"No thank you, Mr. James. TJ. I won't keep you for long."

He noticed her fine pigskin leather gloves, and before he could exchange any further pleasantry, she got down to business.

"You've probably heard the reports. I'm very sorry that you lost Ms. York."

"You cannot be any sorrier than I am, Ms. Holt. She was the best secretary I ever had. Like a sponge, really, the more work I gave her, the more she seemed to absorb. I wondered about that, actually. She didn't seem to have much of a life, apart from family and some rather strange friends. I gather she didn't care to spend much time with her family.

"Can you speculate, Mr. James, as to the reasons for that?"

James regarded this woman skeptically. Probably bright enough, no doubt one of those women's libbers with an attitude. He watched her poise her pen to take notes, then averted his eyes to gaze into the far corner of his office.

"Some trouble with her family in the past, I understand. I thought it best not to delve obtrusively into her personal circumstances. Young people today all seem to have a history of some sort." He threw his hands up, shrugging in a gesture of helpless quandary. "I tried to be of whatever assistance I could to her. It was in my best interests to do so, of course. A happy worker is a productive worker." A useful motto: he grinned at his own quick thinking.

"Actually, Miss Holt, Ali was involved in a lawsuit against her brother, her parents, and a fellow by the name of Billy Corgan. I helped her to advance the claim against them, of course." He noted Holt's look of surprise, misinterpreting entirely. "Oh, I know it seems like I'm stretching my interest, but..."

"It's not that at all, Mr. James..., it's... something else. Don't you feel that there was a conflict of interest involved with you acting as her lawyer with respect to these suits?"

A legal question at last, back to his territory. He shrugged and thought for a moment. "Probably not. She did not have much money and could not afford the cost of protracted litigation. I felt that because of her exceptional capabilities, she might do most of the legal work herself. I expected to do no more than provide appropriate advice, possibly just to supervise her efforts. I would rather not have been involved. I tried to keep out of her personal affairs and of course, I would rather have seen her spend time on office concerns. But there again," he blurted, "none of her responsibilities here were ever left undone. How could I refuse her? If I'd had my druthers, she could have done it elsewhere, to be sure."

"She didn't seem depressed, perhaps,... preoccupied?"

The hot shot lady-detective was fishing, and James' impatience was rising. "Absolutely not. She was a star performer. I picked her up at the top of her class from the legal aide practitioner program. Some great girls in there, you know. Frustrated lawyers, maybe, but all of them ready to offer invaluable assistance to the legal profession." He watched Holt's face darken and her eyes narrow a bit. She stiffened.

Ahh, touched a nerve, have we, Miss Detective?

"I should think, then, Mr. James, that Ali York's

loss to you would be particularly difficult."

Holt was right. Ali York would not be replaced easily. He leaned back in his chair, deciding to express that exact sentiment to this inquisitive woman. "She won't be replaced easily. She was a sweet girl. Always ready to learn from me, eager to take on new responsibilities, exceedingly good-looking..." He paused for breath. "Although I realize that Ms. York's physical attributes probably mean little to this investigation."

"On the contrary, Mr. James, Ali York's looks, while apparently only of peripheral concern, are a clear example of what becomes truly primary to a murder inquiry. At least to some."

Holt's dark tone was unmistakable. He felt himself flush without being able to pinpoint the cause. He decided it was anger. She had gained on him ever so slightly.

"With due respect, Miss Holt, my practice is extremely busy. Moreover, I want to spend adequate time in preparing the eulogy which I've been asked to deliver at Miss York's funeral tomorrow. It seems that she had so alienated her family that I am left with the sad task of doing the honours. I hope that I have answered your questions to some satisfaction?"

"Indeed you have, Mr. James", she assured him, "should I need any further assistance, I won't hesitate to contact you. Detectives McInnis and Sheedy have also been assigned to this investigation. You might be hearing from them as well. I'm grateful that you have been able to give me this much time."

She rose quickly, examining his desk for something.

"May I have one of your cards, Mr. James?"

"Oh, of course, Ms. Holt." James picked one up

and handed it to her. With her gloved hand, she placed it in her purse.

She glanced around his office. He noted her examining his trophies without any disgust. Most women sickened at the sight.

"You're a hunter, Mr. James?"

"Yes, I dabbled for awhile, but my law practice gained precedence over my time. I haven't done any big game hunting for years."

He watched her stride closer to the white-tailed deer head, studying every angle of the taxidermy.

"I get away to do some hunting myself, every year", she disclosed.

He was dumbfounded.

"You don't!"

She gazed at him quizzically. "Why yes, I do."

"Women don't hunt."

"I do."

He didn't believe her. It was a trick of some sort. He decided to test her.

"What sort of gun do you use?"

"Winchester 30-30, model 94."

"No one hunts with a rifle like that! Why, you can't get close enough to a deer to pick one off with a 30-30." He heard himself spit out the comment.

"I can."

"You need a telescope, then."

"I don't have one. Just the sights on the gun. I shot a leaping doe last year at 75 yards. Led her by a foot or so as she ran. It only took one shot to bring her down."

The room was filled with astonished silence.

Holt spoke at last:

"A 30-30 is the gun that won the west, Mr.

James. That's a good thing to bear in mind during Stampede Week."

She stared at him again, this time with a rising pique in her glare. She slapped her notebook shut with her left hand, extending the other one for a closing handshake. She had not removed her glove for this exchange.

"Always happy to be of service, Miss Holt," he said, wincing at the strength of her handshake. She rammed her gloved hand into the webbing of his thumb and forefinger, rendering his hand momentarily impotent. She squeezed, released him, whirling, then marching, from his office.

"God, what a woman," he thought. James was a man of an earlier era. He had neither the time nor the energy to dwell on tackling yet another headstrong woman.

* * *

"What a, a... creep!" I spit, as I walked out of the office of the great Theodore H. James. Guys like that needed to get power from somewhere. Imagine working for him, though. I noticed the hectic pace in that office, everyone scurrying around. And he: Theodore James - king of all he surveyed.

He hadn't liked the fact that I had tits bigger than his balls, and he fumbled with the language he might normally have spoken if I had been a man in charge. I delighted in shocking men like that, which I had managed to do with the deer-hunting conversation. I also had his business card with his fingerprints all over it. A hunch. Maybe the card would yield some useful prints although the paper was not a perfect medium. If it was recycled paper, the chemicals employed in its reconstruction might affect the quality of any prints we could get. Sheedy and McInnis might be able to get some samples from it if we were lucky.

I marched down the sidewalk, fuming and ruminating on TJ. I didn't like that man. He smelled bad in a classy kind of way. It was sort of like dressing up the outhouse with sweetgrass.

Speaking of outhouses, Stampede Week in Calgary was progressing as usual. There was horse dung left over from Parade Day in the middle of Eighth Avenue, still perfuming the street. Straw from hay bales blew out in front of me. I just knew that Richard would invite me to go with him down to the grounds.

I haven't enjoyed Stampede Week since I was a kid. My mother always felt obliged to take us to the parade and the grounds. One day we had entrance passes, but she had forgotten all her money, and my brother and I just ended up walking around with her. She was horribly embarrassed, but hey, there was still a lot to see in the Agriculture and Big Four Buildings. I felt sorry for her; she tried very hard to make a good day of it for us. I have loathed carnival grounds ever since.

But Richard, well, Richard is my best pal. He thinks nothing of dropping $100 on ferris wheels, candy floss and apples, and dancing in the fair grounds. I never want to disappoint him when he asks me to go out. He has even been known to tackle the Silver Slipper on occasion and dance with all the women. They think he's the next best thing to sliced bread.

What made me think of Richard all of a sudden? He's so refreshing next to the suits behind the oak desks. Men like Teddy James make me want to kiss men like Richard. And I guess... well, Richard would never murder a woman. He likes us too well, better than his own gender sometimes, I think.

I slid into my little car when I found it at last. Despite the Stampedey flavour to Calgary, I still felt compelled to play Dan Seals in my car, and bee bop through the streets...

"Brriiing"... my car telephone called me back to reality.

"Hey, boss-lady, can you come down to the station real quick?" implored McInnis.

"What's up, pal?"

"The sarge wants to know where you are, what's going on with the York and Rogers murders."

I sat for a second or so, watching a red light turn green, negotiating my way mentally through this beflagged and bedazzled city.

"Shit."

"What's that, Sam?"

"Never mind. Tell Sarge I'll be right in. I was just interviewing one Theodore H. James, Ali's boss."

"Well, the sergeant will be real glad to hear that, I can tell you."

I flipped the business card at McInnis as I walked into the station, asking him to dust it for prints. I peeled off my gloves and then headed for Staff Sergeant Speirs.

He wanted to see me alright.

"Holt, what the hell is going on? We've got Stampede Week in full fling here in case you didn't notice. 'Mericans from all over spending money like they was really havin' a good time. Love to get their spankin' new cowboy boots dirty, but murders, nonononono, nobody wants to hear about that. We're too friendly in this City, right?"

Speirs flung some paper across his desk at me. I approached when I thought he had spent himself on the Stampede Week tirade. "We've just concluded preliminary investigations at the scene of the York case, sarge."

"Well, what've you got?"

"Nothing concrete just yet. Seems Ali York was taking antidepressants, which means she'll leave traces of a troubled life that will be easy to follow. Her therapist says that Ali was doing well. I just got back from interviewing her last employer: Theodore H. James. He says she was the best thing that ever happened to him. No further leads at this time, sir."

"Well this Rogers woman was a paralegal too. Pay attention to that. There has to be some connection."

Speirs had calmed down considerably. I moved on.

"I've not spent too much time with Sheedy and McInnis in the last two days, sir. We've got to talk this all through. The funeral for Ali York is tomorrow, I want to see all of those characters together."

"Yeahyeah, blahblah. Go talk to them. Let me know how it all goes, wouldya?"

I wheeled around to make for the door while I could still escape. "Oh, and Holt…"

I turned around to face him, expecting another blast. He looked almost apologetic. "You've got a nice a… attitude. I mean, you're too nice for this work. You know, murdered woman an' all. You know what I mean."

I nodded. "Yeah, I know what you mean, Sergeant Speirs".

* * *

I had some planning to do with Sheedy and McInnis, so I shot the main plan at them.

"By the way, guys, we've got a funeral to attend tomorrow. Ali York's. Your job is to stay out of the way at the funeral, but roll some video for me."

"You want me to go to a funeral?" barked McInnis. "I don't do funerals or wash windows. What do you want to do that for?"

I glowered at him.

"Of course I expect you to go to a funeral! You don't have to cry or carry on, okay?" I snarled. The man was exasperating. I had to explain every angle.

"Look up the particulars in the obituary. Anyone who shows up gets filmed. Got it?"

"Yeah, so why do we take pictures?"

"Because I don't know who all the players are, McInnis. Get the video developed into stills quickly and show them to Ali's neighbours, as well as anyone you can find who knew Rogers. Maybe show some stills to that same old block watch lady who wasn't sure of anything. Maybe we can refresh her memory a bit, and maybe the stills will work better than composite drawings."

I was starting to get frustrated, and it showed. Sheedy and McInnis were eager enough, but they were the kind to always want a bit of action. They weren't really thinkers, just scrappers.

"By the way, I hope you guys have suits." I saw them both frown at me.

If not, they would have by tomorrow.

Chapter Six

And they had. McInnis and Sheedy were about the prettiest looking mourners I had ever seen. They were both over six feet tall, maybe 220 pounds on the hoof: burly guys with arms about as big as my thighs. They had suits. Black pin-striped, crisp Arrow shirts, patent leather pimp shoes, and graduation cuff links. I was so pleased, that I pinched their cheeks playfully.

"Ooooh, you guys are so cute, where did you get those suits?"

"Cut it out, Holt, and don't ask. I stole mine," confessed McInnis. "Glad I don't have to wear this everyday. Might start talkin' different."

"Maybe you wouldn't even like girls any more," teased Sheedy.

This was too much for McInnis. "I'm takin' this monkey-suit off as soon as we're outta here. And don't take any dumb pictures of me, or you're dead meat," he threatened. Sheedy grabbed him by the ears and kissed him.

"Alright, you guys, this is a funeral," I reminded them. "Look glum."

"Yeah, and it's gonna be his," muttered McInnis, wiping his mouth violently.

I myself was impressive in a navy blue blazer and knee-length grey charcoal skirt. I had also gone to some trouble to find just the right leather pumps to go with the outfit. I was also glad I didn't have to dress like this every day. I wasn't sure what the dress code was for funerals that took place during Stampede Week, but I suspected that a cowboy hat might have been overstated.

Sheedy and McInnis took a pew seat beside me, digging out the camera equipment.

"Try to be discreet, guys. I'm going to see if I can spot Ali's family. Take lots of pictures of them."

I pulled out the memorial brochure, scanning it for familiar names. Parents: Frank and Wanda York, sister: Tanya York, pallbearers: Luke York, Theodore H. James, William Corgan, and… wait a second. Billy Corgan!

I whispered to the guys: "Take close-ups and a lot of footage of the pallbearers."

Watch reactions, Sam, this ought to be good.

My colleagues down at the station had always thought I was ghoulish, intrusive and insensitive for attending funerals. I was told that women should exercise more delicate behaviour. Bullshit. Business is business. And if murderers are trying to appear nonchalant, the place they will do so best is at a funeral.

I had no desire to inflict needless pain on innocent families of the deceased, but Ali York's family was far from innocent. Incest. Hah, the game the whole family can play. The pickings might be slim at the Rogers funeral, however. I had a hunch that Maureen Rogers' death was linked closely to that of Ali York's, and I just might find as much here as I needed to know.

The family had hired a preacher to make it all

look like a close-knit little group. This cleric had evidently known Ali as a little girl, but hadn't picked out her father for a beast.

Once the minister was through, Theodore H. James took over. This character was a highbrow solicitor, blue suit almost as nice as McInnis and Sheedy's getups, but I had to give him credit. He was a good orator; handled the moment with the right touch of solemn class.

I studied the York clan. Frank and Wanda were the disconsolate parents. Wanda wept noisily beside a stately and beautiful woman who looked a lot like Ali. This was probably Tanya, the sister. A man sat close by them, accompanied by a woman who was clearly his companion. He too, was crying. Good old Luke, no doubt.

The service ended and the pallbearers took their places. I elbowed Sheedy, whispering to him to start the camera rolling as unobtrusively as possible. People gave him some glowering looks, so I pulled him into the back of the room. No point in getting caught in the traffic.

The coffin was placed on the hearse and taken away. With that break, TJ came looking for me.

"Ah, Miss Holt. I am truly glad to see that you and your colleagues are ever concerned about the citizens you serve."

I shook his hand and smiled warmly. His power was a concentrated antagonism designed clearly to embarrass me. He failed.

"And I in turn, Mr. James," I hesitated falsely, pretending to grope for just the right words of condolence: "I am pleased to have heard that moving eulogy. Ali York would have undoubtedly been overwhelmed by your sincerest respects." My eyes remained locked in position with his. Only the smallest cobra would back away.

He bristled, releasing my hand from our viper grip, and clenched his teeth. I wondered how long our look would remain locked, but I didn't flinch. He turned his face to the funeral procession, attempting to appear to all as the properly saddened employer. Very smooth, Mr. James. I'm the bitch, you're the saviour. See who believes that when I'm done with you.

A short, fine-boned, pleasant-looking woman joined him just then. A perfect little legal wife, gently past forty, probably played golf on hot afternoons and joined the ladies at the Country Club for spritzers after five. At least that would be her story. I suspected either a pill or a scotch problem. She was dressed beautifully; a black knit thing with a lovely set of pearls that adorned her tastefully appointed breasts.

TJ at least had the grace to introduce me.

"Detective Samantha Holt, I would like to introduce you to my wife Suzie."

I reached out my hand to grasp her rather cold one. 'Suzie', I thought. You've got to be kidding. Does she skip rope too?

"Pleased to meet you, Mrs. James. Sorry we couldn't have met under more pleasant circumstances."

"Indeed, Detective Holt, it's a terribly sad day for us all. I can't think how my husband will replace Miss York."

Neither could I. But I was sure he'd find a way. She released my hand abruptly.

"Of course, it's a dreadful loss for Ms. York's family. I can't imagine how I would cope if I lost one of my children. The whole idea is unthinkable." She dabbed her eyes gracefully with an embroidered handkerchief that she pulled from her purse.

"Detective…," she continued dramatically, "have you any clues yet as to who the killer might be?"

"My investigation of Ms. York's death is far from complete. We've found no conclusive evidence as yet." It was the usual statement of inertia given to the public for moments such as these.

"If I can be of any assistance… any help at all, please do call, Detective Holt."

"Thank you so much, Mrs. James. Either my colleagues or myself…," I pointed to Sheedy and McInnis, who were busy tripping over themselves rolling pictures of everyone. I winced. "Umm, Sheedy and McInnis are assisting the investigation, Mrs. James."

"Oh, please do call me Suzie, Ms. Holt."

"Why yes, of course… Suzie." I had a feeling that we'd never be friends.

I excused myself and gathered Sheedy and McInnis together. "Got everything you need, guys? Pallbearers. I need pictures of that scruffy one at the end. Did you get his name?"

"Yeah, William Corgan."

"Good, that's all I needed to know. The galloping grief around here is beginning to get to me. Let's get out of here."

We all filed back to my car, but I felt eyes on me, boring into my back. The guys fumbled around with the camera equipment as we walked.

"I can't wait to get out of this suit, Sam," said McInnis. This shift's almost over, want to grab a beer at Ciao Baby's?"

I turned around to have a look at the official mourners just then. TJ was staring at me from a huge chasm, not space, distance, just... a long touch away.

"Yeah, sure, guys, sounds like a good plan," I responded absently.

My shoes squished into something. Looking down, I spied some fresh Stampede horseshit, which had splattered from the tires to my new shoes. It would eat through the leather and probably never come out.

* * *

TJ was relieved when the whole mess was over. The funeral, stupidly polite exchanges, condolences, all the necessary posturing. His eulogy had been brilliant, he thought, he had found just the right tone of life and spirituality from Paul's letters to the Corinthians. The words came back to him now:

> When I was a child, I spoke as a child, I understood as a child, I thought as a child, but when I became a [wo]man, I put away childish things. For now we see through a glass, darkly; but then face to face: now I know in part; but then shall I know even as also I am known.

It had seemed appropriate. The mourners had been impressed. Suzie had sent him an approving look and he knew he had done a first rate job. He was sad, of course, at Ali's demise. She had been a fine and dedicated employee, and hadn't he said so in the eulogy?

Sam Holt had challenged him to think otherwise. It was a good thing he had Suzie to remind him of his unsullied importance. He stared at her wonderingly. She had so much class in the midst of all these peasants, especially those overgrown Holt-henchmen, although he'd follow Holt through the bush any day.

Adaptability. It was all about survival. The capitalist jungle. The unwritten rules that said you had to have a big house in Pump Hill with a swimming pool in the back, and red geraniums in clay pots in the front yard. Never wild flowers. The neighbours would talk. A membership at the finest golf club in Calgary. A network of the old boys, inviting only the most adaptable women into certain circles. The greatest amusement was in watching them posture just like men, believing they had really penetrated the circles. Of course they could never penetrate. It was impossible for women, in more ways than one.

He giggled suddenly at his unwitting metaphor, tired of it all for today. Everything was so completely hysterical, and very, very, boring.

"Anything wrong, TJ?" inquired Suzie.

"No, no, of course not. Let's say goodbye to the Yorks and go home. I need a drink."

Suzie complied, of course, as she always did. Just once he wished that she would say: "You do your thing, Teddy, and I'll do mine." She always took pains to follow his lead. He felt as though he had to baby-sit, although wasn't she just the girl for him? God knows he had looked hard enough.

He pondered his life as they sauntered toward the car. It was Suzie, really, who said all the right things to the Yorks, made all the right noises. They appreciated it, and he could go away, leaving them with the impression that he was far too overcome to participate in their grief, if you could call it that.

But Suzie, ah, she came through again. His youthful hunt for the perfect wife had resulted in a perfect prize.

At Law School, TJ had achieved excellent grades and was near the top of his class, despite his involvement in numerous extracurricular activities. He had worked at a part-time job that had been necessary to sustain him. His peers had dubbed him TJ, and the nickname had stuck.

His own shame of his parents had probably contributed to his high achievements. His people were losers, failures. He had no siblings. The sooner he rid himself of this failing influence, the more smoothly his own career would advance. Or so he believed. When he had picked Suzie as a potential wife, he realized that his own parents would neither understand her nor her family, or the social environment of which he hoped to be a part. His parents were lower middle class, and would hardly have known how to behave at the more stellar events. He did not wish to invest the energy in training them to do so, or introducing them into a world where they would be total aliens.

TJ fancied himself an extraordinary fellow. He was not content to remain mediocre. He didn't sleep much in Law School; still didn't. Work never got done if the boss was asleep. He steeled his body to function and to drive with very little rest, becoming proficient at taking cat naps, little breaks and rests during the day. His determination and resolve overcame any physical or emotional weaknesses, and he prided himself on his wondrous ability to appear fresh and alive for everyone that he encountered.

He hadn't fooled Suzie, though.

He had always made a point of dating the sharpest and best looking girls on campus. The ones who really appealed to him were those with brains, ability, good looks, and those who were impressively nubile. He had searched for a girl who had all of those characteristics. He had wanted her to be subservient as well, the only daughter of wealthy parents. His requirements narrowed greatly the available field of selection, but he had been in no particular rush. Not for him was the adage 'so many women, so little time.' He determined that he needed someone to fit his exacting criteria or he would never be happy.

Then Suzie came along. She was well liked, having the gift of gab: intelligent gab of course. She belonged to the top campus sorority, and she was always on the Dean's List. Suzie was an only child. Her disgustingly rich parents doted on her, and the most athletic young men were always in her company. TJ singled her out. The fact that she was so impressively popular made her a trophy; a prize for the Theodore H. James woman-hunt.

He had made a point of following her to a campus function one night and playing a few male/female games. It was a night when she had been unaccompanied by another male, just her women friends. They were a circle that had no particular loyalties for each other; merely manhunters. TJ was there to entertain them, with one objective: Suzie.

Maybe he had been successful because she was bored with her life on campus. Maybe because he already knew quite a bit about her, and she was impressed. He didn't tell her everything, though. He had checked her background scrupulously, the financial status of her parents, her social history... etc. A suitable wife would be no burden if she brought an extensive financial portfolio into the relationship. Besides, she was pleasant, cheerful, well-liked and intelligent. She would never be a hindrance or an impediment to his career. He believed that she was one of those women who realized clearly that her financial future hinged upon a well-placed marriage to a partner with promise. He even allowed himself to believe that she would do everything and anything to propel his career, and that she would always put herself second to him.

The appointed meet-the-parents night came along soon enough. Suzie's parents, Doug and Mavis Smith, were not crazy about him. They were painfully polite to his charmingly gilded personality. The old man even had the audacity to inquire into his background and family. TJ had answered honestly, hoping to impress Dougie with what he believed was a display of ambition.

"My background is hardscrabble, sir. My parents are hard-working people who never accomplished a great deal. I hope to do better."

"The world would do well to study the intelligence-factor of a hard-working society, Mr. James."

So TJ had been unsuccessful at impressing the Smiths. Dougie clearly had a thing about honouring one's parentage. TJ couldn't figure out why.

For the remainder of that evening, TJ evaded their continuous questions about his parents. Finally, they stopped asking.

For months afterward, however, Suzie resumed those questions, stopping only when she encountered his cold, angry stare. She put it down to an uncomfortable experience of which she might yet discover the truth.

All wedding arrangements proceeded as planned. The Smiths were disappointed when Suzie and TJ informed them that they wanted a small wedding, and given their preferences, would rather elope. Doug Smith was hurt, and Mavis plied the argument that Suzie was their only child and of course they should have an elaborate celebration. Had they not family, friends and associates? The whole affair would make a fine social splash. The Smiths were shocked further when TJ advised them that his parents would not be able to attend the wedding.

"James, son," pleaded Dougie in private, "I don't care to pry into your background if it's a subject of some discomfort to you. However, I am distressed that you are attempting to marry my daughter without a ceremony of which I approve."

The old fart could be tiresome. TJ would have to humour him.

"Suzie and I have plans, sir." He added the respectful form, for good measure. "The money you save from an extravaganza like a big wedding could be a down payment toward our future. I have loans from Law School, and I would like to set up my own practice. With all due respect, a big wedding would be an occasion I couldn't be comfortable with."

His future father-in-law glowered at him, but TJ had won the day. Doug Smith got up and stared outside his front window. He appeared to be thinking deeply, but he didn't turn around to address TJ when he finally spoke.

"I hope you're not a gold-digger, Mr. James. I do not take kindly to predators. At this point in time, however, I am prepared to please my only daughter. Take care not to abuse my favour. It belongs to her alone. In this case, I will not share my affections."

TJ could not bring himself to mention the word love. It didn't belong here, and old Dougie would never believe it anyway.

* * *

Suzie was glowing. Her happiness was radiant, and TJ knew that his future was linked to that happiness. The Smiths had conceded to all their son-in-law's requests. Only the closest friends and family would be invited to this wedding. Mavis decorated the church beautifully with flamboyant flower arrangements. The food and booze were abundant and served up lavishly. The Smiths insisted on doing right by their daughter and that strange James boy. What should have been a wonderful time in their lives, however, ended up being an evening of false smiles and forced bravado. Only Suzie was really happy. TJ seemed suitably gratified.

The hunt was complete. The trophy won. No one even heard the last breath go out of the animal.

SOCIETY OF LAWYERS

society:

1) association with one's fellow men, especially in a friendly or intimate manner; companionship or fellowship;

2) the state or condition of living in association, company, or intercourse with others of the same species; the system or mode of life adopted by a body of individuals for the purpose of harmonious coexistence or for mutual benefit, defence, etc.;

3) an organized community of animals or insects: a society of wasps;

4) an assemblage of plants of the same species not dominant in an ecological community;

(1876) "To the extent men may knowe that they have need one of anothers helpe, and thereby love and society to grow among all men the more."

(OED) - Oxford English Dictionary

Chapter Seven

A lot could be said about TJ, most of it unflattering. No one could argue that he was not hard working and ambitious; maybe even a workaholic. He left the task of rearing the children to Suzie, concentrating all of his efforts on his law practice, business interests and the advancement of his political pursuits. He managed to never be at home, spending little time with his wife and children and racing from one meeting and one client to another. His pace was dizzying.

He prided himself on his affable nature, charm and good looks. His political connections were improving and he had a thriving law practice. He devoted attention to his practice but delegated most problems to legal assistants when, in fact, those matters would be best handled by himself. His personal power and high profile was such that if a senior lawyer encountered a problem on a file with James' name on it, that person assumed that everything was, in fact, copesthetic. What might have seemed like improprieties or problems were most often ignored or left unchallenged. The Old-Boys generally believed that anyone who was as much of a golden boy as TJ, with such obvious political clout, must surely practice ethics at a close and personal level. No contrary conclusions could be entertained at all.

TJ tried hard, but for all his good looks, charitable donations, and visibility at public meetings, he could not seem to translate his efforts into votes. He was a consistent loser in mayoralty and any other electoral spots he took a shine to pursuing. His sole claim to fame was that of a Public School Board Trusteeship and a few insignificant Corporate Directorships.

He knew exactly what he wanted from life, and he would stop at nothing to achieve those goals and objectives. The game was really just like Law School. You worked almost nonstop, did without sleep, and subjected yourself to tremendous pressure, strain and anxiety. No pain, no gain. He wanted to be enormously rich, self-sufficient and if possible, secure a plum political position. He hoped to cease practising law as soon as he could. Dougie Smith had secured the finances necessary for TJ to begin a law practice. The cash flow from that practice was vital, but the time demands and requirements to keep it all going, well, that was overpowering sometimes. TJ believed that he was worth more, and should be able to earn more, than the minimal monies which he received from his practice. He imagined that most peons would be pleased with the money he earned, probably they would be even envious, but it was insufficient for him. His wants and needs were insatiable.

He invested as much as he could borrow or otherwise secure, in the hope that his investments would make him more self-sufficient and less reliant on the rigours of his law practice. Those investments ranged from real estate and property holdings, to interests in a variety of businesses and limited partnerships. The tax ploys went on and on as well, utilized via oil drilling funds and real estate trusts, in an attempt to avoid or postpone income tax payment. TJ was satisfied as long as the pain of payment could be temporarily delayed. The long term consequences and implications were never a chief consideration; the prime intent was to retain as much money as possible to recycle into other ventures.

Sometimes his imagination was titillated by an investment and its possibilities. When that happened, he would try to own as much as he could. If the investment was faring poorly, he would piece portions of it to unsuspecting friends and clients, thus diluting his personal interests as much as possible. If it improved, he would try to reacquire it from that client or investor associate, for a reduced rate. He had to keep a careful watch on those little surprises, and to remake the acquisition, prior to the other party realizing that its value was increasing.

The slipstream of conniving never slowed down for a minute. He could never afford to let that happen.

These were TJ's reflections as he drove home from the funeral.

Suzie sniffed quietly beside him. Oh, the frustrating perfection of that woman. Never a hair out of place or a blemish on her skin.

He had even encouraged his in-laws to invest a considerable amount of their savings in a risky venture, for which he received a substantial brokerage and consulting fee. The investment had failed, and when he had had to give them the bad news, he apologized with some cliche like "you win some, you lose some." He had watched them both turn quite pale and exchange glances with one another. Most of the conversations he had had with them took place through clenched teeth on all sides, but he had known they would do nothing to disappoint their daughter.

Suzie, too, had much to think about now that Ali York was dead. Despite her simmering anger against her husband, she felt truly sorry for the Yorks. A sniff here and there was genuine enough, even though she was well aware of Ali York's relationship with her husband. Suzie couldn't have cared less about TJ's shenanigans any more. She'd been married to this wiley snake for too long. You bed them down, make babies with them, and you're stuck. Especially when they're rich, pompous, and own all the right memberships.

It wasn't that she was as shallow as that lady detective supposed. Oh sure she had read the contempt in Sam Holt's face while they talked. It was just that Suzie had been raised to believe in all the fairy tales; the wealth and position that she took largely for granted. She had thought, when she met TJ, that he was different from the rest. He had seemed to value her truly, as an individual. She had certainly never deluded herself about what she had to offer; she was a valuable commodity. TJ had made her feel as though the commodity part was not as important as her person. She had been thrilled, and fancied herself in love. It was the first time.

Well, she had been deceived. She couldn't really even blame her husband as much as she blamed herself. She should have seen through it all, but now there were children, charities, and a life of sham in the public sphere. She hadn't made the Dean's List in Dramatic Arts every year so that she could waste it on useless activities. Her children, Holden and Jessica, were important to her, but she realized that they were destined to be victims of the same privileged life from which she had come. How to protect them? She hoped to turn them into contributing citizens and warm human beings unlike their father, but, if pressed, she conceded that she simply didn't know how to go about it. All she could do was lavish them with love, affection and attention. She didn't know if that would be enough.

Suzie realized how important it was for her husband to be in the limelight. His political aspirations demanded his visibility in community activities, so her role was augmented to stand behind and beside him to highlight his acceptability. Well, she didn't mind so much: it was her job. A Political Wife for a Political Being. This was the public sphere.

On the private level, she knew she would have to ignore TJ in order to survive. To see Walter whenever she could. To be in a space and place with him. To be where she could ensure some happiness for herself. To live. To be.

TJ had been her prince in the fairy tale. It hadn't been long before she discovered that he was the overgrown frog who wasn't worth kissing. She covered for TJ with their two children, becoming so skilful at it that everyone except herself believed that he was an excellent father. She tried to keep him informed as to all their activities and to seek his input, disinterested as he was. When he came up with something useful, she took pains to advise the children of how their father thought or felt. No point in trying to raise them alone. Sooner or later they would go looking for him and expect some fathering. He might as well get used to the job.

Suzie knew that she held things together at home. Nothing was disjointed. Dysfunctional, maybe, but who really knew what 'functional' was all about anymore? Maintaining cohesion and superficial happiness seemed necessary. You couldn't hope to impress anyone without it. Even her parents thought more of their son-in-law, given his apparently skilful discharge of parental duties. Although they gave Suzie credit for being the wonderful mother that she truly was, they never suspected the extent of her highly manipulative role.

The picture was so complete that Suzie hoped no one noticed the flaws. Ali York had been an irritation; a defect in the total dynamic. Suzie had no trouble liking most people even superficially, but Ali had scratched the surface of her patience. It was not her husband's screwing around that had caused the irritation. She had long ago ceased to deceive herself that she loved him; he was now merely a means to an end.

No, it wasn't love. Ali had caused a lot of extra work. Suzie felt that the juggling act of keeping her foolish husband from stepping into traps was a full-time job. The whole affair was downright embarrassing. Wasn't it reasonable to expect that he could exercise a bit of intelligence on his own? And now Ali was dead. What would the police discover? Who would they interrogate?

TJ swerved to avoid hitting a jackrabbit.

"It's mating season again for those critters. They're out on the road in the middle of the day. Messy when you hit them. Just goes to show you: never lose your head over a piece of tail."

Point taken.

Chapter Eight

TJ liked to golf. He got away as often as he could, and shot a ninety-something most days. He practised golf in order to think, not being able to do much of that in the office. He often paired up with a buddy just to chew the fat about some legal tidbit. Stampede was a good time to get on the golf course, as the cowboys were otherwise amused.

He whacked a ball clear down the fairway, and reflected on the fact that he was a truly modest and self-effacing kinda guy. He was capable, his mind was sharp and alert. He attacked a problem and spit out the answer. He had so many balls going at the same time that his mental agility amazed even himself. He prided himself on having time for everything that he deemed important, and for acting so promptly that no one could accuse him of dragging his ass.

Patience was not one of his virtues. Nor was honesty. He didn't feel the need to cultivate virtue. Surely the ability to manipulate investment potential was a more practical skill.

One of TJ's best and favourite investments was a mortgage firm and corporation formed by himself and six of his friends. Over brandy one night they had named themselves The Group of Seven. The prime function of The Group of Seven Corporation had been to seek individuals or firms that required immediate funds, and who were prepared to pay interest rates of 24% to 48% per annum. These people would hold real estate that would be offered as collateral and security for the mortgage loan. Creditworthiness was not really considered by The Group of Seven; their sole interest and lending criteria was the amount and percentage of the advance. The Group of Seven loaned funds against the security of real estate, provided that the amount of the monies advanced did not exceed 75% of the appraised value of the property offered for security.

TJ found it all exceedingly stimulating, for he was entirely in charge of the Corporation, its lending practices and policies. He received, for his efforts, a monthly administration fee. Most borrowers or mortgage brokers who dealt with The Group of Seven Corporation believed that TJ was the sole principal and shareholder. TJ said nothing to correct that belief. If head honcho was what they expected, then head honcho was what they got.

Not only did he receive an administration fee, but he also did the legal work for the Group. That work entailed drawing and preparing of mortgages, foreclosure proceedings and so on. The costs were borne by the borrower. He also received another sweetener that formed part of the ambiguous administration agreement: inducement fees respecting a good many of the mortgages that were funded by the Group. With a free hand and no outside interference, TJ had a good thing going with the Corporation and the other investors, mostly doctors and dentists who were quite happy to receive a good rate of return on their funds. All the inducements and legal fees were charged to the borrower, and the mortgage corporation had no responsibility whatsoever for the payment. The Group of Seven Corporation showed healthy and substantial profits. Everybody was happy, including TJ.

He loved the fact that he was treated with the utmost deference and respect by the borrower, the brokers, and even the Mortgage Corporation's bankers. He would have done all that work anyway, whether he was paid or not, but his position with the Mortgage Corporation placed him on a cushy pedestal.

The arrangements that The Group of Seven held with the bank were quite standard. The bank matched two for every dollar, so that each dollar invested into the Mortgage Corporation would be doubled. The bank's security was an assignment of the Mortgage Corporation's interest in the mortgage loans and personal guarantees of all the shareholders in The Group of Seven Corporation. Each shareholder in the Group was actually responsible, at any given time and on demand, for the entire amount of the bank line of credit and indebtedness, with the right of indemnity being available to each shareholder from the other six. Consequently, the bank never worried about the loan or even the security per se, because they held the Personal Guarantees of seven people: seven professional and extremely creditworthy individuals. In addition, the bank also insisted upon and received, monthly reporting materials and a statement of the mortgage loans with The Group of Seven. The lending guidelines were supervised and administered solely by TJ.

It was his responsibility to make the monthly report to the bank, advising as to the status of the loans. The bank automatically imposed the standard that any loan had to be in good standing, or performing. Any default resulted automatically in the bank requiring the injection, by The Group of Seven, of the amount of mortgage loan that was in default. Failing that injection, the bank would lower the doubled line of credit by two times the amount of the mortgage loan in default. If the loans were in good standing and performing, as was the bank's expectation, the Corporation could function at full clip. It was TJ's responsibility to see that the loans were not of the type that would be in default. He ensured that any non-performing loans were dealt with right away via foreclosure, so that the line of credit would not be reduced and cut back.

TJ saw to it that the partners in The Group of Seven received glowing reports, albeit on a somewhat intermittent and infrequent basis. TJ advised them that the Corporation was doing exceedingly well, generating large profits, and so forth. All the shareholders in the Corporation seemed wonderfully content to leave all the profits there to revolve and increase through compounding. Some of the investors looked upon the Mortgage Corporation as their retirement plan, and TJ felt that they couldn't be more pleased with their golden boy - himself, and his tireless devotion to their investments.

The shareholders were happy to allow TJ a free hand as long as things remained 'peachy.' They left themselves at his mercy. Some of them felt queasy about charging exorbitant and even usurious interest rates. The qualms were only temporary, however, passing quickly when they distanced themselves from it all. None of them imagined for a minute, in their greedy naivete, that they might not only lose their investment, but be called upon by the bank, on demand, to repay funds borrowed by the Corporation.

TJ depended upon the corruption of the human spirit to garner his success. Aggression. Strike the ball at 80 m.p.h., your whole body taut and poised.

He was particularly pleased with the balance sheet of The Group of Seven. He was proud of the baby he had stroked and nurtured to life. After several years, they held $2,800,000 outstanding in mortgage loans. Of that sum, $2.1 million was the bank's borrowed monies, $700,000 represented the shareholders' initial investment and profits realized over the years, ploughed back into the operation. TJ's monthly administration fee and funds received for bonuses and inducements were substantial and sizable. He had no intention of having anything encroach on his good fortune. Besides, he fancied that he was regarded with awe by the other shareholders.

In addition to being their lawyer and friend, he was their personal and confidential financial advisor. The majority of them were relying on him to move their outside investments. The trust placed in him and the confidence, never mind the possible financial rewards, were uplifting and satisfying moments in his life.

Thanks to a buoyant economy, the mortgage company had lost no monies since its inception. Substantial profits were reaped, in fact, with all of it reinvested into the Corporation. TJ knew that the surging economy had made him look better than he actually performed, but he also realized that he had considerable skill in the evaluation of mortgage loans. He could evaluate the borrowers, as well as their ability, and that of the capacity of the project to repay the mortgage indebtedness. Over the years, some loans had gone into default. Sales, refinancing, or straightening financial affairs ultimately resulted in no funds being lost and full interest monies always received from the borrowers. Unlike others in The Group, TJ had no queasy moments with the excessive rates and bonuses charged. He adopted the viewpoint that there was a law for the rich and one for the poor. The rich were easy to deal with. The poor were not his problem. He had no sympathy for the downtrodden, or those who were so desperate to borrow funds that they would pay whatever the price sought from an unscrupulous lender. The capitalist system predetermined what your choices would be. His had been made.

Reflections before a sand trap. He had been so busy reviewing the Mortgage Corporation process in his mind that he smashed the ball in the wrong direction.

The sand trap. He sauntered to the edge, taking off his shoes and socks and sliding into the hot white silt. He stood very still for a moment, savouring the feel of his unprotected skin against the sand. Then he remembered himself and his place. Looking for the errant ball, he covertly looked around to see if anyone was watching him. Presuming himself unseen on a flourishing golf course, he picked up the ball and carried it out of the trap.

Chapter Nine

TJ straightened his body in front of his bedroom mirror, drawing in his belly in order to evaluate his masterful look and handsome physique. He slid his fingers through his black wavy hair. It was greying like pepper over his ears, but he thought this a rather charming feature. Men always improved their looks with age. Theodore H. James had long been convinced that he was no exception. The notion that he might not be desirable to women never entered his mind. Too many women, frequent social and professional successes, and his wife's clever strokes kept his self-esteem in the bank, compounding with interest.

TJ fancied that he had a way about him. He was quick-witted, charming, suave, and held an influential stature amongst a wide circle of people. He believed that other lawyers were envious of him. His legal practice was wide; touching the ordinary citizen, to that of a high powered executive head of a major corporation. His work affected numerous corporations, and his efficient, pragmatic approaches garnered the unabated approval of his clientele.

A fine individual, he thought, gazing warmly at his mirrored reflection. Good-hearted, generous, forgiving and willing to overlook the shortcomings he saw so frequently in others. He was even fond of his wife on occasion. She was a prize, after all. His children were also fast becoming little citizens that he could be proud of.

A devoted father, too. What more could the world expect of him, TJ the magnificent? So what if he was a bit of a Lothario at times. Faithfulness was a rather dull state of consciousness. He knew that his wife dreaded his dalliances, for of course she adored him. A woman so hopelessly in love would forgive his sins easily. And he always came back.

He had a fine-looking receptionist, an accountant, and the loveliest stable of full-time secretaries that a successful man like himself could possibly want. Throw in a number of part-time employees and his office was a maelstrom of activity most days.

He wiped his hands together briskly. Mr. Success. The purveyor of a positive attitude at all times. Life was rosy, and when the flower looked a bit frayed, he would toss the old one out and pick another. Defeat was an insufferable concept to him. He was always upbeat and ready to flash a charming grin to just about anyone, whether he liked them or not.

He plucked his briefcase from the hall table and marched confidently out to his BMW. A man of means. King of all he surveyed, or so he had managed to convince Ali.

He slid in behind the wheel of the car and plopped his forehead against the wheel. Ali. The only diversion he had been unable to control. She had brought so much fun into his life and now it was over. His shoulders sagged as he allowed himself the best of his memories.

* * *

The office was always a zoo. Activity was like feeding time, with the lions roaring for their share. The employees were generally happy with their arrangement; some esprit de corps existed. TJ's infectious resilience affected everyone. The days passed quickly, but the pivotal point in his life, the moment of discontent, had begun and ended with Ali.

It seemed to him that it had all started with paper. He had needed an assistant, but not just any paper-pusher out of secretarial school. He wanted a legal assistant who could absorb the job by osmosis, and second-guess his next and necessary moves.

He had taken an instant liking to Ali, fencing with her during the interview. She had taken it well. All she had really had to do was just sit there. After he set eyes on her and listened to her silky voice, he couldn't have cared less whether she could walk and chew gum at the same time.

But she could.

"Miss York," he began formally, "I am what you might call a mortgage lawyer although that description is quite restrictive in terms of what I do. I engage in commercial, corporate and business proceedings, and I am involved in various corporate matters, real estate and conveyancing, mortgage preparation and foreclosure. I also manage and operate a Mortgage Corporation called the Group of Seven Corporation. Most of the loans in the Mortgage Corporation's portfolio for which I deal are rather mundane. Some mortgages are registered against houses, land, commercial buildings and the like. In terms of mortgage and loan approval, I rely generally upon appraisals prepared by an accredited appraiser, and then I determine the worth of the security in order to decide whether the loan will be granted or not. I am far too busy to actually view the security property. I know that I should, because I am vulnerable to faulty or exaggerated appraisals, but that's where you come in. You'll relieve my office presence requirements so that I can do the property inspections."

She had raised her lovely eyebrows at that one. Everything about her had been so statuesque, he had felt as though a portrait was coming to life before him.

"I understood that the job was secretarial, Mr. James. I'm perfectly willing to start at that level in order to learn your business."

"In fact, Ms. York, it's more than secretarial. I selected a short list of people from your classmates. Your grades impressed me."

"I was particularly good at actuarial mathematics and investments, Mr. James. Legal matters relating to real estate also interest me."

"I know I'm not supposed to ask the following questions, Miss York, but I'm afraid I'm still from the old school. Are you in a relationship right now that might lead to a more permanent commitment? Marriage, children?"

She had only looked amused. "No, Mr. James, you're not supposed to ask those questions." And without answering them directly, she responded: "My job will be my life. I'm ambitious. Clever, I think, and I have a great deal to offer."

Well-spoken. He had persisted. "A boyfriend?"

She had laughed then. A lovely rich giggle that had surprised him for its honesty and unfettered amusement at his prying.

"You can never tell what's around the corner, can you, Mr. James?"

He had returned her smile, and the moment was one of merger, of complete understanding of each other's intentions. Oh, he had been captivated, indeed.

"I think you'll be perfect for the position I had in mind, Miss York. It will be a combination of secretary, legal assistant, and junior accountant, I expect. Can you handle it?"

"Indeed I can, Mr. James." Her eyes had glittered strangely at that point. He had had no idea what that sparkle was all about.

"I've decided to offer you a bit more than the advertised salary."

She had only smiled knowingly.

* * *

Ali's memory faded into the whiteness of the paper before him.

A loan was generally approved by TJ where it represented a low advance and where a high interest mortgage rate could be secured. One of the prime considerations for granting a loan was if the borrower was prepared to pay a usurious interest rate, like three or four percentage points a month, and also willing to part with a substantial bonus or inducement fee. The monies upfront would be retained by TJ, separate and apart from the Corporation's monies. He was more apt to do a mortgage where the bonus or inducement fee was substantial, even if the interest rate was not as good as it might otherwise be, or if the security might not be considered prime.

The clear conflict of interest, not monitored nor checked by the other shareholders, was certainly known to TJ. He gave it barely a second thought. He trusted his own abilities and intuition, assuring himself that he needed to only answer to himself, not the other shareholders. What did concern him, however, was the legal requirement that an interest rate of 60% per annum, counting bonuses, inducements, and so forth, could not be exceeded. To seek an interest rate payment in excess of that amount was criminal and against the Interest Act of Canada.

The moral and ethical implications of what he was doing, or the monies charged and received, did not concern him at all. He just didn't want to spoil a good thing, or get dinged with a criminal sanction.

Most of his business came from mortgage brokers. Those vermin were calling him constantly with mortgage proposals. He had no use for most of them. They were entirely unscrupulous and prepared to sell their mother if the price was right. His own tenuous connection to ethical behaviour remained unevaluated in his mind. He passed judgment on people who could outmanoeuvre him in the dishonesty game. Still, a great deal of his practice, as well as the Mortgage Corporation's business, relied on vermin. TJ was polite and charming to all. He believed that others thought he was a wonderful human being.

One loan that really caught his fancy was the Lazy Valley Project, a large commercial enterprise involving an Amusement Park, pads for Motor and Mobile Homes, a Water Slide, Miniature Golf and a playground. The second phase of development was dedicated for the construction of multi-family and single-family dwelling units. TJ thought that the concept was brilliant. If the owners of the Project had wanted a partner, he would have sold all he had in order to be involved. As it was, they needed secondary financing, with the funds to be repaid at such time as the Project was completed. Long term financing, pre-arranged and in place, would then be drawn. There was a large first mortgage registered against the Project, on an interim basis. The owners required a second mortgage investment of $400,000. The Project, TJ believed, was excellent, and there was considerable equity of funds already in place. The long term financing had been pre-arranged in this case, and the principals of the Lazy Valley Project were exceedingly strong and creditworthy.

Furthermore, and equally important to the low advance, TJ was advised by the mortgage broker that there was a 10% bonus that the broker would share with the lender. He could hardly resist! The sweetener was one-half of 10% of the contemplated second mortgage advance of $400,000.

TJ examined all the information and documentation before he committed himself, because so much money was involved. The more he pondered, the more he became excited. His enthusiasm overflowed to the broker and the principals of the Project. They figured it was only a matter of time before TJ would issue a formal commitment and agreement to fund from The Group of Seven.

Their best instincts were correct, of course. The commitment letter appeared before long. The $400,000 second mortgage was approved, the paperwork stamped, and TJ had received an inducement of $20,000. The Group of Seven Mortgage Corporation had a second mortgage charge against the entire Lazy Valley Project. None of the other shareholders of the Mortgage Corporation had the remotest clue that The Group of Seven was involved in the Project.

* * *

TJ had installed a smoky mirror to line the wall behind his office bar. He could pour himself a congratulatory drink and admire the man before him. He was doing so remarkably well, he thought. Everything was hunky dory. A lot of money had been made for relatively little effort and grief. His partners, of course, believed that he worked a lot harder on the Mortgage Corporation loans than was actually the case. Whatever they chose to believe was fine by him. He was happy to allow them the notion that he was underpaid and overworked. Far better this delusion than the contrary. The less they knew, and the more misinformed by their own judgment, the happier was TJ.

His first alarm came around the first of one month, when the Lazy Valley Project second mortgage cheque was returned, dishonoured. A quick check with the first mortgage holder revealed similar default on that mortgage. He called the Project Manager immediately and was told that the guy was out, but then called one of the principals of the Project. This fellow was a millionaire, or so was the general belief among those in the know. In any case, he reassured TJ that there was just a slight glitch and temporary imbalance with payables. The money problem would soon be rectified.

Could he have a few days to remedy the problem? He assured TJ quite earnestly that both his mortgage corporation and the first mortgage holder would soon be in receipt of replacement funds. Sure enough, within three days, TJ received monies for the default. Another quick check with the first mortgage holder confirmed that their arrears had also been cleared. The Man offered TJ the explanation that the whole occurrence was just one of those 'shit happens' things. Not to worry.

The ease and speed with which the default was cured, and the relaxed attitude of the borrower, calmed TJ somewhat. He would be in a fine mess if the $400,000 loan crashed to default. The arrears would alter badly The Group of Seven's line of credit with the bank. No end of consternation or of fast-talking soliloquy would have much effect.

His sigh of relief had been audible to the then alive Ali, who was working just outside the inner sanctum.

"Anything wrong, TJ?"

"Nope, just cleared away another boulder."

Chapter Ten

The phone rang while Ali was getting coffee one morning. TJ had no choice but to answer it, and thanked whatever potent deities there were within earshot, that he had.

The call was from Bill Cooper, the lender in charge of the first mortgage on the Lazy Valley Project who, dispensing with platitudes, asked the leading question: "What are we going to do about the Lazy Valley Project?"

The pause was quite pregnant. "What do you mean," spluttered TJ. "everything seems alright with the development. They appear to be making acceptable progress and honouring their obligations."

"You've got to be kidding me," spat the voice on the wire, "we haven't received a payment now for two straight months, and if the default isn't dealt with soon, well, we were thinking about the possibility of a Receiver or something like that. Thought we'd first talk to you to find out what your position was. Guess you haven't got one, hey?"

God, he'd better have one. "I didn't know there was any default on the first mortgage loan, and why am I just being told about it now, why didn't someone tell me immediately when the default occurred?" He didn't like Cooper's attitude. He'd played enough golf with the guy to expect a little more deference.

"Sorry, TJ," replied Cooper, only a touch more politely. "Someone here must have forgotten to tell you, but no big deal. We've been riding this borrower regularly without any break. They are having almost insurmountable problems. Seems that they will be able to do nothing at all with the default. The lenders will have to deal with the problem. And I'm warning you, it doesn't look like it will get better, just worse."

"I'll get back to you on this," mumbled TJ, "just promise me not to move until I'm notified first. I'll need to investigate the situation."

In truth, he hadn't the vaguest idea what to do. The shock kept pulling him back into his chair. He had no idea how long he sat there, mulling the mess before him.

The Lazy Valley Boys had kept the second mortgage loan current, just to keep him off their backs, he guessed. They had obviously been in default with all other creditors, trades, you name it, not to mention the serious default with the huge first mortgage loan. He wasn't terribly concerned about the unpaid trades, because the Group of Seven mortgage had priority. The first mortgage was a major concern. If that default remained intact with interest accruing, it would not be long before the second mortgage was in serious trouble, and all equity in the Project eroded and extinguished. TJ knew he had an ugly problem on his hands. He had to move quickly, and even though his options were limited, his mind kept running on the treadmill.

Over and over.

What would be over would be his career. It was clear, from his conversations with the principals of Lazy Valley, that they were in dreadful financial trouble. They required a substantial infusion of cash, and that was not forthcoming. TJ pressed all of the principals and guarantors of the Project, urging them to pledges of certainty. What would they do when foreclosure proceedings were initiated and when they were all sued on their personal guarantees? All of them indicated that they would walk away from the Project. After all, their considerable funds had been expended. You can't get blood from a stone, so piss off, Mr. high-browed lawyer. Besides, all the personal guarantees were virtually worthless, as the guarantors were all overextended, broke, busted, penniless, judgment free, and just plain out of luck. Assets had been transferred long ago to wives, children, and great-aunt Alices, for immunity purposes. And if TJ wanted to take on Aunt Alice, well then, he could just do so. She'd scrapped with uglier lenders than him during the depression. Good Luck.

Aunt Alice not withstanding, TJ was prepared to make a decision on behalf of The Group of Seven. He advised all the principals of the Lazy Valley Project that he immediately required the provision of their financial statement materials. He advised them that he intended to compare what they were going to submit with what they had provided at the onset of the loan, and prior to its grant. The Lazy Valley Boys had no problem with TJ's request. Within several days, he had received a detailed breakdown that outlined the financial status of the Corporation and its four principals. It was the first moment in his life in which he wondered whether he would have a breakdown of his own.

* * *

TJ retreated in solitude to examine and evaluate carefully just what was going on with this Project. The exposure of The Group of Seven and their loan was uppermost in his mind, along with the consequences of the default and the havoc it would wreak on the Corporation's line of credit.

All the submitted materials were professional. Documents had been prepared by people who knew what they were doing, or at least had a good grasp of the situation. He examined the costs incurred, money expended, and the price of completion. There was no doubt in his mind that the Project had a tremendous upside.

He smelled tremendous profit potential. Insofar as concerned the four principals of the Lazy Valley Project, he carefully scrutinized the financial statements and other materials presented. All of these documents showed that, when the loan was approved originally by The Group of Seven, all investors had been creditworthy and substantial. If any of them had thought, by a fraudulent or improper conveyance to a wife, cousin, or even an Aunt Alice, that they might hide assets from The Group of Seven, TJ would find their livers and rip them out. He would take all steps available to set aside the fraudulent or improper conveyances, so that all assets might be returned to the point of original holding. The guarantors would then have to stand good for their guarantees with The Group of Seven.

Even Aunt Alice would be surprised.

TJ noted, however, that the financial statements given originally to the four principals were almost exactly the same as that originally provided at the time of the loan approval. One didn't have to be Einstein to know what now needed to be done that hadn't been done initially.

TJ ordered a search of various of the party's properties, especially the homes that he had believed the principals held in joint ownership with their wives. Most of the properties still had the same equity, as was the case previously. However, as originally unknown to him, all four houses were owned clear Title by the wives of the principals of the Project. James knew that he would not be able to advance against the principals on their guarantees to take advantage of the equity. The houses and various properties were all owned solely by the spouses or family members of the principals. No assets or property were registered in the name of any of the principals. In fact, even though their credit records were all impeccable and they were all so creditworthy they could make a TV banking commercial, they had nil assets to advance or support any judgment that The Group of Seven might secure with regard to the mortgage loan.

Proceedings taken by James against the four parties would, in all likelihood, result in four acutely embarrassed reputable businessmen being faced with the spectre of personal bankruptcy. Most of them, no doubt, would prefer to file for bankruptcy than to encroach upon assets owned by their wives or children. The personal guarantees, unfortunately, were not worth a coyote's carcass.

James had omitted to note, at first instance, that the financial statements that were submitted by the borrowers to secure the second mortgage loan, and which stipulated right at the top that the financial statements were true and correct to the best of the party's knowledge and belief, reflected assets and property held by the principal and their spouse. Nowhere was it written that the principals owned nothing and that their spouses, in turn, owned everything.

He had been sloppy. Maybe negligent was a better term. He could kick himself for his stupidity and failure to follow through and examine the statements more carefully. The error and negligence were a fait d'accompli: irreversible and uncorrectable.

TJ was embarrassed. He wouldn't want the other members of The Group to know about his bungling or the default. Even if that were not the case and the insurer was appointed, coverage would probably not be available. He had, after all, acted for himself. This reality alone could nullify his personal insurance coverage and quite likely that of the other members of The Group of Seven. There was nothing to show that he wouldn't have done the loan anyway, whether or not the principals of the borrower corporation were exceptionally strong and had assets. The Project would have stood by itself quite nicely, even had he attached relatively little weight to the personal guarantees. He had believed that default would not likely transpire; the fact that the individual guarantors held substantial worth had been a bonus, and the loan would probably have been approved regardless.

TJ was in a quandary. He liked difficult problems and eagerly accepted challenges, but this was one mess that he would have avoided gladly. He didn't want to deal with it. Time was not in his favour; he had no immediate alternative but to deal with the difficulty. He began to scribble the available alternatives on his worksheet:

1. call a meeting and advise the other shareholders of the precarious situation with the Mortgage Corporation, their loan, his error, ad nauseam. Can't do that. No way. It's best that they remain in the dark. When the matter is resolved, I'll let them know. They can't be of any use at all in a time of crisis. Advice from them is worse than useless. Get on with the job.

2. call the bank and let the manager know of the loan's default. Buy time. Don't tell them anything bad. Obligations? Forget 'em. At least until another alternative is found. Put the bank in the dark with the rest of them. Bank officials snooping about will be injurious to the Mortgage Corporation. Bound to cause skittishness amongst the shareholders. Line of credit might even be pared dramatically. Further cash infusion might become necessary.

3. call first mortgagee (good plan!) have them hold all foreclosure proceedings in abeyance on the understanding that help is on the way. Solutions in hand shortly. First mortgagee to be advised that the second mortgagee shall ensure that their position does not deteriorate. How? Best interests of all concerned that the first mortgagee not advance foreclosure. Don't panic. Rely upon The Group of Seven to extricate both lenders from the financial mess, to reduce and mitigate against exposure. Cavalry on the way.

TJ decided to chat with Cooper again, assuring him that matters were fine and that their equity would be increased without the resulting deterioration of the Project. Cooper was tickled and agreed to sit back and relax so long as TJ kept him apprised of all happenings, and as long as TJ was taking steps to rectify the default and clean up the mess.

The first mortgagee had no desire to assume responsibility for the Project, or to transfer the loan to permanent non-performing status. Cooper was hopeful and optimistic that a payment in full would happen quite shortly.

More notes

4. initiate foreclosure proceedings against the Project. Sue the four principals on their personal guarantees. Ultimate result: judgments (of dubious value) against four parties. Ownership of the Project by The Group of Seven, subject to the huge first mortgage loan. Problem: who wants to assume responsibility for the Project, first mortgage? Implications are ugly. First mortgage payments relentless, the need to infuse fresh capital in order to advance Project to completion. Oversee trades, attend to payment... yuk. Too much. Scary. Same feeling shared by principals of the Project.

5. strike deal with same principals. Take a Quit Claim of their interest as against the Project in return for a release being granted and no action taken on personal guarantees. Advantage: avoidance of the requirement and need for foreclosure proceedings. Disadvantage: waiver of all rights as against the principals pursuant to their guarantees. Costs & hassles associated with the foreclosure probably overweighing the worth of the guarantees. Bottom line: The Group of Seven would become the owner of the Project, and would have to move it along to completion, bearing all the hurdles.

6. secure the Quit Claim in return for Releases. Different catch would be that The Group of Seven would not be the owner. New party would be found, maybe a bona fide purchaser for value, to assume the first and second mortgages, complete the Project, keep the mortgages in good standing, and reap the profits associated with Project completion.

TJ was certain that there would be as much as one million dollars profit on the table for such a purchaser. The trick was to find that person and to do it within the restricting time constraints.

Chapter Eleven

He knew exactly what he was going to do. How to go about it was another matter entirely. Deciding not to tell the other shareholders and partners in The Group of Seven was easy. He hadn't considered them for more than a few wasted seconds. The next hurdle, however, was the bank.

Strong monthly reporting statements were essential for satisfying the bank, and to preserve a healthy line of credit for monies borrowed to the Mortgage Corporation. TJ clenched his teeth and began to smile, not unlike the grin of a cornered coyote. He plucked the phone from the cradle, mentally preparing to execute The Plan:

"Mr. Denison, please. Tell him it's TJ."

An unusually long pause, thought TJ. Didn't bode well. Telephone etiquette, or lack of it, was a tool worth mastering. After a horribly long wait, TJ heard a welcome voice:

"TJ, how's the game?"

"They're all going well at the moment, Den." He chuckled that particularly macho chuckle between men. It was a bonding thing.

"Cleared that nasty score of 80 yet?"

"No, I seem to be riding the plateau at about 95. But I don't like my chances of hitting better than 90 this year."

Bullshit, garbage, let's get on with it.

"Say, Den, you know how well the Mortgage Corporation is doing."

"No, but you're going to tell me. Hopefully it's better than your golf game."

Needling from the head buck. He would play along. Locking horns would come later.

Another macho chuckle, just to show there was no offense taken.

"You better believe it, Den. The returns to The Group of Seven and the shareholders are nothing short of phenomenal. But, Den, I thought I'd call and let you know that there may not be monthly payments made to the Mortgage Corporation on the Lazy Valley loan for several months. They've made a request that, in return for a further bonus," bullshit baffles brains, he thought viciously, "we allow them a couple of months to use the mortgage payment funds so that the Project might be completed even sooner. Don't worry about anything. The Project is going to be completed for sure, and the second mortgage loan indebtedness is secured. You know old Bill Cooper? Well, he represents the first mortgagee. That group will not require mortgage payments on the first charge, and they'll hold matters in abeyance until the owners deal with and complete the Project. When it's all done, they'll proceed with sales. It's clear to me that there will be more than enough to pay off both mortgage loans with lots left over for the owners."

He had spoken at length: too long, with no audible response from the banker. When in doubt, keep talking.

"The excellent equity position, the strength of the Project, its principals, bonuses, blah, blah, blah, need I say more? Well, our Corporation has no problem at all with the request and the accrual of interest owned. I need your approval with that scenario. I want you to say that you can live with limbo on the payments for awhile, on the understanding that I have made a deal with the project owners so that they can proceed to completion and sale.

He was beginning to beg at this point.

"I just wanted to let you know why no payments will be reflected on the monthly reporting statement for the next couple of months. I'm sure the bank will have no problem with it, and things will tick right along nicely."

An uncomfortable lull was heard on the opposite end. TJ mused for a moment, thinking that the great flaw in the invention of the telephone was the inability to watch body language in the verbal duel. You had to know what the enemy was doing with their strengths. He had no idea on this one.

Denison responded finally. "That should be no problem at all, and if it is, I'll let you know." His voice was tight, lower. "Please keep the bank apprised and notified as to the status of the Project, and when you believe you will receive full payment for the loan, or alternatively, when you will require the Project to resume payments to The Group of Seven." The sudden change in diction alerted TJ to Denison's unstated attitude. No more golf talk, no more banter. All business, thank you.

TJ signed off pleasantly. The line of credit with the bank would not be reduced for The Group of Seven. He anticipated no difficulty with the bank, and

The Group of Seven shareholders would not be made aware of the problems. For all appearances, the first mortgagee was happy to do nothing and just sit back. The Group of Seven banker was prepared not to receive mortgage payments and TJ, well... He could proceed to plan A.

He had the word of the first mortgage holder agreeing not to further proceedings so long as The Group of Seven was attempting to resolve the default. He had also examined all the contingencies and alternatives quite thoroughly and deliberately. His action was quite clear. It was the same one he'd had in mind when he learned of the initial default by the Lazy Valley Group. The only unresolved issue in his mind loomed large. How was he going to do it? No matter. Decision made. He wouldn't be stopped, regardless of the consequences. Still, rhetoric and resolve were one thing. Action and implementation were quite another.

TJ leaned back in his great chair again, rubbing his brow. His smoky mirror caught the gesture and he stopped, catching himself.

He shut his eyes, wondering where it all had gone wrong. At one time, he had wished and wanted with all he had, to be a lawyer. The trophies of his success lined his office, decorated his home, adorned his wife and children.

He had tried hunting once. It was the sport of some of his colleagues, and he had found those associations useful. He had the head of a five-point mule deer buck on his office wall, a prize cock pheasant with a 24-bar tail, a trophy moose head at home, and a plush black bear skin to warm his feet.

He had stopped hunting when the trophies had come too easily after awhile. Once the desire was achieved, he couldn't figure out why it had been so all-consuming. Something quite fundamental was missing from the formula.

He no longer liked being a lawyer. Some of the work was interesting, to be sure. The rewards were reasonable, but the prestige associated with the position had waned over the years. Now it was minimal. There no longer existed a clear line between them and us, the privileged few and the marginalized everybodies. Women had infiltrated the Old Boy's system. He didn't really mind them, in their place, of course. He had always made it abundantly clear, however, that no legal ladies would challenge his world.

Lawyers had become abundant in Calgary. Clichéd. A dime a dozen. The work was shrinking due to recessionary times, and the plethora of solicitors willing to do anything for a buck were on the rise. The fees decreased dramatically while the costs increased.

No doubt most people would have been pleased, even overjoyed, to take home the monthly salary that TJ enjoyed. The only problem was that TJ didn't really enjoy it. He didn't think it that much, really, considering his perception of his own worth and the tremendous hours and effort he expended. He often looked at less talented people, clients for instance, who made far more money with considerably less effort. He was always working, thinking, going and doing, and for what? So many of his friends and clients had more free time, less responsibility and earned far more while enjoying a happier lifestyle.

Opportunities to make a substantial sum came far too infrequently. TJ could smell money from ninety paces, and he could see clearly that there was at least a million dollars or more at stake in this Project; it would be available to the person who had the moxy and guts to grab the proverbial bull by the horns. The trophy would be the Lazy Valley Project, its completion and sale. He knew the trophy was his, if only...

He would get that Project, make the money. He would save the second mortgage loan for The Group of Seven. He would make enough money from the Project so that he would be free, able to do what he wanted, no longer a slave to the law or its constraining practice.

It certainly hadn't seemed that way at first, but the easiest part had been making the decision to assume the responsibility of the Project to its completion and sale. The difficult part would come later. How would the Project be done? Who would pay the trades? When would everything be ready for sale? The sole barring issue and question was, of course, where would the money come from?

He pulled the papers out of his desk and began to review the figures again. Documentation, materials, paper, cost projections. He estimated that approximately $600-750,000 should be required to complete the Project. Upon expenditure, the sales could occur and expended funds recouped.

Where to find a banker? He couldn't very well go to his own. That banker was retained by The Group of Seven. The mere mention of his involvement in the Project, never mind a loan application, well... it would be catastrophic. He really could not go to another banker or lender for funding. Too many questions would be asked. Alerts would be out as to his involvement and the default of the first and second mortgages. The usual safe routes were impossible to consider.

So where would he get it?

He got up to pace. Thinking came better on his feet.

Aggression. Fight or flight.

He seized the telephone and began to make the calls that would alter his fate. TJ heard an echo from some Shakespeare he'd learned in school: Henry V, he thought, and couldn't shake the notion that he, like Henry, was preparing for battle: "once more unto the breach, dear friends."

* * *

He concluded the deal with the principals of the Lazy Valley Project, accepting a Quit Claim from them and a transfer of their interest in the Project in favour of his own Corporation. Mutual Releases were exchanged. The Midas Corporation was now the sole owner of the Lazy Valley Project, subject to the first and second mortgages. The Group of Seven had no further rights against the principals of the Project. The four principals were of course relieved to get their releases in exchange for the transfer and divestment of their interests in the Project. They assumed that TJ was acting as solicitor on behalf of an undisclosed principal. No one guessed that TJ was stroking TJ. Had they known, they would simply have looked the other way.

He sat placidly in his great chair now, his hands clasped, rubbing his lips. If he cleaned out his Retirement Savings Plans and those of Suzie's, maybe if he took another mortgage on their house... yanked their savings, odds and sods of other available funds, well, he just might come up with about $200,000. It didn't even come close to what he would need to complete the Project. Two hundred grand would get things going, though, and he had a good idea where he could get the rest of it. All available surplus funds would be committed and allocated to the Project.

When it's scary, don't look down. He couldn't afford to. He might fall. Most of the tradespeople assumed that James was acting on behalf of a client. There was no reason why they should believe otherwise. No reason at all.

Chapter Twelve

TJ was terribly frazzled: his pace was frenetic. It was impossible to juggle as much as he did, to maintain a busy practice, some semblance of a family life, and to devote his whole-hearted efforts to the Project and its speedy completion. That particular list of jobs would have been manageable, except for the glaring fact that he was running desperately short of money. The trades, suppliers, and creditors were unbelievably bothersome.

The time had come for action. He attempted to relax, but his head was full of details and dollar signs.

TJ surveyed his wife from across their back yard. She was clipping some sweet peas, releasing a pleasurable aroma from the flowers; a scent he enjoyed almost enough to deter him from his intended course of action.

He permitted a fondness to enter his voice. "Suzie, would you please call your parents to see if they will loan me some money for a project of mine? The interest is terrific. Maybe they would rather be involved on a profit-sharing basis. Tell them I know that things haven't gone all that well, business-wise, in the past, but I would like to make amends. It's a wonderful venture and they can double their money in no time. Tell them how important it is to me, and to us, of course, and that I'll be in a real tough position if they can't help out."

She didn't turn to look at him, allowing the rigidity of her back to speak what she would not say. She paused in her snipping until he'd finished his lines, then resumed cutting, just a bit more viciously.

The voice that returned to him sounded like sweet peas gone bad in water.

"How much money were you thinking about, honey?," countered the false sugary sound.

"I would think that somewhere in the range of $150,000 would be ample. If that's too much, I might be able to scrape by with a little less. Maybe something in the range of $125,000, or possibly even $100,000".

"I won't call them tonight, dear."

A pause.

His teeth clenched. He knew the pause was calculated, but the power was hers. How he hated that!

"If the matter is so important and sensitive, then of course, I'll meet with mom and daddy tomorrow. We have to look over some things that they wanted me to check for them. I'll raise the matter at that time."

Another pause.

He waited expectantly.

She still refused to look at him. "I will push gently for it, TJ, but I don't think they are interested in loaning you any more money, or to be involved in any more of your deals. They've lost too much money in the past. I'll tell them how important it is to you, of course. I will even tell them it's important to me.

That ought to make some difference." Her tone was unmistakable: a 'don't mess with me, babe.'

He swallowed his irritation. "I knew you would do your best, honey. It's very important to us, of course. Without the money, quite frankly we'll be in a real bind." He shifted his weight in the lawn chair and waited for the move of fear from her that he knew would come.

It did. She looked at him straight in the eye, stopping her scissor-cuts in order to evaluate his veiled threat. He refused to return her gaze. He didn't need to. She knew well enough that her future was tied inevitably to his; her survival hinged upon the almighty dollar, a fact of which he reminded her constantly.

* * *

The Smiths had realized their sweetest moment with their son-in-law. It was their distinct and un-equalled pleasure to categorically and unequivocally reject Suzie's request for money. Any possibility of their participation and investment in another one of their son-in-law's cockamamie schemes was perfectly ridiculous. They didn't trust him, didn't like him, and he was unreliable. Even if the venture were successful, they would achieve little more than the return of their invested funds with a bit of extra. The inevitable stu-pid explanation of why their share was not greater would also accompany a disappointingly small return. If the venture were a bust, as it was likely to be, TJ would get all his money back, and they would surely lose their shirts.

They shared none of this with their daughter whom, they were beginning to believe, was not as na-ive as they had supposed. She had been different lately. A sunny glow adorned her features in a way they had not seen on her in years. They didn't suppose it had anything to do with TJ. The glow was difficult to identify, but it evoked a different tone from them as they gave her the bad news.

"We can't encroach on our savings, luv," said her father. "As much as we want to, we depend upon all of it and the interest earned on the principal to provide us with a reasonable living income."

She caught the tact, of course. Suzie was embarrassed to have put them in this position. She knew their feelings about TJ; shared them in fact, so she didn't push hard. She knew they loved her and their grandchildren unreservedly.

The truth of the matter was that they were beginning to suspect that they would have to come to her financial rescue before much longer. They had made a pact to be there for her when that time came.

As for TJ, well, he could rot.

He was livid when Suzie relayed the news. Her back was turned to him as the words were emitted. That habit of hers was beginning to make him crazy, and all he could do was shout at her.

"Look at me, dammit!"

She whirled unexpectedly, meeting his attack. "Don't you dare bully me! My parents have given you money for years, just so you could piss it all away." Her voice lowered now to a hiss. "Naturally they loved everything about the venture. They wanted desperately to be involved, but they just didn't have the capital. I was the one who told them not to take a chance. What they have left of their savings will be theirs. And mine."

He was taken aback by her vehemence. He had never seen it before. Never knew she had it in her.

Where had he gone wrong? What had he failed to give her? He had thought their relationship was secure, never dreaming that any imbalance existed. And she, she had told them not to give him anything? He was astounded.

Her eyes narrowed at him, like a cat ready to claw. He retreated, if for no other reason than the fact that his in-laws needed no further discouragement from supporting him. TJ knew that the Smiths would rather have had their fingernails ripped out than give him anything.

When the initial shock subsided, he was beside himself with desperation and rage. The refusal was not unexpected, but the very idea that Suzie had defied him, had flown in his face... the reality was unbearable. Whatever had happened to that feckless, insipid female he had married? She would have been the only one who could have saved his hide, and now what? He wanted to punch her, and didn't know why he stopped himself.

Suzie ran out of the room, and TJ watched himself in the hall mirror, rubbing his brow again and thinking. He was juggling far too much, attempting to do what felt like a million things at once. The Lazy Valley Project was only sputtering along with minimal funds; it was in grave danger of stalling. The trades and creditors hounded his office relentlessly, demanding to speak directly with the individual behind the Project. TJ was reminded of Sisyphus, the god condemned eternally to roll a block of stone to the top of a steep hill, where it rolled inevitably down to the bottom again. He felt now that he might not reach the top of the hill, or even descend on the other side. The massive stone might well turn and crush him. The angle to the tale that TJ had forgotten was the part about condemnation. Sisyphus had been guilty of fraudulence and avarice. The gods had condemned him for it.

TJ didn't believe in gods. He was his own master, and while he had never before capitulated to despair, he would have been a fool not to know that things were collapsing around him. All would surely be lost unless something positive could happen.

The trades and creditors were one problem. The bank was another. Denison was wondering, loudly and regularly at that, what was happening and when the mortgage payments might be resumed. Maybe even payment in full? No more platitudes about the golf game. Denison was calling him James, now, forget the TJ bit. TJ's advice was no longer accepted by the bank. Further and full particulars were being demanded, along with demands for an infusion of capital from The Group of Seven shareholders in order to maintain the existing credit line.

In other words, get your act together, TJ. The bank was not receiving any answers. Written advice of its concerns, requirements and demands were sent to TJ's office, and most annoying of all, with a copy sent to each of The Group of Seven's shareholders. Not only did TJ have to placate trades, creditors, the bank, you name it, but now he was also deluged with calls of concern from each of the shareholders. This angle to the game had never before happened. He was able to dispel most of their concerns and queries, but there was an air of uncertainty that now dogged his relationship with them. They no longer accepted his statements and advice without reservation.

To make matters worse, if that were possible,

relentless pressure was now being applied by the first mortgagee. TJ was feeling the heat on all flanks, and being advised that continued nonpayment and non-advancement of the Project would result in foreclosure proceedings. If he didn't come through, and quickly, the first mortgagee would foreclose and the second mortgage charge held by The Group of Seven would be struck from title. Ownership would be vested there-after, solely in the name of the first mortgagee, and The Group of Seven would be left to freeze in the cold.

Things were far from tidy at the office, as well. His credit line was maxed-out. Pushing the ceiling. The bank was extra cautious with him and his credit facility, given the ongoings with The Group of Seven Mortgage Corporation. His practice and cash flow were being cut and hurt, in that TJ was not devoting enough time to his legal affairs. The bulwark of his efforts and time were committed and diverted to the Project and all the garbage arising from that mess.

He was fast approaching a saturation point. He had no one to turn to. He had canvassed all his friends and solicited all the gullible parties that he could think of, to no avail. It crossed his mind to visit a solicitor or Bankruptcy Trustee to discuss his affairs, in the strictest of confidence, of course. Maybe it was the only way out.

No, dammit, he was a fighter. No bankruptcy was going to be declared, not while he was still in charge, just to rescue a $400,000 second mortgage loan on behalf of The Group of Seven Mortgage Corporation. Even if the rescue would save his own personal ass.

Maybe there was another way. A way he didn't like, to be sure, but the transaction would be quick and clean.

* * *

Mom had kept herself rather well. TJ was surprised at the respect and tempered warmth of her greeting. Communication between them had been infrequent, and he had not bothered to visit. He'd been far too busy to come to his father's funeral and he had expected his mother to understand that. He knew that by dint of hard work and scrimping and saving, she was quite well off. Maybe even wealthy, if his dad's pension had been substantial. Her meagre surroundings and frugal lifestyle attested to the fact that any wealth had not been frittered away, but increased substantially. The wealth would be his of course, some day. He was an only child. Why not now?

He made small talk, admiring her flowers and wallpaper. She was gracious, and could have been far harder on him. As it was, she asked him a lot of questions.

"How have you been keeping, Ted? It's been so long. I know you're busy, but mothers worry. Why not bring the children over? I'd love to see them."

All the questions he had wanted to avoid. It was hard to ignore your mother and then come asking for money. She was not part of his existence, really. How could he explain?

"Umm, they're in school a lot, mom. Piano lessons. Suzie's part of the parent-teacher association. You know, busy, busy."

"Yes, I remember, Ted." It was all she had to say. What was it about mothers that could rip the guilt up from your gut and make you chew it thoroughly?

He hung his head, feeling again like the little boy in the schoolyard. The one with the funny clothes and running shoes that hadn't quite contained his feet.

She noticed his abjection, and smiled.

He didn't return the smile. Instead, heaving a sigh, he began to sketch briefly the business opportunity in the Project. The proposition positively glowed when he was through.

"Could you see your way clear, mom, to loan me some money? I need to repay some contracts. I could promise that the money will be protected and returned with profit." He watched her face pleadingly. Her love for him was obvious in the searching look she returned him. The desperation in his voice was quite believable as well. He knew that there was no way she could deny him what he needed.

He watched her open her mouth a few times and shut it again, searching for the right words.

"Ted, my only dear son, I will not give or loan you as much as one cent, and you can be assured that you will never, ever, see one dollar of my money, if it's the last thing I do. You may not know it, in fact I'm sure you don't, but that blessed wife of yours, Suzie... God knows what she sees in you, has brought your children, my grandchildren, Ted..." her voice had risen to a powerful pitch, "to see me on a regular basis. They visit, boy, and I know them. You I do not know. I brought you into this world, but I should have taken you out of it before you could do any real damage. My money you will never see. It will all go to your children, Ted, in trust for their exclusive use, only after you are safely out of their lives."

Her voice lowered to a raspy whisper then. "You are a bad seed. You will have to rely on your own demented wit to get you out of the mess you have created."

Chapter Thirteen

What was with these hysterical women all of a sudden? Suzie, Mom, who next? The whole business was simply not to be endured. Where could a guy go to get some security in life if not to his wife. Surely his mother?

He could feel the treadmill speeding up.

There had to be another way. Had to be, had to be. He admired himself in the smoky mirror again, swilling back some well-aged scotch just to get his thinking going.

It was just remarkable how things came to him when he was desperate. That quick, agile mind rescued him yet again.

Of course the decision to embezzle old Mr. Jensen's account was not really intentional. TJ held so many accounts, and stealing from them never crossed his mind. Until now. And was it really stealing? Would old Jensen really miss it? The temptation to take those funds was wonderfully compelling and he was surprisingly calm about it. He wasn't overly pleased about being in this desperate position. He felt somewhat embarrassed, and maybe just a little furtive, but didn't the end justify the means? When it was all over, only TJ would know what had been done. He would cover his tracks well, of course. It would be so easy to pull off.

Jensen's account was worth $100,000, and it was quite dormant. The old farmer had sold some property several years ago, and for some reason, had let the net proceeds remain in TJ's trust account to earn interest. TJ had never received instructions to transfer the funds to Jensen's bank. The old guy was really quite ancient, and TJ had expected to deal with the funds as part of an estate. There was no harm in letting the monies remain in trust. The old coot had not contacted TJ in a long time, so he thought he could probably use the money as he wished. No one would be any the wiser when the funds were returned. It was just too bad that Jensen did not have more money. If there had been enough, TJ could just rely on one lender to complete the Project.

TJ knew he had to be extremely cautious. He could only use money from places where it wouldn't be missed. He had to be able to return them without garnering any suspicion. He was confident that there would not be a difficulty with targeting the right client base and funds, but he also knew that there was just one more thing he had to do to ensure that the plan worked to perfection.

Ali. Time for her to show her stuff.

* * *

Mrs. Smidge had worked for TJ a long time: ten years or so. She would have buttered his bread and cut his meat for him, or so TJ thought. He relied tremendously upon her to keep his bookkeeping and financial records straight. He knew he'd be lost without her. His accounting department, as it was, would crumble in her absence. In fact, he was hoping for that very thing.

Mrs. Smidge knew too much about everything; she would realize immediately what was up. He would get no sympathy or assistance from her. He knew he had no other options but to get rid of her. Friday afternoon at 5:00 would be Smidge's last moment with his firm.

She didn't even protest. She was just crestfallen, deflated, her tears about to drop on his desk. Well, he couldn't just fire her without some sort of package. She had, after all, given him some good years.

"Now, now, Mrs. Smidge, this has nothing whatsoever to do with your ability or loyalty. Business is down dramatically."

She just stared at him, unable to respond. He tried another tack.

"And actually, Mrs. Smidge, my personal life is taking a terrible beating. Everything is so fouled up for me…" He let his despair reach her. "I am not sure when I will be able to get things back on course. My legal business will have to slide a bit, I think."

It worked. He noticed a turn of sympathy in her eyes.

He tried to affirm that loyalty. "I really have no choice but to pare things down, Mrs. Smidge. You have been absolutely wonderful. I so regret having to do this." He made himself sound sincere.

"I'm giving you an excellent letter of recommendation and a substantial severance package to help you out. If you ever need anything, do not hesitate to call me. I'll give you a wonderful endorsement. Any enquiries from a new prospective employer, well, they just won't be able to shut me up." He was beginning to sound silly now, but the deed was done.

* * *

TJ was quite pleased with himself. His little unpleasant chore had not been as difficult as he had imagined. Of course, he had no choice but to get rid of her. Anyway, she could be quite bossy and overbearing sometimes, not to mention her occasionally rude behaviour to some of his clients. He really wouldn't miss her that much. Funny how you could come up with all sorts of useful reasons to rationalize behaviour when necessary. It was especially easy to do so with someone whom you had just fired.

He would miss the accounting skills, though. If he waited an appropriate amount of time, anyone who stepped in would have a great deal to clean up. Any muddle would go unnoticed.

He knew exactly who to get. Someone who was capable and did precisely what she was told to do, no questions, no funny looks. Intelligent, obedient, pleasant and not too experienced. Ali York was perfect.

The Project was stealing large chunks of his time, occupying every facet of his life. He barely had time for the rest of his practice. Clients were becoming increasingly disenchanted as they wanted their demands met immediately and consequently cash flow from his practice was dwindling. The financial demands of the Project were even more consuming than what he had supposed it would be. TJ realized that he had no alternative but to secure more funds, not only for the Project, but also for his own living and office expenses. He was confident that he would be able to repay everything when the construction and sale of the Project were complete. He also entertained his private thoughts with speculation on all the profit. He knew that he had to spend most of his time on the Project. His para-legal staff would have to attend to the demands of his unhappy clients.

The bank roll would be in place because of his daring and fearless action concerning the Project. TJ was not unhappy with his course of conduct, and the game and its stimulation was rewarding in itself.

Money, money, 'k-ching, k-ching'. He could see it, hear it, almost smell it, but he couldn't put his hands on it easily. Or could he? Surely there was more than one old Jensen. The trick was simple. TJ truly thought of himself as a kind of wizard. Funds could be taken from accounts and places where it would not be missed, and where replacement could occur at a later date. No one would know. It was all so simple. He proceeded to withdraw funds from all sorts of accounts and wondered why more trust breaches didn't happen. Well probably they did, and no one ever found out.

His other action concerned Suzie. He kept original Wills, General Powers of Attorney, and Enduring Powers of Attorney in his office vault. Luckily, he also came upon an unexecuted blank Transfer of Land which had been signed previously by Suzie. He thought he might have retained it when he transferred his interest in their home to her in the early days of their marriage. That sort of exchange was done all the time. He could be judgment proof and the house, if nothing else, would be in his wife's name. In case any creditors took a fancy to going after him, he would still have a roof over his head.

He took the piece of paper as a good omen; one that encouraged him to pull off what he had planned. He claimed the original Power of Attorney documentation as drawn by his in-laws subsequent to his marriage. Suzie had been named her parents' attorney for all lawful and unrestricted proceedings. He could execute a title of land without even involving Suzie. He had his real estate paralegal complete the transfer, wherein Doug and Mavis Smith transferred their residential property by their attorney and daughter, Suzie, in her favour, and with Suzie's transfer of land, from her to Theodore H. James, Solicitor.

Once TITLE to his in-laws' house was registered in his name, it was an easy matter for him to place a mortgage against their property for $175,000. Suzies' folks were none the wiser, of course. TJ would make the mortgage payments on the loan from his office until such time as he could get around to its repayment from the Project proceeds. He chuckled when he imagined his father-in-law's possible reaction to the shenanigans. Doug Smith would blow a gasket, and then promptly blow a hole in TJ's head. But the old busybody would never know.

TJ's next move was to call four mortgage brokers to arrange for $100,000 first mortgage loans against four separate properties. He advised them that it had to be an excellent rate, he was personally vouching for the safety of the mortgages, that all were first charges against properties, and the total advance would be less than 50% of the appraisal value. It had been so easy to pull off. Not surprisingly, each broker shortly reported back to him that it was a done deal, and the individuals who were providing their funding had given instructions to solicitors, so that mortgage documentation might be prepared and submitted for execution, registration and funding. TJ knew the four lawyers who acted for the four different lenders. He contacted each of the lawyers and gave them the same shpiel about the safety of the loan and its low advance. He told them that his client was buying the property in question, and would be using the mortgage funds to complete title acquisition.

TJ knew that when the solicitors for the mortgagee looked at the title and noted that it was not in his client's name, they would assume that the client was buying the property. The mortgage, therefore, would be registered against the property taken, and would represent a first mortgage charge with a substantial equity cushion.

He would be ever so grateful if the funds would simply be provided to him on the trust condition and requirement that appropriate title documentation could be issued in the immediate future. All of the lawyers acting for their funders were only too pleased to oblige TJ. They knew him, respected his ability, and all were quite confident that nothing could possibly go wrong with such an established and respected practitioner.

Each of them forwarded the would-be mortgage monies surprisingly easily. Not one of them even questioned him. They acted on the trust that he provide TITLE documentation as soon as it became available, within a reasonable time period, of course. The understanding was that insurance and post-dated cheque documentation would be provided immediately before the release of funds. TJ had no difficulty with the provision of post-dated cheques and insurance. The mortgage brokers were paid from the advance, and the remainder of the funds were utilized for his purposes. He was hopeful that he wouldn't need to swing any more deals until he was in a position to have the Project completed. He could then begin to repay all the borrowed and stolen money.

Chapter Fourteen

Ali was like a sponge. The more work he gave her, the better she coped with it all. She was truly the best thing that had ever happened to him. It was almost as though she needed the extra load in order to feel good about herself. He knew that he would have to be extremely careful with all the accounting, otherwise, she might well realize that something was amiss; she was just bright enough to do so. She might not even accept his explanation for doing things in a certain fashion.

All things considered, she made his life tremendously easier. Things were awfully hectic, but orderly enough. It was that order and planning he wanted, in order to make his life seem controlled in the teeth of chaos.

The Project sucked more money than he dreamed possible, but it was nearing finalization. TJ felt that he had done a good job. Superb, you might say. He had dealt expertly with the trades and creditors. He had managed to assuage the concerns of his clients, all the while siphoning money from dormant trust accounts.

Of course he knew that he was treading a wide

road that some people called Wrong. His actions were unethical and entirely unlawful. But so what? The end justified the means.

Strange, thought TJ, that everyone would be so happy to see a lawyer get hammered and punished beyond requirement or reason. People were always more concerned with the punishment given a lawyer than the redress and compensation offered or given to the injured party. He figured that this aspect of human nature went a long way to explaining why stoning was still an accepted form of penalty in some cultures.

The Lazy Valley Project was almost complete, but it would be awhile before the subdivision would be at a stage where sales could commence and money received to pay the numerous outstanding obligations. Although TJ could see the light at the end of the tunnel, he had to get there in one piece. That might be difficult. Oh, he was sure it was all downhill, of course. He only had to placate the parties that were clamouring for payment until funds were available and in hand.

The problems were crazy, but the worst of it was the other six parties in The Group of Seven and their incessant complaining. The telephone calls and demands for meetings to deal with the loan were a chronic source of irritation. The guys at the bank were not terribly concerned about their position from an enforcement viewpoint, but people get into a mob scene without knowing why. The bank was making demands on all the Shareholders of The Group of Seven, stipulating that each of them had to inject funds into the Corporation, payable to the bank, in order that the credit arrangement and facility might be stabilized. TJ had advised them that they need not be worried, that the bank was only flexing financial muscles. The whining was positively not to be endured. 'We're worried,' snarled one partner, 'we're not used to receiving threatening letters from any credit institution. Satisfy the bank, appease them. We've always enjoyed smooth sailing. We don't know what it's like to be burdened with financial difficulties and demands. Fix it, TJ." They vented their frustration and hostility on him all too frequently. Peasants. There was no other word for the lot of them.

It was clear to TJ that the bank would not initiate legal proceedings against The Group of Seven or the shareholders. The bank felt that it was well secured and that all of the shareholders, with the possible exception of himself, were financially strong. There was little doubt in the minds of the players at the bank that payment would be received eventually. Any of the six shareholders, excepting TJ, could probably write a cheque right now, or at least make arrangements to deal with the indebtedness, without even breathing heavily.

What TJ did not know was that the bank had made an inspection of the Lazy Valley Project in its capacity as lender to the second mortgagee. Consultations had been made with the holder of the first mortgage and a bank representative. These guys were pleasantly surprised to note the near completion of the Project and its readiness for sale. The new owner had done a remarkable job, to be sure. The equity position of both the first and second mortgages was secure. There was little doubt that the Project was viable. Abundant sale proceeds were expected to discharge both mortgages, with a substantial surplus anticipated. All things considered, the bank was not terribly unhappy with the second mortgage loan or the creditworthiness of most of the principals of The Group of Seven. Demand letters and menacing correspondence continued to be submitted, simply because no suitable war would be quite the same without these trappings. Besides, those actions were the business of the bank. It was kind of like the snarling of a hungry coyote, teeth bared. Don't trifle here, bub. The Group of Seven Corporation was definitely in default, and if one cared about the future, one took care of defaults. They were messy. The guys at the bank took counsel that advised them to toss correspondence back and forth on occasion. It was hard to get into the game unless you could demonstrate the ability to manage the ball. It was dangerous to imply that the default or the conduct of The Group could be condoned. If the worst happened, the bank would need to demonstrate some real muscle. One didn't need to be accused of agreeing to the default, or approving of it. Any inaction or non-movement of legal proceedings by the bank might be perceived as weakness. Couldn't have that.

The other Group of Seven shareholders were miffed, to say the least. There was a lot of muttering going on in the wings. TJ's name was mentioned unkindly. All this unnecessary difficulty, not to mention the imposition and insult to their integrity, caused each shareholder to seek legal advice in order to deal with TJ. There is nothing quite as vicious as an offended dentist or doctor who perceives himself to have been diddled or ignored. The rhetoric around TJ was that he had dealt with the whole matter in a most unsatisfactory manner. Meaning, in lay terms, that he had screwed them. They sent their lawyers to tackle him.

The independent lawyers that were retained by the six men did not receive what they deemed to be an acceptable response from TJ. He either ignored their letters or served them platitudes. The lawyers suggested that a meeting be held between all parties and their counsel. Of course, TJ was invited to attend and thereafter, any steps that might be deemed appropriate would be taken by these parties.

TJ received formal notification of the lynching. He preferred not to be in attendance, but what was the alternative? He thought it best to try and quell the concerns of these lawyers and their clients, his former friends and other shareholders of The Group of Seven. He also decided not to appear intimidated at the meeting. He had planned his strategy quite well, he thought. No belligerent or abrasive behaviour. Just a firmness and strength about his position. And never, never, show any weakness.

He was, in fact, calm and polite. He greeted the other shareholders and their esteemed solicitors with graciousness, and proceeded to hear their concerns. Nothing that was said was unexpected. In fact, they were all a lot more civil and gracious than he had anticipated. He had not retained his own solicitor, which was a risky position. 'The lawyer who represents himself is a fool,' says the maxim, but it was clear to him that there was no way that he could be represented by anyone. Who would he tell, and what could he tell them?

So he listened, patiently and politely, until all the lawyers and the shareholders had their say. He then graciously advised the Group that all the shareholders had been friends for a long time, and that of course he realized that the proceedings were not personal, merely something that had to be dealt with for business and practical reasons. He went on to explain that he had always operated the Mortgage Corporation with little or no assistance from other shareholders. The books were always open. Anyone was free to be involved. He pointed out to them that none of them had ever chosen to take anything more than a passing interest in the Corporation, as long as profits kept pouring in and no difficulties arose.

His attack stance got better.

He indicated that everyone seemed perfectly happy to have all the benefits of the Corporation, but no one, apart from him, was willing to expend the time and effort needed to ensure a prosperous and successful enterprise.

"Now, after all the years of success and prosperity, one difficulty has arisen, and everyone gets worried just because the bank is telling them that they ought to be. This distrust occurs, even though I have expressly assured everyone and proved that there was nothing to fret about." TJ made himself sound quite injured.

He went on to recount how the subject of mortgage problems had come about, and what was being done to resolve it. He retraced his movements back to when the second mortgage loan for The Lazy Valley Project was first approved. He gave them all the details, which he believed they needed to know, that had prompted the loan's approval. He assured them that the Project was great, the principals were extremely creditworthy, experienced and strong, and that cash infusions on the part of the borrowers were substantial and the equity advance was low.

"There was never any doubt," he insisted, "that the loan was excellent in all respects. Unfortunately, and for varied reasons, some of which I was not privy to, the borrowers and investors in the Project ran into problems and difficulties. They tried desperately, but they could not surmount the obstacles. The Project took over, wresting control from them. Soon, and even though the Project was excellent and viable, the borrowers panicked and became unglued."

He paused for a moment, trying to gauge the emotions of his audience. He couldn't. Best poker faces in town.

"When cohesion and strength of mind were essential, the borrowers and investors failed to maintain their business composure, and from that point onward, the Project, with them at the helm, was doomed. Soon, the Project halted as trades and creditors got antsy about nonpayment. Default occurred with the first mortgage. Shortly afterward, payments stopped coming on The Group of Seven second mortgage loan."

TJ pressed home the advantage he thought he had at that stage.

"At that time, The Group of Seven was at a crossroads. The substantial and non-performing loan of $400,000 rocked the portfolio. What to do?" He waited only a few seconds. Some of the guys exchanged glances.

"Well, it was a tremendously large responsibility and a question that had to be dealt with immediately. Should I call the other shareholders in The Group of Seven? Would they wish to hear from me, or would they simply wish that I deal with the problem as I had always done in the past. In other words, 'do what you have to do, TJ, as best as you can. Don't involve or bother us. And of course, don't forget, we're 100% behind you.'" TJ couldn't resist adding the sarcasm.

"I had a mandate," he declared vehemently, "to do whatever I thought was necessary, proper and correct, for The Group of Seven Mortgage Corporation. The management and administration of the mortgage company was my responsibility, for which I was paid handsomely.

He was aware that he was being strong and aggressive. He felt that his brazenness and directness might be perceived as arrogance, or at least received in the wrong fashion, but there it was. He had no alternative but to forge ahead. All the other shareholders were present with their high-powered lawyers, and they would all have happily ripped out his innards. If he allowed himself to be attacked and censured without aggressively speaking on his own defence, it would be his own fault that he hadn't been able to diffuse the onslaught. When he paused to consider all the other hurdles that he had overcome and the sacrifices that he had to make, he knew that there was no way that the other inept shareholders and their buffoon lawyers would stand in his way.

He folded his arms across his chest in a gesture of defiance. To get to where he was, to have accomplished what he did, spoke for itself. He was quite prepared to let them know where he stood.

"So let me get this straight. You are all here today to voice your concern over the status of the mortgage company and its portfolio. You are also concerned, primarily, because you are receiving threatening letters from the bank, demanding a further cash infusion from each of you."

He stood resolutely, examining the faces of his peers and judges. He had made his attack one of a linear progression; it was the tack that these weasels understood best. Once he had glared at them all equally, noting who of them could look him in the eye, he went on.

"I don't really have anything further to add, but I would suggest that the floor be open to whomever would like to ask questions or voice their concerns."

He was most pleased with the manner in which he had dealt with the assault on his management and administration of the mortgage company. He tried to keep the smirk off his face; he wasn't safe yet. He almost expected a warm round of applause, some guffaws, some weak or back-handed apologies. Maybe even some good-natured backslapping. But then again, he knew that such displays would not be forthcoming because the lawyers who were retained by the other shareholders were far too arrogant to acknowledge the capability of another solicitor.

He never expected what he got: complete silence, a good deal of fidgeting, and the passage of considerable time after he had finished and sat down. One of the older and more respected of the lawyers stood up at last to address the gathering. Even if you didn't like Frank Martinson, you would have to acknowledge his integrity, and the fact that his conduct as a solicitor and an individual were entirely above reproach, $300 an hour notwithstanding.

Martinson was a lawyer's lawyer, power stitched in every seam of his suit. He was brilliant, analytical, and possessed a keen, incisive mind. He had been at the bar for almost forty years, but he was still a relatively young man at sixty-four. Martinson was the senior partner of the downtown law firm that bore his name: MARTINSON SMITH. TJ had not had much to do with Martinson over the years. In those instances where they had worked together on files, all matters had gone smoothly, and TJ had been impressed with the efficient, proper, and orderly fashion with which Martinson had conducted the practice. Martinson was generally regarded as a work horse, and continued to work much as he had as a young man. His stamina and productivity were often the subject of conversation and abundant admiration in the MARTINSON SMITH offices.

Martinson raised himself up to his full height, made larger by his barrel-chested voice. He spoke clearly and distinctly:

"TJ, I have been designated by the other solicitors to give you our position with respect to all the ongoings that have occurred recently. We have numerous concerns, and unfortunately, your position and explanation do little to allay these concerns. Before I go on, I will say on behalf of the group that we are presently uncommitted to any particular or single course of action. Much of what has come forth in the past and to date, is extremely troublesome to the other shareholders and ourselves as their solicitors. To the extent that your position has been outlined in point form, I will attempt to match that conciseness. I want matters to be easily followed by everyone present, with no possibility of misunderstanding. I will put forward our position in a forthright fashion, without malice or hostility.

I must say at the outset, that myself or the other solicitors and shareholders present are neither pleased nor satisfied with what has transpired respecting the Mortgage Corporation.

Second, it has always been the position of the shareholders that you have been well paid for the management of that portfolio. You continue to collect that salary come what may, regardless of what is happening with the portfolio.

Third, in addition to that salary, we also note that you receive considerable additional funds for mortgage preparation, foreclosure work and other corporate affairs attended to your firm on behalf of the corporation. With that in mind, I think it fair to state that you are the sole lawyer for the mortgage company and that you reap considerable fees on a monthly and annual basis as a result of your association with the mortgage company. It might also be fair to say that you gain far more, and possess many more advantages from the mortgage company than the other shareholders. Not only do you receive your salary and fees for services rendered, but you share in the profits of the mortgage company, not to mention the glory that attends it. As well, you do a lot of the work for the shareholders of the corporation, and your work and association with the other shareholders is strengthened by your management and administration of the mortgage portfolio.

Fourth, I have reviewed in some detail the decisions that were made by The Group of Seven company over the past years. I have discovered, though you chose not to reveal this point, that you took a substantial bonus from every borrower with every mortgage loan. Almost unbelievably, every loan funded by The Group of Seven provided for an extremely large bonus payable to the lender, resulting in a greatly increased percentage yield to the lender. Unfortunately, and unknown to the other members of the mortgage company, none of the bonus monies was ever paid to the company. In fact, every one, large as it was, was kept by you and never accounted for, to the company or any of the shareholders.

Fifth, it seems trite to say that you would never have approved a mortgage loan for the company unless there was a large bonus payable to yourself. At least two deductions flow from that premise. One: that you were more concerned with the amount of the bonus rather than the quality of the mortgage security. Two, the interest rate payable to the company was undoubtedly prejudiced, or less than it would have been to a large extent by virtue of the bonus, and the fact that only a certain amount of funds was available to the lender from the borrower. Naturally, we understand that the latter required a certain amount of net mortgage proceeds. In other words, money that belonged to the company was retained by you. In reality, you placed your own interests ahead of the company's, notwithstanding your position of trust and fiduciary obligation to the mortgage company and the shareholders.

Sixth, to a novice in the mortgage business such as myself, one would not have thought that the Lazy Valley Project loan was a good one, or even one that The Group of Seven should have taken on. The interest rate was only average; respectable, one might say. Even though the appraisal seemed to confirm a reasonable equity advance, the fact of the matter was that the $400,000 loan was far too large a mortgage to be given by a small company like The Group of Seven. It wasn't even a first mortgage loan. It was second to a dangerously large first mortgage. The Project was not even finished, involved various complicated stages of completion, and required expertise that the principals of the Project did not appear to have, given their documented inexperience. The loan looked like instant trouble right from the onset.

TJ, a prudent lender or lawyer always looks at the possibility of default. If you had exercised that intelligence when the loan was first approved, doubtless you would never had made the same imprudent decision. The Group of Seven would have had little option in the event of default than to complete the Project; hardly a viable alternative. To foreclose and hope for a third party to bail them out was not practical. To sue on the guarantees was also impractical, as the parties that gave the guarantees were likely judgment-proof, or else they wouldn't have given them, being smart and experienced businessmen.

Seventh, why was the mortgage loan granted to the Lazy Valley Project, given the numerous warning flags associated with it? It was clear that there were lots of other sources that required mortgage funding. The answer must be simple. The bonus, payable to the lender, or yourself, in this instance, amounted to 5% of the loan amount, or $20,000. It all went directly to your pocket, and not the mortgage company's coffers, by virtue of your approving the mortgage loan. I am hardly surprised that you approved and funded the loan. You had a vested interest and you were in a clear conflict position. Even if the loan and your intentions were honest, which does not appear to be the case, you should not have allowed yourself to be in a position where your intentions or good faith might have been questioned. For that alone, if nothing else, you have erred.

Eighth, what I have said to date is damaging and bad enough, but it gets worse. The second mortgage loan, not surprisingly goes into default, and all parties start clamouring for payment. The bank quite rightly makes a demand on the mortgage company and the shareholders to restore the line of credit. This is done to infuse capital into the company if the default continues with the Lazy Valley Project. Everyone is yelling, no one knows what to do, and the responsibility for a decision is directed to you and only you, on behalf of The Group of Seven.

What should you do? Or perhaps I should ask: what should you have done? Without a doubt, you should have convened a meeting of the shareholders to discuss the situation. You should have advised them that they could or should obtain independent legal advice, given the default, their guarantee exposure to the bank, and so forth. What you next did was exactly the opposite. Instead of calling a loan and getting some sort of consensus from the other parties, you decided to act unilaterally and arrogantly. The issue, of course, is for whom it was prudent. Namely yourself, or the mortgage company."

Martinson slapped his enormous hand on the conference room table as he beat time to his next words:

"You claim that the mortgage loan with the Lazy Valley Project is being saved, and that payment to The Group of Seven will be along shortly, with all interest owed to date.

You claim that you should be held as a saviour or hero, in that the loan is saved, the portfolio is intact, the bank is happy and everyone able to go on with their lives.

What you don't mention, and what you pointedly fail to say, is who the unknown third party is that came to the rescue to complete the Project. What is your involvement with that third party? If you were involved, the mortgage company and shareholders might rightly and properly ask some leading questions. Such as, was that the overall design when the loan was first approved? If your intentions were only noble and altruistic, why didn't you reveal them immediately? Shouldn't the mortgage company and the shareholders be able to share in the Project completion? If there is money to be made, the very least obligation was incumbent on yourself to fully disclose everything going on with the Project.

You remain consistent, however, you reveal nothing, you cloud and obscure matters, and you make everything so murky that no one but yourself knows what's going on. You placate the other shareholders. You take unsophisticated clients, your shareholders, leave them in the dark, tell them nothing, and act in a conflict of interest position as though you have no accountability to anyone. With all of that in mind, it is truly no great revelation that you and only you, are apparently the sole and moving force behind the completion of the Lazy Valley Project. However you have done it, you have moved without telling the other shareholders that you are the individual who has assumed control of the Project. You have opted to complete the Project and to reap a substantial profit for doing so. If our speculation is not correct and there is, in fact, a party behind you who is responsible for concluding the Project, you are bound and obliged to tell us so, here and now. You might also provide us with details confuting or disproving our thesis.

The proceedings would appear to have been handled so improperly by yourself, with such a flagrant breach of solicitor/client responsibility, that we are hoping, for your sake, that you are not that party, nor personally or financially involved in the conclusion of the Lazy Valley Project. Speak now, and save yourself."

The verbiage that had come from Martinson halted with his great sigh. He lowered his burly frame to his chair, clearly spent with the exercise of his attack. All parties turned to TJ for his response.

Chapter Fifteen

He gave them none. He merely sat resolutely, his hands folded on the conference table before him. He took time to look each one of his accusers in the eye. Many of them looked away, but not all. He rose then, slowly and deliberately, tapping his fingers solidly against the oak table.

"Gentlemen, this inquisition is over." He gathered his papers and marched out of the room, leaving them all with their anger.

The whole scene was wonderfully dramatic. The only point he regretted was his inability to judge what his fate would be after that meeting. Leaving powerful professional men with their anger is never a good plan. In that brief moment, however, it was the only plan that came to mind.

There was nothing he could do now but wait. Return to his office, take up the business of law yet again, and wait.

* * *

The mail came in. Stacks and stacks of it that required sorting like a baby needed milk. Redirection here and there, but if you left some of it long enough, the problems would go away. TJ was certain that if he didn't have a heart attack or stroke, given all the pressure on his nerves, he would surely live to a poverty-stricken old age. On the other hand, he felt confident that Alzheimer's wouldn't get him, because the strain and abuse to which he was subjecting his body right now would ensure his early demise. His thoughts jumped haphazardly. Living to be an old man was a nasty fate, he decided. You were stuck with little old ladies at tiresome family parties. Then there was Christmas, funerals, etc. He'd have to sit and listen to everyone relate stories of their recent gall bladder operations, or worse yet, prostate surgery, if you had the good fortune to find another old fogey who hadn't been able to get it up in twenty years.

TJ didn't want to have to see that day. A heart attack would do just nicely, thank you. His morbid movement of thought stopped abruptly as he spotted a letter on his desk, a letter marked with the all too familiar insignia of the Alberta Law Society.

Funny thing about legal letterhead. It was like warpaint: a shock of meaning that instantly forced your heart to race. As if his heart was not palpitating enough. The envelope with enclosure caused him to develop a migraine right then and there. The letter was marked to his attention: "Personal and Confidential". He reluctantly pried it open.

Dear Sir:

We enclose herewith letter of complaint as received from several solicitors and their clients, its contents being self-explanatory. Kindly provide our office, prior to the elapse of seven (7) days, with a complete and detailed response. If you have materials or documentation to support your position, we would ask that copies of this accompany your return letter.

Your immediate attention is appreciated and required.

Thank you.

LAW SOCIETY OF ALBERTA
WILLIAM FRANKS, SECRETARY

TJ was too busy for this crap; he had a thousand things to do. Whether he liked it or not, his primary livelihood was the practice of law. He had no alternative but to direct his immediate attention to the letter and to respond to it as quickly as possible. With that in mind, he delegated as much as he possibly could to Ali. That done, he proceeded to compose his thoughts so that he would not be tardy in the required response to the Law Society. He did not need to be reminded that failing to respond in a timely, diligent, and candid manner was deemed as unbecoming conduct, and sanctionable.

He ran through his defense strategy. It was foolhardy to write something immediately without evaluating its consequences. It would be prudent to bear in mind that subterfuge and evasive language was clearly a no-no. The less said, the better. The answer should be concise, straight-forward and prompt. Rambling or circumlocutory language was just as dangerous as an evasive answer. It was important to deal frankly and openly with the complaint, and expeditiously.

TJ had never really evaluated, philosophically, how legal letters operated. The exercise helped him compose his response. Letters were two-dimensional text. Words that creep like large viruses on paper are the insidious weaponry of the law. When you're in trouble with the Big Boys, they don't invite you to any old-fashioned joust in order to settle the matter. Trouble meant exposure for lawyers: a challenge to a life of privilege. Letters were the battle-style of social class.

The mental joust replaced a physical battle, and the phallic pen (although TJ would never have acknowledged that metaphor) replaced the audible voice of pleasantries... or, one could say, bullshit.

TJ poised his pen carefully to make the right marks.

Dear Mr. Franks:

I acknowledge your recent correspondence and appended materials with thanks, and I confirm that I have reviewed the contents. I have been the solicitor for, and a shareholder in The Group of Seven Mortgage Corporation since its inception. This Corporation has been extremely successful. I have been responsible for granting loan approvals, administration of the portfolio, reporting to the bank, accounting and reporting to the shareholders, auditors, and so forth. A salary and compensation is payable to me for those services, and all legal work respecting the Corporation is attended to by our office, involving mortgage preparation, foreclosure and related proceedings.

At all times, I have been the sole party attending to the requirements of the Mortgage Corporation. All the other shareholders are extremely busy professionals. They had requested expressly, or by implication, that I do whatever had to be done, prudently and practically, and that their involvement be minimal, given that they do not have the time nor expertise to be involved in the Corporation and its operation.

A substantial mortgage default involving a second mortgage in the portfolio has occurred recently. The other shareholders are concerned as a result of the default. I have assured them that matters were under hand, and as advised numerous times on previous occasions, they should retain independent solicitors and accountants to satisfy their concerns. I would, of course, be pleased to deal with any of these inquiries.

As a result of the referenced default and attendant consequences, all the other shareholders retained solicitors, and a meeting was held recently between myself, the other shareholders and their solicitors. Everyone's apprehensions were voiced at that meeting.

The concerns of the shareholders were transmitted through their solicitors. I gave what I believed was a satisfactory response to all of them. The primary thrust of the meeting was that the shareholders and their lawyers were advised that rectification of the default would be made shortly, as well as all costs and interest owed.

The Project, representing the security for the loan in default, was deteriorating; both the first and second mortgages were outstanding and in substantial arrears. No one was doing anything about this deterioration and default. I felt that I had no alternative but to make arrangements with the first mortgagee and the Bankers for The Group of Seven Mortgage Corporation, as well as the owners of the Project. Ultimate responsibility for the Project's completion would be undertaken by myself. At that time, my sole consideration was to rescue The Group of Seven Mortgage Loan, its continued unrectified default and possible loss. That possibility seemed devastating to me. I did not want that reality to be suffered by the other shareholders. I felt, wrongly, I can see now, that they depended on me: indeed, looked up to me. I felt that I couldn't let them down. The project had to be completed regardless of personal financial consequences.

The meeting adjourned, and all the parties went on their respective ways. Suffice it to say that they did not appear to be happy nor pleased with the Mortgage Company and its operation, even though it has always been profitable, and a full accounting has always been made. The books and files were open to all, whenever requested.

Given the lack of confidence in my ability and management of the Corporation, at such time as the loan in default has been remedied, I propose to resign from my position as Manager of the Corporation. I shall advise the shareholders and their solicitors that I no longer wish to be involved with the Corporation. It should be disbanded and dissolved, the portfolio sold and profits distributed. In the alternative, my interest should be purchased at the face value, or one-seventh of the mortgage portfolio, less liabilities, the exact worth of one-seventh to be determined by auditors appointed by the shareholders.

I respectfully trust that you find the foregoing in order. A copy of my letter to the shareholder's solicitors is appended for your reference.

THEODORE H. JAMES - BARRISTER AND SOLICITOR

ENCL.

"WITHOUT PREJUDICE"

TO: The shareholders of The Group of Seven Mortgage Corporation via their Respective Solicitors:

RE: THE GROUP OF SEVEN MORTGAGE CORPORATION

Further to the above matter, and in light of events that have occurred recently, in good conscience and inasmuch as it is clear that I no longer have the confidence of the shareholders of the Corporation or their solicitors, I no longer wish to be associated with the Corporation as the Administrator of the portfolio, as a shareholder, or otherwise.

Kindly arrange for alternate solicitors to assume immediate conduct of Corporate materials, and for a party or firm to be appointed to attend to the management of the Corporation's portfolio. The bank and auditors must be notified of the change.

In addition to the foregoing, I wish the Corporation to disband, and assets sold such that the net profits might be realized and profits disbursed in equal shares. In the alternative, my shares in the Corporation can be purchased for one-seventh of the audited worth. Determination of said value will be set by auditors appointed by yourselves.

In the event that this request is not dealt with in an expeditious fashion, I shall retain solicitors and initiate proceedings under the Shareholder's Agreement in place. Should that be necessary, I shall offer to purchase all of the other shareholder's interest in the Corporation, subject to specified terms and conditions. Reluctance or unwillingness to sell on said terms will result in your being compelled to buy my shareholding interest on the same terms. It is, of course, understood that this letter is being forwarded on a 'Without Prejudice' basis and that it is my intention to deal amicably, if possible, outside the ambit of the Shareholder's Agreement. Failure to achieve resolution in a timely and cordial fashion shall result in steps being taken to exercise the shotgun provision in the buy-sell agreement.

I require your response no later than twenty-one (21) days from the date thereof, and I shall meet with the designated parties to ensure that an orderly transference of control is achieved.

Yours truly,
THEODORE H. JAMES
BARRISTER AND SOLICITOR

TJ was certainly not happy about having to write the letter to the shareholders and their solicitors. He clearly had no wish to kill the goose that laid the golden egg. He perceived that he was left with no alternative, however, given the letter received from the Law Society. TJ believed that he had no other choice but to take the offensive stance, to throw all matters back to the shareholders or their solicitors. There was a possibility that they would yield on bended knees, genuflect and beg him to reconsider the portfolio's management. They might even withdraw their complaint to the Law Society, but that was a doubtful possibility. He knew that the shareholder's solicitors, though perhaps not the shareholders themselves, smelled blood. They would want an accounting via the Law Society, and so he knew that he was left with little alternative but to turn the battle around in his favour. If he were a general, he would have thought that his strategy was brilliant. He would carry a fight to its laborious, dying end.

Chapter Sixteen

So what if his life and practice were hectic and virtually uncontrollable? So what if the cash flow from his practice was awful, his clients disappearing? Those who were still with him were grumpy and belligerent, complaining that he was overcharging them and even ignoring them. So what? Too bad if he couldn't spare the time to return phone calls, or give the kind of service to which they had been accustomed in the past. He was almost at the top of the mountain. From there, all this petty stuff would seem quite insignificant.

Some complained loudly, but most of them just began to shop for a new solicitor. TJ wasn't too concerned. When you made calculated financial risks, you had to take responsibility for the outcome. He had manoeuvred through all the land mines successfully thus far. He saw no reason to think he would be blown to bits in the near future.

His calculations had been careful, and his cost controls were cautious, but two things were abundantly clear. First, he was still shy some funds to complete the last leg of the Project. Secondly, and far more sadly, cost overruns were encroaching on his hopeful megaprofits. When the dust settled he would see a profit, but the amount might be minimal compared to his exaggerated fantasies. He might well wonder if the profits would be worth the changes he had made to his life, not to mention the havoc wreaked upon his professional and social life.

Potential funds had run as dry as a prairie spring in July. No other family funds or trust money could be found. His only remaining source of income was his practice. There had been no repercussions whatsoever respecting the trust funds from which he had temporarily borrowed. The reason for that was the care and caution he had utilized in selecting the right sources. He was hoping he could find another similar account, largely unutilized and dormant, so that final funds might be borrowed to complete the Project. TJ knew that he was living dangerously by encroaching on his trust accounts one last time. A spot audit by the Law Society was even more likely in the wake of the complaints filed by the shareholders of The Group of Seven. But he felt the need to finish what he had begun, and to finish well.

Having rationalized his decision, he withdrew $175,000 from the Charitable Trust and Arts Foundation, which belonged to the Society for the Advancement of Education and Culture in Third World Countries. He knew that there would not be any demand for these funds until budget determinations were made for the Society. There would be a six month breathing space for the return of the monies, possibly longer. Millions of people in third world countries would die of starvation and disease before anyone could point a finger at Theodore H. James.

He felt that his juggling and strategy had been brilliant to date. He was aware of other factors, however, one of which he had no control, and the other of which he only had partial control. There was nothing he could do if the Law Society made a spot audit or swooped down on his office for investigative purposes. He just had to hope that the worst would not occur. Spot audits took place all the time, regardless of who or where the law firm was. Well-connected, well-oiled, well-heeled. It didn't matter to the Law Society. One bad lawyer made everyone reek.

The other factor was Ali York. She was so wonderfully smart and perceptive. He caught her watching him from time to time, studying his every move. He was flattered by the attention, believing her to be quite infatuated with him. She was something to watch, too. Ali York was more than just a lovely face. The questions from her were relentless, and she was always making perceptive inquiries of the rest of the office staff. TJ had tried to give her enough work to bamboozle her, but she was a driven woman. No obstacle was insurmountable to her. The more work he gave her, the better she performed. He conceded that she must be dragging files home with her, working through the night.

Her gaze at him, he believed, was completely star struck. She had no idea of what was going on, he felt sure of it. He had hired her primarily because she was worth looking at, although her sharp brain had also been a major consideration. It might turn out to be an unfortunate one. He knew he would have to occupy more of her time outside the office. She would be an exhilarating diversion. In turn, she would become so tantalized by him that she would be blind to his failings and balk at questioning his brilliant and necessary finagling.

* * *

The Secretary of the Law Society received TJ's response to the Great Complaint. The next correspondence was automatic, statutorily prescribed:

Dear Mr. Martinson:

With respect to your recent complaint levied against Mr. Theodore H. James, Barrister and Solicitor, we enclose herewith the response of Mr. James to your complaint. Matters shall be further reviewed by the Law Society, and you shall shortly be advised as to the proceedings to be taken, if any, respecting the complaint.

We trust that you find the foregoing in order, and we shall report further shortly. Thank you.

William Franks,
LAW SOCIETY SECRETARY

cc: Theodore H. James
Barrister and Solicitor

TJ opened the correspondence from the Law Society as directed to Martinson, almost holding his breath in anticipation when he first received it. He hoped the matter would just go away, so that he would be allowed to complete the Project in peace. He could repay everyone and then get on with his life and the rebuilding of his practice.

William Franks was a revered member of the Law Society. Pondering the complaint that was forwarded by the esteemed Frank Martinson, and the response submitted by Theodore H. James, Franks decided that he had two choices. He could simply write Martinson and tell him that it was the position of the Law Society that the complaint had been dealt with by Mr. James, that the explanation seemed acceptable, and that no further proceedings would be taken respecting the complaint. That action was his prerogative, and he was leaning toward exercising it and so closing the matter.

The problem was that Frank Martinson was well regarded, possessing such an honoured track record that the man was unlikely to let go of the prey while he thought he had it in his teeth. Martinson would probably roar at such a response, taking it as a slap in the face. He might even appeal the Secretary's decision. Then he might become persnickety, demanding that the matter be heard by a panel of three benchers, or senior solicitors, a procedure that was followed when a complaint was rejected at first instance by the Secretary. It was an action that Franks wished to avoid, since it tended to undermine his own authority.

He sighed. He would have to demonstrate some respect for Martinson, no doubt. Linear authority must be obeyed, particularly among the sharks in the revered Legal Profession. Appeals could be embarrassing. They could spoil the fun at the next reunion, make things tense the next time a few of the Boys decided to drink at the Country Club. One tried to avoid appeals. Franks decided to take the latter approach.

Mr. David Dark
BARRISTER AND SOLICITOR

Dear Mr. Dark:

RE: Theodore H. James - Complaint

We enclose herewith letter of complaint documentation as received from Mr. Frank Martinson as directed against Mr. James, along with the response of James. We have advised Mr. Martinson that his complaint is presently being investigated. Pursuant to the provisions of the Law Society Act and the Legal Professions Act, we would ask that you make investigations and take proceedings as you deem necessary. Your position respecting the claim is to be reported in our favour at your earliest convenience, and preferably, no later than thirty days from the date hereof.

Respectfully yours,

William Franks
LAW SOCIETY SECRETARY / TREASURER

cc: Frank Martinson
    BARRISTER AND SOLICITOR
cc: Theodore H. James
    BARRISTER AND SOLICITOR

Chapter Seventeen

David Dark, or "Ducky", as he was known to his friends and colleagues, was an affable guy. He was exceedingly popular with his fellow practitioners and most members of the judiciary. He had political savvy and was well-connected. Through the years he had held various positions with the Law Society, which included its Presidency for a two-year term. He was the type of individual who got things done, even though he didn't appear to work exceptionally hard. He had time for everyone and everything, often acting as an advocate and solicitor for individuals and other lawyers, when proceedings were brought against them by the Law Society. One of his better clients was the Law Society itself; he was quite regularly engaged in acting as an investigator for that Body. He determined whether complaint proceedings that were initiated by another lawyer should be acted upon or merely dropped.

Dark had reviewed all the correspondence and communications that passed between TJ, the Law Society, and Martinson. He tried to keep an objective mind when assessing and evaluating the submitted materials. He was not the prototypical lawyer, being much too nice for that role. The steps he determined to take in these kind of proceedings often reflected his compassionate nature.

Dark knew that there could be a lot of trauma associated with receiving a complaint from the Law Society and having to respond to it. When he was retained by them for disciplinary matters like this one, he tried to be as fair and impartial as possible. It was always easy, in hindsight, to see where something should or shouldn't have been done, but he liked to act in time with the old cliche: 'to err is human, to forgive: divine'. Wherever the alleged misconduct or improper action was not too serious or reprehensible, it was generally Dark's recommendation that no further proceedings be taken against the accused. At most, a letter of warning might be issued, or the charged party simply receive a directive to exercise more caution and responsibility in the future.

As Dark received complaints, he liked to reflect on what he knew of the players involved. Dark had hardly known a time when TJ hadn't been part of the legal profession's furniture. He and TJ did not socialize or hang out together, but they had always been friendly, serving on several boards and organizations together. Dark had a healthy respect for TJ and his ability as a lawyer. He had admired TJ's contributions both mentally and physically to the community at large, the local bar, and to other worthwhile causes or endeavours.

Thus, the general rule applied here. The investigating lawyer would write a letter to the lawyer charged. Dark dictated the following letter for transmission to TJ:

Dear Mr. James:

<u>RE: Frank Martinson Complaint Against Theodore H. James</u>

I wish to confirm that I have been retained by the Law Society to investigate the referenced complaint. Accordingly, materials and documentation have been submitted to the undersigned for examination and consideration.

In order that I might be assisted in the furtherance of the investigative proceedings, I wish to have a meeting with yourself, in order that you might outline your position in greater detail to the undersigned. To that end, please contact the writer's secretary to arrange for an appointment in the near future.

The matter at hand is governed by strict time constraints, so I would appreciate the meeting set at your earliest convenience.

Yours truly,
DAVID DARK

TJ received and read Dark's letter with considerable relief, for if there was one individual that he would select to review the complaint amongst the powers that be, it would be Ducky. He and Ducky went back a long way, and even though he knew the meeting would not really be a casual outing, he felt strongly that Ducky would give him the benefit of the doubt. TJ might even be able to persuade Ducky that everything was in order, and to dissuade him from requiring that the claim be advanced any further. Its summary dismissal was certainly best for all concerned, especially for himself.

TJ wasted no time contacting Ducky. A meeting was scheduled for the following afternoon. He knew how much the meeting counted.

He was cautiously optimistic as he was ushered into Ducky's office by the officious secretary. Ducky slapped him on the back, exchanging warm greetings. TJ eased himself into a fine, comfortable chair, and was urged rather gently, to tell the story. TJ started to relate his version as simply as he could. He was only interrupted a few times by Ducky, who seemed to have an excellent grasp of what had transpired. Ducky almost seemed to be leaning toward favouring TJ's explanation and siding with him. The lengthy discourse took almost forty-five minutes. He felt the unpleasant attachment of sweat under his armpits, even though he had exercised his best acting ability to hide his nervousness.

Ducky cleared his throat. "Well, have you anything more to add?"

TJ shook his head.

"With respect, TJ, I don't want to appear smug or holier than thou, but it is my humble opinion that you have acted in an abominable fashion. There has been a clear breach of your fiduciary duty. Amongst other things, you had no business nor any right to take the bonuses or inducements without sharing them with the mortgage company, unless all of the shareholders were in full agreement. All loans should have been approved by an independent body other than yourself, in order to remove any spectre of conflict if you were, in fact, to secure the bonuses. In addition to the fact that everyone should have received regular reminders of their right and obligation to seek independent legal and accounting advice, you had no right and no business," Ducky glowered, shaking his head vigorously, "to take over the Lazy Valley Project without all the other shareholders agreeing to that action or without full disclosure being made. At the very least, you are guilty of not revealing what was happening within the Mortgage Company to the shareholders. Your conduct is far below the level and standard expected of a solicitor in our ranks."

TJ left Dark's office in a state of shock, never mind a forlorn and demoralized mood. He hadn't expected Ducky to drag him over spikes. He had hoped that Ducky would look kindly on his evidence and presentation. None of that had happened.

If he were in the mood for wager, he would guess that Ducky's letter to the Law Society would go in the form of an invitation to a very special lynching party. It would direct the venerable Body to launch a further investigation into the conduct of one of its members. 'Whatever happens, happens', he rationalized. 'Let the chips fall where they may. You never know what's going to happen. It's not worth dealing with a problem until it's really a problem. No point in expending energy for nothing'. With these cliches reverberating in his mind, he brushed off the meeting with Ducky. There were lots of things he could do something about. This situation wasn't one of them.

* * *

Dark's letter to the Law Society required little thought or preparation on his part. He purposely refrained from submitting his report for several weeks. The natural inference from that delay would be that he had devoted his expensive time to considerable rumination. This is the letter that went, after a suitable amount of time had elapsed:

LAW SOCIETY DIRECTOR

Attention: Mr. Franks

Dear Mr. Franks:

RE: Frank Martinson - Complaint Against Theodore H. James

Further to the above matter, and the letter of instructions, I have reviewed all materials and documentation submitted at length.

A meeting was scheduled and held with Mr. James, and the latter was afforded the opportunity to provide me with his position and explanation respecting the matter and facts at hand, as well as the complaint advanced by Mr. Martinson. At the meeting, in addition to Mr. James presenting his position, I subjected him to a vigorous and prolonged examination in order to satisfy myself as to the defence and propriety of that position.

After considerable review, analysis, consideration and soul-searching, it is my unequivocal and objective position that the member, Theodore H. James, acted at all times with the best interest of his clients and the other shareholders in the Company. I am satisfied that he had no intention of taking advantage of them, or to unfairly or otherwise utilize his position of trust. Throughout all his dealings with shareholders and clients, said parties were always directed to obtain independent legal and accounting advice. If they neglected to do so, the fault should not lie with Mr. James.

There is no doubt that Mr. James could have attended to matters in a more professional and thorough fashion. Given the circumstances at hand, however, I believe that he attempted diligently, honourably and honestly, to discharge his obligations and duties as a solicitor.

Though seemingly improper on the face of it, I conclude that all the other shareholders in the Mortgage Company knew and approved of what Mr. James was doing and receiving and that all inducements and bonuses were being retained by him. Similarly, there is no doubt in my mind that the other shareholders had no interest in the day to day management or operation of the Mortgage Company or its portfolio. They implicitly delegated that task to Mr. James, along with the proviso that they should not be bothered nor called upon at any time, for consultation or otherwise. The other shareholders made it quite clear that they wanted nothing to do with the Mortgage Company except to share in the benefits.

When a difficulty ensued, and the bank began to place pressure on the other shareholders, then and only then, was Mr. James brought to task. His response was to the effect that he had always done an honourable job, and that he had always directed the other shareholders to obtain independent legal and accounting advice. He indicated that he was, in fact, resolving the problem with the Lazy Valley Project, and the loan in default.

I find that Theodore H. James was foolish to have allowed himself to be and to remain in a position where his good faith and credibility might well be impugned, and where his evident conflict of interest would be utilized against him. Even though I find otherwise, and believe that Mr. James acted in good faith and exercised honesty, he has been, and should be, censured for allowing himself to be in such a position. Mr. James should be directed by the Society to ever refrain therefrom in the future.

The complaint also deals with the issue of lack of full disclosure. In response thereto, I find that the member was, in fact, remiss in this regard. Mr. James should be directed to always yield full disclosure in the future. The complaint proceedings to date find that Mr. James failed to make this disclosure respecting the Lazy Valley Project as an oversight, or alternatively, due to the fact that the other shareholders would not have taken an interest. The other shareholders were interested only in the delinquent loan being brought into good standing.

In point of fact, the Group of Seven Mortgage Company has performed admirably in the past, with the shareholders realizing an extremely good rate of return, notwithstanding minimal or even nil involvement. Furthermore, Mr. James confirms that the Lazy Valley Project loan is shortly to be fully paid. The major issue in the dispute would appear, then, to be resolved satisfactorily.

I recommend that the complaint against the member, Theodore H. James, be held in abeyance until such time as determination might be made whether the Lazy Valley Loan is fully paid or otherwise. Mr. James has, in fact, dissociated himself from the Group of Seven Mortgage Corporation to the fullest extent.

In due course, if the Lazy Valley loan is fully paid, and the member, Theodore H. James, is no longer associated with the Group of Seven Mortgage

Corporation as its administrator, I would recommend that the complaint against Theodore H. James be dismissed. I recommend that the member be admonished to act with more caution and care in the future. The complaint proceedings to date, embarrassment, and so forth, are sufficient punishment for Mr. James. With respect to the complaint lodged by the respected member, Frank Martinson, I note its merit. I also note, however, that the other shareholders and clients have a certain responsibility to look after their own affairs. They should simply not be able to vent their wrath or anger upon another solicitor simply by virtue of the Law Society's intervention. In those instances where the complainants might well have been more diligent and watchful, the Law Society should not be asked to intervene in circumstances such as these.

Respectfully yours,
David Dark
BARRISTER AND SOLICITOR

Ducky had a pet peeve about his legal colleagues. He believed, although it was left unsaid in the formal exchange of battle, that shoddy practitioners certainly existed. He just didn't believe that it was either fair or reasonable to allow some whimpy party or querulous individual to allow a lawyer to be castigated simply because the complainant didn't like the other guy. Maybe there was jealousy involved, some rough personal problems, who knew? Ducky, however, felt that it was a foolish waste of time to involve the Law Society in petty grievance issues. He acted accordingly when he was called upon to exact judgments that smacked of such ignoble motivations.

It was William Frank's mandate as the Secretary for the Law Society, as he received Dark's report, to direct the following letter to Frank Martinson. A copy was sent simultaneously to Theodore H. James.

Dear Mr. Martinson:

RE: Frank Martinson - Complaint - Theodore H. James

Further, and subsequent to an extensive and lengthy review and investigation by the Law Society and independent appointed member, I confirm that we have been directed by Mr. Dark that the Law Society's complaint file should be held in abeyance until such time as the Lazy Valley loan is fully repaid, and Mr. James' dissociation from The Group of Seven Mortgage Corporation is finalized. Thereafter, the file will be closed. A recommendation has been made that no further proceedings or steps should be taken against Mr. James. Mr. Dark found that Mr. James' conduct was not as it should have been. He allowed himself to be in a conflict of interest position, whereby his motives and intentions could be impugned. Mr. Dark determined that Mr. James had acted in good faith, with propriety, and that his conduct, though not entirely above reproach, should not be sanctioned further. Mr. James has sustained considerable embarrassment, expense, and loss as a result of the complaint and proceedings.

As you know, you have fourteen (14) days to appeal the foregoing finding. If notice of said appeal is not received by our office prior to the elapse of said time period, we shall proceed to close our file.

Yours truly,

William Franks, Secretary-Treasurer
Law Society of Alberta

cc: Theodore H. James
BARRISTER AND SOLICITOR

Frank Martinson received the letter from the Law Society and shook his head in utter disbelief and disgust. He immediately dictated a letter to the lawyers who were acting for the other shareholders in The Group of Seven, outlining briefly the findings of the Law Society, and recommending that the appeal not be advanced.

TJ was euphoric about the response. He read the letter submitted to Martinson, disbelieving his good fortune even as he read. He felt certain that the lawyers for the other shareholders would not appeal the findings of the Law Society. He was tickled that matters had gone the way they had. He knew he had received a stroke of great luck when Ducky was appointed as the independent investigator. He knew that Ducky had given him the benefit of the doubt, but TJ had been able to convince him that things were not as black as painted by Martinson. Foolishness or naivete may have prevailed, but not improper, deceitful or dishonest conduct. Dissociating himself from The Group of Seven Mortgage Corporation had been a stroke of genius. In combination with his assurance that the Lazy Valley Project loan would be paid shortly, the starch washed right out of the white collar complaint. 'One down' thought TJ, 'and one to go'. There was surely a pot of gold at the end of the rainbow.

* * *

His sanction from the Law Society infused him with new energy. He could now carry his plan to completion. The Lazy Valley Project would be ready for sale soon. So far, luck had helped him along. The market for new homes in northwest Calgary was terrific. TJ was optimistic that the Project would sell out completely and quickly.

He had crunched the numbers so many times that he could do it all in his head and visualize the dollar signs. There would be sufficient funds from the sale of the Project to repay the first mortgage, The Group of Seven mortgage charge, all the trades and creditors, provide replacement money for the funds that were unlawfully taken, and those borrowed from trust. He hoped that anything left over would compensate him royally for the hell he had gone through in the past months, but he could not be entirely sure of that. He still allowed himself to dream.

He deserved some perks. The completion of the Project would get those perks for him. He was entitled.

A lesser mortal would have given up a long time ago. He had persevered. He was tenacious. The past chapter that he had written for himself would never be regarded as a dubious achievement. It would always stand as a glorious exploit. He felt invincible. There was no chore or project that was insurmountable. He now knew that if he wanted to go out and do anything… anything, he would, and nothing would stop him.

Lesser mortals could not have accomplished what he had. The euphoria that was invading his sensibilities told him that he had overcome terrible obstacles to achieve the nearly impossible. True, he'd had to do some things that many would have called improper, but that could all be fixed, and no one would be any the wiser. Sometimes a dirty job had to be done. One just had to find the right person for the job.

TJ had one regret: the severance of his relationship with The Group of Seven and the other shareholders. The Project had made them all some good money. He would miss that part indeed. Perhaps, he surmised, the shareholders would dismiss their lawyers once the Lazy Valley loan was paid. They would then be at his office door in droves, begging him to come back, assuring him that they had erred in their misjudgment of him. He could hear the apologies for all the trials and tribulations to which they had unnecessarily subjected him.

He would protest, of course, feign indignation, even hurt, over the lack of trust they had shown in him. After much begging and cajoling, he would allow himself to be persuaded to once again assume stewardship of the Corporation. He could hear them all declaring that only he, the Great Theodore James, could take it to new and exalted heights. He would be forgiving, of course. He would assure them, like any good father, that he would not hold their past rebelliousness against them. He could let bygones be bygones, just to show them what a fine fellow he was. He would make it quite clear that he was more stalwart than anyone or anything else. They could rely on him absolutely. A guy could dream again, once he had awakened from a nightmare.

Chapter Eighteen

The trouble with being a God in your own mind is that there is never anyone around to do the worshipping. No one else knows the litanies, the ceremonies, the strategies of worship, quite like yourself. TJ had worked out the acceptable access to his person. The trouble was, no one cared but him. In addition to that little complication, he had not yet worked out how to see the future.

Today, that trick could have come in handy.

'Wouldn't you know it', he muttered.

Just when things were on the mend, out of nowhere, Ali advised him that the Law Society auditors had arrived for a spot audit. He hadn't even had a chance to open his fan mail.

He glowered at her absently. She was so calm and innocent that he was amused by her.

"TJ, what do you want me to do?", she beseeched him.

"Oh, show them in, of course, spot audits are not unusual. It's probably just my turn."

She looked at him quizzically.

"I mean, let's go to greet them, Ali."

He thought his front was quite brave. Forced

confidence would win them over. They would find no wrongdoing, he felt sure.

After the flamboyant welcomes and the introduction of the auditors to the rolodex files, Ali quietly inquired of TJ: "What happens now?"

"They'll be here for at least the morning, probably the better part of the day. They'll select twenty or thirty files from the rolodex and pore over them with our accountant. That's you."

She looked pleasantly surprised. "Oh, well, what am I doing here, then!!?" and off she hurried.

He chuckled to himself. Every so often he snuck around to see how she was handling them. She couldn't have been nicer or more compliant. A total innocent. If the auditors thought that she was hiding something or knew that anything was amiss, they must have been impressed with her acting. She was as pleasant and cooperative as he expected her to be. Her professionalism would ensure that no suspicions would be raised.

TJ was surprised, then, when the auditors announced that they intended to spend yet another day at his books. They finally left after spending almost two days in his office. He debated about asking Ali some questions, but he didn't want to alarm her. Her inquisitive nature would be alerted. She ventured nothing, even after he took her to dinner and enchanted her with wine and his banter. She made no comments on the auditors or their disclosures to her during the informal audit.

He decided that it was best to let matters lie, and to await the formal report from the Law Society. That might well be dastardly, but perhaps not. It would arrive, in all likelihood, preceded by certain other authorities, who might say everything was okay. He might be patted on the head, maybe some irregularities would be pointed out, who knew? No point worrying until there was something to worry about. He figured that the longer the lapse between the audit and the advice from the Law Society, the better his chances of escaping unscathed.

A formal letter arrived three weeks later from the Law Society, advising that all matters appeared to be in order. A few filing and procedural requirements were discussed, that was all. He could have danced, but decided instead to call Ali in to his office. He showed her the letter and advised her that it provided confirmation as to the excellent job that she was doing.

She beamed. Ali was proud, grateful, worshipping, and he was so lucky.

She took the opportunity, however, to ask him some ugly questions. He couldn't believe his bad luck. Of course the questions were innocent, she didn't have the slightest inkling that anything was wrong. It was rotten luck that she would have tripped on two or three entries out of a bizillion that were involved with his trickery. Appear calm and collected. Don't look upset.

He was concerned, however, and assured her that the matter would be resolved without delay.

"Will you at least look at some of these ledgers, TJ? I just can't figure them out."

"I'm sure you've got everything under control, Ali. You're diligent, careful…"

"But, I'd feel so much better if you'd take a look, please?"

Very well. Soothe her concerns. He knew what was in those ledgers better than she did. He examined them cursorily to assuage her misgivings.

"Greek to me, dear. But I'll contact the firm's Chartered Accountants. They'll be happy to review the ledgers and tell you what adjustments to make."

She seemed relieved. He figured the C.A.'s would turn up in two or three weeks, maybe even a couple of months.

"Let's get out of here and go have a drink someplace," he suggested. "What do you say?"

He needed a drink more than she did. He sauntered to his private office to retrieve his coat, thinking to himself. When the diverted funds were replaced, after proceeds had been received from the Project's sales, he would do what he had to do. Concoct the required entries, whatever. He would simply advise Ali that several improper entries had been made to the wrong files, and corrections had been made. He would also tell her that the C.A.'s were unusually impressed with her astute eye. He'd throw in a little laughter and a small bonus as well... tell her that if he wasn't careful, the C.A.'s would try and lure her away from him. He snickered quietly. He could make something so major disappear with a flick of his wrist, a twist of his mind.

PRIVATE [I]YE

I: the person who is speaking or writing;

Eye:
- the organ of sight
- the ability to see small differences in things;
- a way of thinking or considering; view; opinion; judgment;

the pronoun I is written with a capital simply because in the old handwritten manuscripts a small i was likely to be lost or to get attached to a neighboring word, and a capital helped keep it a distinct word.

(Dictionary of Canadian English)

Chapter Nineteen

"Sam, Sam"... I heard them calling. "Sam, look what we caught!"

I watched them coming from half a mile away. Six boys, three on either side of the great load they carried between them. A long pole suspended the carcass of a doe deer. It was a kill they had tried hard to manage between the six of them, and might have been easier had they known how to gut her out. Rope had been strung around her hoofs and the pole. The boys laboured to bring her as far as the field in front of our house.

One of the boys was my brother. Another was Norm Svensen from next door, and Billy Thompson from down the street, and, oh, I had to look more closely.

Her head hung at a weird angle, tongue lolling futilely from the side of her mouth. I was overcome with pity and horror. She was dead, so very dead...

I heard myself moan through my dream fog. I had that recurring dream again, the one that hadn't troubled me for years. It was really a memory, of course, and it had often come back to haunt me during times of stress in my life: the awful day that my brother, with the boys in the neighbourhood, lugged home a dead mule deer.

They had told me to get lost. I was a girl and they, the boys, had killed. Girls and killing didn't mix. They had killed with the deadly homemade bows and arrows that were okay to use in Calgary back in the 1960's. They could become grown males who would use weapons which hurt, maimed or killed unsuspecting females.

I was now sufficiently awake to stagger to my bathroom and splash cold water on my hot cheeks, wiping the cold sweat from the dream. My heart was pounding off my chest wall like a racquet ball. I could feel my fingers coldly wet as I stroked them over my face.

* * *

Sheedy was fumbling around with the video equipment. The lab had processed the funeral film, and we were all set for replays, only this was no game.

"Sheedy, you turkey, quit the fine surgery and let's roll 'em." McInnis could never resist needling the kid.

I ignored them both, allowing my fatigue to move over me like a wave. God, if I didn't get my fifteen minutes of sleep every night, I was just useless the next day.

"You had a fun night, Sam?"

"What makes you say that?" I snapped at McInnis. "Don't I look glowing and rested to you?"

"Sorry, you could have warned me you were having PMS".

"Chill out, McInnis," I retorted. "I understand it's worse to live with residual semen buildup. They call it RSB in clinical circles."

He flushed quite noticeably in the dark room. Six days into Stampede Week and McInnis hadn't got lucky yet.

"Okay, I guess I had that coming," he muttered.

"We'll accomplish more if we keep our minds on the film and off the gonads, thank you very much." What a bitch I could be, and I didn't even feel guilty.

Sheedy finally figured out how to use the equipment, and we all tried to concentrate.

TJ featured prominently in the film. I was beginning to think it was his natural tendency to dominate the bigger scenes in life. He made no move to avoid the camera, but he did look haggard.

"Sheedy, pause it here."

Theodore James hung suspended in time.

"Have the lab cut this to a still. In fact, we'll take a look at all these characters and do some snapshot stills."

TJ was followed by sweet Suzie.

We hadn't missed anyone.

Frank York appeared with his wife on his arm. The son, or brother, a tall, clean-cut preppie; Luke York. Tanya, the darker model of her sister Ali, emerged from the funeral home after the rest of the family.

Interesting. Tanya kept a certain distance. She was alone.

I instructed Sheedy to have stills made of all the family members.

Then William Corgan emerged. He was handsome in a brutish kind of way. Bushy, wavy hair and a massive moustache. He was clearly uncomfortable in a suit, and kept rubbing the tight collar under a strangulating tie-hold. I couldn't judge him on that quirk, or his obvious discomfort in a suit. Even

Sheedy and McInnis were looking like overdressed cossacks.

The odd thing about Billy Corgan was his stare - right at the camera.

"Sheedy, pause. What do you guys make of that look?"

"What do you mean?" snarled McInnis. "He takes a good photo."

"Sure he does, but it's like he's looking for us. Challenging the camera."

"You're imagining things, Sam." McInnis dismissed my insight. Did McInnis ever have gut feelings? I took the liberty of asking him that very question.

"No, I don't, but since you ask, if a guy stared at me like that in a bar, I'd probably pop his face."

"That's what I mean. Gut feeling. Reaction. McInnis, there's hope for you. You've got the primal makings of Woman's Intuition."

He glowered at me. I wish I knew someone I disliked enough to fix him up with.

"Sheedy, cut that last still of Billy Corgan."

"What do you want us to do with the stills?"

"You visited some of Ali York's neighbours, right? And those of Maureen Rogers? Take the stills with you and ask again."

"Great!" beamed Sheedy.

"What are you so excited about, kid?" badgered McInnis.

"Well, old Mrs. Schultz makes terrific banana bread. She invited me back for some when I had a day off."

"Sheedy, what is it with you. It's Stampede Week. Check out some bars, meet some women. Get with the program." McInnis punched the kid softly in the belly. "Take some fat off".

They started to wrestle, nearly toppling the video equipment.

I watched them try to maul each other. Sheedy conceded mastery to the dominant ape, and then felt the need to explain himself.

"My mom used to make this great Irish soda bread, you know. I kinda miss my mom."

McInnis had the grace to shut up.

"Mrs. Schultz seems like the type of woman who would be everybody's friend", I told him. "Buy her some old bananas. They make the best bread."

"Really? I didn't know that. Maybe I'll try to get her recipe."

"Guys, let's work on gleaning all the information we can about the victims: who they knew, family, friends, bad habits, what they ate, noise level in their apartments. You know. The works. You were going to have some composite drawings made from Mrs. Schultz's recollections. Have we gone anywhere on those?"

"Nothing concrete, Sam," revealed Sheedy. "I think the stills might work better."

The guys left the room and I was left to meditate, alone in the dark.

Some puzzle pieces were starting to fit together. I had discovered from enquiries to the Registrar at Red Deer College that York and Rogers had been classmates in the legal aide program there. They had each graduated with honours. The Registrar at Red Deer had been most co-operative with the investigation, expressing horror at the news of the ladies' deaths. I believed that the murderer had been much more interested in Ali, judging from her state of undress. Rogers was, as I had noted at the crime scene, an afterthought.

The scientific arm of forensics was all over the evidence, poring over prints, DNA, hair, you name it. A sensible approach to investigation, but only one approach. There had to be another, but what? A few leads had come up and I had a few hunches, but no real credible motive.

Neither woman had been sexually assaulted. There was no robbery or theft. Only a past, a connection that was common between them. That past had cost them their lives. So it was premeditated. Had to be. The same individual had probably snuffed them both. Whoever it had been, he was good; very good, and he had some sort of plan. Why a he?

Both victims had been shot in the back of the head, with little damage to the facial features. These elements suggested a male murderer. Generally, women murderers killed with direct aim at the torso. Men shot through the head.

We had found the bullets that we hoped we'd find in the walls of the apartment, but the type was inconclusive. Average .22 shells.

A general plea for public assistance had been made but so far, no concrete leads had developed. I could not comprehend what would possess anyone to take the lives of two young women. Rogers and York had not gone looking for trouble. I supposed that if the victims were two lawyers, rather than secretaries or clerks, the public might not have been quite so interested in bringing justice to bear on the perpetrators.

Mental notes. Make sure all the other evidence moves around these clues. I knew I would solve this one eventually. There was so much to know about Ali and Maureen. Eventually the truths in both their lives would intersect. We had science on our side, not that I believed wholeheartedly in that tool. The murders were almost certainly planned. In fact, the answer might end up being far too easy.

Had I missed a turn somewhere? Sat in the wrong spot upwind of the prey? Sexual assault was relatively easy to spot. There had been none in this case. I was also assured that there had been no forceable entry to either apartment.

It was so dangerous to proceed in the wrong direction. You could dislodge all sorts of valuable clues if you moved too quickly. By the time you realized you were heading the wrong way, retracing your steps was almost impossible. The wind would shift, blowing all the tracks away. Next week there might be another murder.

My only answer to myself was to watch and wait. Eventually the wind would turn in the right direction.

Chapter Twenty

I was checking addresses, places to go and people to see about Ali York. I was breathing, sleeping (sometimes) and living the York and Rogers cases. I found it easier to work at home. The office was crazed with media, all trying to press us to verbiage about "The Cowboy Cutter", as the York and Rogers murderer had been dubbed. The local bars had placed extra watch dogs at the door. Some folks were more sober than usual. Stampede Week brought out the crazies normally, but this year was different in that respect. Things seemed quieter because of the murders.

The press, try as they might, didn't have a thing to go on. Everyone concerned had kept quiet, and as yet, I could only be accessed by people who counted. Like Sheedy and McInnis. Sergeant Speirs. And fortunately, Richard.

I heard the front door slam. "Halloooo, you!"

"Out here, Richard, admiring the flowers."

Normally, I spend a lot of time on the flowers. The earth was hot and dry this week, and I had neglected to water my precious blossoms. I thought I might as well fix that problem.

Richard found me lugging the hose around.

"My, aren't we energetic for someone who's been suffering from insomnia."

I stopped to look at him wonderingly. "Not energetic, Richard, just a slave to routine. Besides, the flowers haven't been watered."

"Neither have you. Feel up to some entertainment one of these evenings?"

"I'm not going Stampeding with you, so forget it."

He was undaunted. "Okay, so let's have an el-cheapo Stampede barbecue over here. I've already invited Mark and Greg."

I frowned at him.

"Greg… hm… you know, Richard, he borrowed my black satin top with the rhinestones and he hasn't returned it yet."

"You're kidding. Wasn't that last Halloween?"

"Yes, about then. Eight months is long enough to borrow a rhinestone top."

Richard cozied into the patio chair. "I must speak to him. He's taking this Cleopatra disguise too far."

"Never mind," I replied, "I hadn't planned to wear it again. Trust me. By the way, Greg didn't strike me as a plausible Cleopatra. Doesn't he have a tiny beard? A five o'clock shadow most of the time?"

"Oh, yeah, but we shaved his chest hair and made boobs from stockings filled with birdseed."

"Really? That's quite creative. What's this cross-dressing all about anyway, Richard?"

"Think of it as gender-resistance, Sam. You do the same thing as a woman, by shooting defenceless wildlife."

This time I glowered at him before I spoke. "I don't think it's the same thing at all." I didn't see his point, and I didn't want to pursue it. Instead, I batted my eyelashes at him imploringly. "Are you going to get me a drink, buddy?" I wanted to change the subject before he introduced some other issue that might tax my brain.

"Oh, yeah, sure." He disappeared for a minute.

Insomnia. Richard had mentioned it. I wondered how he knew. When he reappeared, I asked him. "You should be the detective, Richard. How did you know about the insomnia?"

"I do have ears, sweetie. You splash the meanest cold water at three in the morning."

"Sorry, I didn't realize I was waking you. I can't face the office these days."

"What's on your mind?"

"I have this recurring dream. It's nothing, really."

"It keeps waking you up. You want to finish the dream, where it breaks off for you?" He handed me my soda and lime.

"Nothing to finish, I can't remember what happened after."

"So it's not a dream."

I put the hose down, then turned to him. "No, it's a memory."

"What made it ugly?"

"It's about a dead deer. It wasn't just that the deer was dead, the boys took such pride in what they had done. I never shoot a deer without some ceremony, which acknowledges that I've taken a life that I must use with respect. Those teenage boys didn't care. They carried her back on a rotisserie pole. No dignity in the death. They just wanted to cut her open to see what was inside. Maybe it was a male/female thing. I just don't know. All these bodies, the blood, brings it all back."

"Would it have been different if you had helped carry her?"

I thought about this question. What a curious way of framing it. If I had helped carry her? Included myself in the kill? How would things have been different?

Perhaps I could have been the part of the team that ensured dignity.

Extrapolate.

What about Ali and Maureen's deaths? What part would I play in the closure of these women's lives? I knew it would have to be ethical; I could afford to believe nothing but my own instincts.

He was watching me carefully. I didn't feel like being the guinea-pig. 'I'm a tough officer of the law', I reminded myself, picking up the hose again, to water... absently.

"I'd love to help you entertain the guys, Richard." It was the only response I could make.

* * *

Red Deer was an hour and a half drive north of Calgary. Good thinking time. I had called ahead to make an appointment with Wanda York. I had discovered a fair bit about Ali and Maureen, but rather than point to solutions, my discoveries only ended up as soup. A fairly tasty soup, no doubt, but certainly not clear. Frank and Wanda York lived in Red Deer, where Ali had grown up. Sheedy informed me that Luke and Tanya had moved to Calgary, so they would be next week's project. What did I know for certain about Ali's family? She had been suing her parents and brother for psychological damage, according to

James. They could not have been too enamoured with her while she was alive. Her death would have ensured their peace.

She had also initiated a Restraining Order against Billy Corgan. Who knows what a potentially unstable personality would do in the teeth of a Restraining Order? Spurned boyfriend and all that. Maybe a single or double murder would be a natural consequence. Lord knows it had happened before to a lot of women who thought they were safe from abusive husbands. But that didn't explain Maureen Rogers.

They all seemed to have at least an emotional motive for eliminating Ali. It was unlikely, however, that family members would go to such lengths, and anyway, how would that explain Rogers? I knew only one thing for sure. There was little real evidence to link anyone specifically to the murders, or to either of the women, actually. The fact that there had been no forceable entry at either York's or Rogers' apartments would indicate that both the deceased girls had recognized their murderers. The culprit had been let in by the victims.

God only knew.

With a little bit of searching, I found the York homestead. Nice little yard. Pansies, marigolds, hanging baskets of beauty. Primed for looks. It only lacked the white picket fence.

I stepped up to the door and rang the bell. Mommy Wanda answered.

"Mrs. York, I'm Detective Samantha Holt from the Calgary City Police."

She looked positively miserable. I started in gently. "I'm sorry, I know this is a dreadful time for you." She nodded, fixing her eyes on my shoes.

"Come in, Ms. Holt. I don't know how we can help, but we'll certainly try."

We? I stepped over the landing and noticed that Frank York was at home. Easy now, Sam. Carry Ali, the dead doe. Start to privilege her. You can take a swipe at daddy-bear later.

He stood up defensively. "Ms. Holt. I recall seeing you at the funeral." I flushed slightly at the memory of Sheedy and McInnis taking pictures.

"Yes, Mr. York. I was there. It's a practice of mine to include attendance at funerals in investigative procedure." I decided not to apologize to the slime-bag.

Mrs. York invited me to take a chair. Daddy remained standing. Grizzly bears often stand on their hind legs to survey their prey just before they decide to maul. I refused to meet him head on. Not just yet. Mrs. York interrupted the moment.

"Frank, sit down. Ms. Holt is trying to help. It's part of her job."

For some odd reason, he decided to take her advice. I thought I heard a low growl.

I commenced the interview, taking out my notorious notepad. Frankie glowered at me. Not good.

"Did Ali have any enemies that you know of?" I addressed the question to both of them. Wanda looked at my shoes again. I took a moment to check if the horseshit was gone, but not before I noticed Frank change his countenance. Good poker face. Emblazoned innocence.

"Of course not, Ms. Holt. Ali was a star student at the college. She had many friends. I encouraged her to try for law school, although I thought it was beyond her capabilities." Frankie wanted me to know what a terrific guy he was, ever in support of his daughter.

"She had many boyfriends, as well," commented Wanda. I detected a poignant strength behind her words, but I wasn't entirely sure they were intended for me.

They weren't. Frank glowered. "She had a particularly difficult acquaintance by the name of Billy Corgan. He was an undesirable, in my mind. Billy had been around since Ali was quite young. Wouldn't leave, even when I strongly encouraged him to do so."

"Yes, I've heard of him." I decided to ask the leading question.

"Mr. and Mrs. York, where were you on the night of Ali's murder?"

They did not even exchange glances, but Frank York went quite red. I watched his teeth clench as he responded:

"My wife and I were at a church meeting, a pot luck supper." I took down the name of the minister and the church. He was the same guy who had spoken at Ali's funeral. I might yet look him up, but in the meantime, there was no point in preserving this happy little home thing any further.

"Mr. York, what was your reaction to Ali's lawsuit against yourselves and her brother Luke."

His roar was quite threatening indeed. "Ms. Holt, when I agreed to speak with you, I had hoped not to be insulted."

Wanda stared fixedly at my shoes.

I pressed my arrow home. "How do you feel insulted, Mr. York?

"How dare you cast aspersions about my character. Ali was clearly under the influence of that...

lawyer, or that half-assed therapist she spent time with."

His knuckles grabbed the armchair he was only partially raised out of. "I cannot imagine how she could have contrived such a ridiculous idea. Why, I can hardly speak the word… incest. The notion is completely abhorrent!"

"Indeed it is, Mr. York. But it's important to my investigations that I determine who the players are, and to what purpose they may have played Ali."

"Ms. York, I am a member of a support group that deals with these things. As you may know, many parents have been falsely accused of incest, and the group is quite large. That should give you a clue as to the validity of accusations concerning my relationship to my daughter. Ask yourself why only one of my daughters accuses me of such an atrocity."

Of course he wanted me to apologize for my question. He was a bully. I can smell them from ninety paces. They are the only human beings, if you could call them that, which I become totally out-of-order about.

"I'm not certain that only one of your daughters accused you, Mr. York." I refused to call him sir. Not this guy.

He blanched considerably. I kept my eyes on him. Another snake. Meet his gaze. Smirk if necessary, but don't let him intimidate you.

"Ms. Holt, I would appreciate it if you would leave my home. It is completely unconscionable that you would come here to insult me and horrify my wife."

I stood up nonchalantly. The manner infuriated York even further. He actually stamped his foot.

"Get out, get out, you bitch!"

Oh, pleeese, I thought, I've been called worse than that before.

"If... there's anything you need, Ms. Holt..." Wanda looked at me directly, imploringly. I nodded at her.

"Wanda!!!!" was the last shout I heard from Frank York, as I stepped none too quickly out the door.

Chapter Twenty-one

One should always de-brief these crisis situations. I was able to do that on the way home from Red Deer. Wanda had seemed... beseeching, somehow, had wanted to help me. How intriguing. But what did that mean? Had she been trying to annoy her husband? Was Wanda trying to tell me something? What?

I got back to the cop shop about two in the afternoon. Sheedy met me at the door. "Where've you been, Holt? We've got all kinds of information!"

He was fairly hopping around in his excitement.

"So, Sheedy, let's grab a coffee and you can tell me all about it." I did so, while he scanned the office for the cream and sugar, which always seemed to go missing.

I took off my silly shoes and wiggled my toes. The coffee steamed comfortably over my face as I tried to focus my thoughts. "Have you talked to Mrs. Schultz about the pictures?" I inquired.

"Yeah, she's been great. Seems that Ali liked banana bread too. Mrs. Schultz claims that she saw a woman enter Ali's apartment in the afternoon and early evening of her death. She can't be sure that it's any of the women in the pictures, though."

"Not even Wanda York?"

"Mrs. Schultz just wasn't sure. She did say, though, that a tall middle-aged man, well-dressed, showed up at the apartment the same night. She thought the guy just might be Theodore James. I showed her a picture. She also said that she heard arguing and yelling coming from the York apartment. She couldn't be sure, but she believed that the yelling was the result of a confrontation between two people, both of whom sounded like women."

None of that made sense to me. Although what seemed obvious here was that everybody was mad at Ali, and TJ was as likely a suspect as anyone else.

"Did you check with other witnesses?"

"No, but McInnis did." I looked around for the big guy, wondering if he had yet experienced a successful Stampede in the manner to which he was accustomed. I spied him from across the office. He seemed preoccupied. A good sign. Eliminate RSB, and you have a functioning man.

"Sam," offered McInnis, unusually pensive, "it seems we have two additional witnesses here, one that claims she saw Wanda York at her daughter's apartment on the day of the murder. The same witness identified someone that she said looked like Luke York at Ali's apartment on the day of the murder. Another old guy, who prides himself on being the neighbourhood block watch, claims that he saw someone identified as Billy Corgan on the day of Ali's murder."

"Not only that", interrupted Sheedy, "but a motel registration clerk from the Robin's Nest motel phoned us to let us know that the lovely Ms. York had checked in with someone matching TJ's description some days earlier. He has the exact date. The clerk said he'd seen her picture on T.V. and the papers, and wouldn't forget such a beauty."

"Good work you guys, but any defence lawyer who's awake will have both witnesses fumbling about the identity, confirming that they would be hard pressed to state with certainty that the parties they saw at the York residence on the day of the murder were in fact those named and identified. I could also make moves for Frank and Wanda's fingerprints, and those of Luke, maybe even Tanya, but we can't just ask out of the blue. Their lawyers would be all over us like sweaty T-shirts. We've got to work with anything we have, build a suspect profile. If anything starts to look like someone we know, we can start following tracks."

"Great," announced McInnis, with a note of frustration. "Where do we go from here?"

"I don't know, guys."

We were all three silent for a minute. Then Sheedy announced: "I've got that coffee mug, the one I picked up at the murder scene. It's got prints all over it, I just don't know whose. They don't belong to Ali York."

I frowned over my own coffee cup. "Try Billy Corgan. We have his prints on record, surely. We've got everything else on him. And TJ's. I brought that card back from his office.

"Sure, I'll try them both," muttered Sheedy, "but Corgan seems like the most likely suspect."

"And Sheedy, could you check out the Yorks' alibi? Some minister at the local Lutheran church in Red Deer. Same guy who was at Ali's funeral." I gave Sheedy my notes, and he sauntered away towards the phone.

I hardly knew where to begin. The whole business just seemed so overwhelming.

"Guys." They both looked around, waiting for a break in my sombre mood. "We've got Luke York's address and place of employment, right?" They both nodded.

"Think you guys could encourage him to come in for an interview?" I asked.

McInnis grinned happily at me. "Say no more, Sam."

They left so fast that I reckoned they were just as frustrated with the non-action as I was.

* * *

The culprit, Luke York, came in all right, with a defiant sneer and a smirk that could cause volcanoes to puke. Sheedy and McInnis were enjoying the muscle, bringing him directly to my desk in a 'take me to your leader' kind of gesture. I thought I played the part rather well.

"So, Mr. York." I said pleasantly. "Glad you could make it."

"I'm not sayin' nothin' until my lawyer gets here."

"You're not wanted for murder, Mr. York. I just wanted to ask you a few questions about your relationship with your sister. Do you see any need to phone your lawyer about something as innocent as filial connection?"

"Picking me up at my job and hauling me in here isn't a friendly act, lady." He growled, wiping invisible lint off his pin-striped suit.

I stood up. "The name is Detective Samantha Holt, Mr. York. I do apologize if my colleagues ruffed you up a bit." Bad cops, Nice Lady.

Sheedy winked at me.

"Shall we move into a more secluded place to discuss some issues respecting your sister?"

He grunted, following me to the interrogation room. Sheedy and McInnis followed quietly, their roles as bodyguards quite unmistakable. I threw open the door to the interrogation room.

"Sit down, Mr. York", I invited, not too pleasantly.

He took the seat, glowering malevolently at me. Sheedy and McInnis took a comfortable position in a corner.

"Now then, Mr. York. I understand that your sister, Ali, was suing you for all kinds of nasty things that happened, allegedly of course, in her younger years." I added 'allegedly' so as not to alarm him too much. I didn't need a cocky lawyer in here.

"Those allegations are unbelievable."

I raised my eyebrows. "Indeed? Allegations of incest often seem quite shocking, Mr. York. Could you shed any light on your family's response to them?"

I knew full well what her family's response had been.

"Tanya told me what Ali had in store for me. I couldn't believe what she was up to."

"Did you ever give much thought to what your parents might be going through?"

"'Course not. Dad can take care of himself."

Hmmm. No mention of mom.

"The financial consequences of a lawsuit, well, it would have bankrupted me. Laying criminal charges would have ruined me. I didn't need my wife to learn of it, either. I didn't need that headache. Besides, I might like to see my kids, you know. What if people thought I was a molester? I'd never see them. Just because my sister said I was a pervert doesn't mean that I am. I had to try and stop her." He looked me straight in the eye, waiting for my approval.

He was asking the wrong person, and he knew it.

"I never did what she said I did, or anything close to it. Maybe some minor little 'things', you know. Kid stuff. Playing around. My sister was batty, and she blew everything out of proportion. Maybe I made a few mistakes, but Ali was short a few raisins in her fruitcake."

He waited again for my approval, which didn't materialize. "You don't believe anything I'm telling you, do you? It figures. Women. You're all going to fry me. You can't possibly think that Ali's murder is linked to the incest charges!"

"I don't believe I said that, Mr. York." He flushed.

"You, you... bitch!" he spat.

I sat quite still, waiting for the right moment. "You can't do anything to me! You're a cop," he roared, "you wouldn't try anything without checking your rules and regulations. Better yet, you're a lady cop. You don't have the balls! Just try and muscle me around, lady! I want my lawyer present!" He vaulted upright, shrieking. "I'll have you and your lackeys over there sued so badly that you'll be writing out traffic tickets for the rest of your career. If you're lucky!"

I hurled my body over the table, knocking over the chair behind me, grabbing him by the lapels of his pretty little suit.

"Don't mess with me, Mr. York." I fastened my eyeballs on his. "In the first place, I'm not a good enough cop to concern myself with legal details. In other words, your lawyer means fuck-all to me."

That slowed him down, but it didn't stop him.

York tried desperately to disengage my glower. "Your cronies here will report you," he spat.

McInnis volunteered: "I didn't see a thing, did you, Sheedy?"

"Nope. Detective Holt always behaves like a delicate flower when conducting an interrogation."

Luke York knew he'd lost the battle. I released my viper-grip on his suit, smoothing the crinkles for him.

"You run along, now, Mr. York. I'll send for you if I need you again."

"You don't understand, Detective. Incest is a terrible charge. A blemished reputation tarnishes permanently. I didn't know how to stop my sister, I..." he was pleading with me now. The power differential had shifted. "I didn't kill her."

"Didn't you, Mr. York?" I didn't want to let him off. "Incest is not only a terrible charge, Mr. York. It's also a terrible crime. Perhaps you'd also like to share with us where you were on the night of your sister's murder?"

"I was at my son's little-league softball game. I'm the assistant coach, so I have to be at the games. All the other parents know me."

"Perhaps you'd like to provide us with a list of names, Mr. York?"

Concern finally registered in his eyes. I tried to remember that he had been a boy once, and that ultimately, Frank York was the culprit. Daddy had abused the boy as much as the girls.

"I'll drop it off for you tomorrow, Detective."

I refused to look at him. I was becoming quite ill with all this suburbia, good-people, 'can't happen in our family' kind of garbage.

"Get him out of here." I sincerely hoped that I would have no further cause to speak to Luke York.

I stared at the wall as Sheedy and McInnis led him out. They glanced at me, trying to read what I was thinking. I wasn't thinking about anything. Just dead air.

* * *

Richard made me set the table. He always insisted on fine linen, flowers, the works. I reminded him that it was just a barbecue.

"Nonsense. Only plebeians have barbecues. You and I have dinner parties", he sniffed.

"Oh really. Then why did you heat up the barbecue?"

"Don't argue with me. Forks on the left, Sam."

"Oh, please. I know that. So tell me more about this Mark guy, besides the fact that he has a great sense of humour."

"Ohh, I met him at a party last week", replied Richard, casually stirring his drink.

He was unusually nonchalant. I suddenly realized why the best dinnerware was on display.

"So, am I your best friend, or what? How come you don't tell me about your new love interests?"

"Because you always behave boorishly. You'll grill him mercilessly, and before I know it, the man won't have any secrets from any of us."

"So what's wrong with that? One can't be too careful these days. And what about Greg? Is he chopped liver?"

"No, I just haven't seen him in awhile. Besides,

he's great at dinner parties and I told him to bring back your rhinestone-thing."

"You didn't, Richard! He'll be embarrassed. It wasn't that important, really."

"Cut some flowers, would you", he ordered, changing the subject impatiently, "they'll be here any minute."

I had been dismissed. With that, I wandered outside to cut some snapdragons and pansies to grace our lovely dinner table. No sooner had I arranged them than the doorbell rang.

Richard leaped for the door. "Hellooo, hellooo, guys!" Kisses were exchanged all around, and good wine was quickly added to the festivities.

A delicious meal awaited us after much laughter and good-natured ribbing about Richard living with a woman. He wasn't at all embarrassed, I was proud of him. And could he cook! I took pains to point out that Richard was quite a catch.

I noticed him flush, and realized I would pay for that one.

I decided to open up some useful conversation. "And what do you do for a living, Mark?"

"Well, a number of things, Sam. My day job is a waiter at Ciao Baby's. The one I really enjoy is my acting job."

"Really! The theatre?"

"Nothing that fancy. I do murder mysteries with Borealis Productions. It's a lot of fun, and besides, I get the opportunity to write my own mysteries. The actors often take turns writing the script."

We spent some time talking about the nature of those scripts. They were creative and talented pieces of work, to say the least. Richard interjected.

"Sam's working on her own murder mystery these days."

I started. That stuff was confidential. Was this his way of getting back at me? No. He wasn't that vindictive. I glared at him, but he completely ignored me. He was too far away from me to kick under the table.

Greg perked up. "That wouldn't be 'The Cowboy Cutter', would it?"

"Maybe".

"Geez, I knew the lady who was killed. Ali York."

I nearly fell off my seat. Where would this go?

"I know who was boffing her, too."

"Boffing!? Now you guys call it boffing?"

They all exchanged glances. I recognized the stares. WARNING. RED ALERT. Foaming feminist on the rampage. I would have to let this one go if I wanted to know more.

I attempted to take the irritation out of my voice. "Tell me more, Greg. How did you find this out?"

I counted on Greg being too gossipy to refuse feeding me the tidbit. I wasn't disappointed.

"I'm a golf pro at the Country Club. I saw Ali York there once or twice with Mr. James the lawyer."

I gulped. This was perhaps the connection I needed.

I steadied my excitement. "So, anyone could go to the golf and country club with Mr. James, the lawyer. How do you know he was 'boffing' her, as you say?"

"You know, Sam. You just *know*. There is really only one thing you need to know about class. Them and us. That's all. We can wait on tables, hand them their golf clubs and gold cards, and they truly believe we're deaf. Ali York was some babe, and James knew it. All you have to do is listen to people when they believe you're least conspicuous. Oooee, if I was so inclined."

The conversation deteriorated at that point. Thankfully, Richard brought it back on track. I knew now why he had tried his diversion. He was hoping that talking about this would save my mental health.

"Well, okay, you're not so inclined..." a conversational nudge from Richard.

"Hey, what's the difference between a lawyer and a sperm cell?" challenged Mark.

"The sperm cell has a billion to one chance of becoming a human being." Hoots and laughter.

"Say," says Mark, "did you hear the story about the lawyer and his two clients, a bishop and a nuclear physicist who went out fishing? They were some miles at sea when their engine failed. Sharks began to circle the boat.

When neither prayer nor science could get them out of their difficulties, the lawyer dived in, fastened a towrope around his waist and swam ashore, pulling the boat behind him. The sharks formed lines on each side of the boat and escorted it to shore.

The bishop and the scientist congratulated their lawyer and asked him how he had been so successful with the sharks. 'It was nothing', he said, 'just professional courtesy.'"

They would have gone on, but I yawned. I think Greg was disgruntled with my impaired sense of humour. He tried to explain himself.

"Jokes are important cultural rhetoric, you know, Sam. If there's a glut of jokes about some particular issue, it's because we in the marginalized classes find that rhetoric to be a good way of challenging the status quo."

"You mean like blonde jokes?"

"Well, yes. Blondes have always been privileged females. The jokes brought them down a notch or two. Of course, guys like me never really cared." He wanted to be careful that no one got the wrong impression.

Mark commented: "So lawyers have always sat in the seat of privilege, and we tell jokes to erode that throne?"

"That's it exactly," continued Greg. "A sure sign of success is when lawyers stop taking themselves so seriously that they can afford to repeat the jokes. What they don't seem to realize is that they are taking up the rhetoric of the lower-middle classes. It shows we've won. It demonstrates that we've dismantled legal arrogance. The joke is on them."

I nodded. I could think of a few pedestals that needed dismantling. The privileged legal profession had been collapsing for a long time.

Suddenly I knew who that mug belonged to. Just as surely as if his name had been imprinted on it. And really, it was.

Chapter Twenty-two

I left the dinner table quite abruptly, leaving Richard and his buddies to wonder what had become of me. I suppose they thought they had offended my feminine sensibilities, but so what.

I decided to try McInnis first, just to prove to him that I still cared. I hoped he'd be at home. I waited impatiently for his voice.

"Yo, McInnis here."

"Hi, it's Sam. Sorry about interrupting your evening."

"God, I should be so lucky. What's up, Sam?"

"Did you get the print results from the card I brought back from TJ's?"

"No, Sheedy had them. Do you think…?"

"I'm pretty sure, actually. I'll bet that the prints on that card and the mug are an exact match."

"I think I can get on that right away. Call you back in an hour?"

"Yeah, no problem. I'm not doing anything either. See ya."

I returned to the guys at the dinner table. They all looked at me like one of those weird pictures in a haunted castle, you know, the ancestor whose eyes follow you everywhere. Only here, there were three pair of eyes.

* * *

I read far into the night, long after the guys had left. I shouted at Richard once, to ask him if he needed help cleaning up. He yelled back 'no, I don't need any help. You're always messing up my kitchen.'

Ali kept me awake. It was clear to me that I would have to use her diary as the tool for cracking this case. I flipped ahead in her diary to the recent past. Ali wanted me to pay attention to her. She told me so in no uncertain terms:

November, 1993: I'm really beginning to get off on this Theodore James guy. I can't get over how lucky I am to have landed a job where there is so much action and never a dull moment. Of course, I don't have much of an outside life, but then I never did. My job responsibilities are immense. TJ seems willing to let me do everything but climb into his bed, and it won't be long before that happens, either. Around the office, he acts like I'm the senior secretary. I meet with clients, I have a stack of files on my desk that I look at myself and what's really weird is that I have control and responsibility for the office's accounting. I get all the cheques, send out billings, do bank deposits, and reconcile all trust and general funds. You bet I'm capable. TJ says I'm enthusiastic, diligent, and smart. I learn quickly, I know, and I don't mind working long hours. The future? I'm not sure. I can't deal with the future until I've dealt with the past.

If I had to make a plan, I think I would open up a school for legal aides. It doesn't need to be accredited. Better yet, go to law school. TJ says I can handle it. I'm prepared to work as long and hard on it as necessary. I know that TJ thinks that I'm doing a great job, so maybe… just maybe.

November 10: I really want to know everything, and make myself indispensable to TJ. I rely on him a lot too, says Leslie, when I tell her about the job. She says that's okay. I've never trusted anyone before. It's a new experience. I don't always know what he's trying to do, or what he's saying, but I pretend to. In any case, I'm used to following directions exactly. Frank trained me well. I never allow myself to second guess TJ. Sometimes I think that something could be done better but I ignore my inclinations. Better not to upset the apple cart. I worry sometimes. TJ sees my concern but assures me that I am doing an excellent job, and that he will monitor my work and let me know if everything is okay.

December: I am angry. Leslie says I have been that way for a long time. It just didn't seem like it to me. I have always been ambitious. Accomplishing things made up for the pain, I guess, and channelled the anger. Now I want to channel it in a new direction. Sometimes I think I am most angry at my mother. She knew. She knew what Frank was doing and just let it happen. She knew what Luke was doing and let that happen too. Frank ruled. Maybe Wanda cried, but if she did, I never heard, and I would bet money that she never cried for me.

December 12: The revulsion I feel for the lot of them could make me puke. Maybe I should. It's all been buried for so long. I just can't figure out why my mother could allow Frank to do what he did to me.

Oh sure, it must be a terrible thing to live with, but I had the worst of it. I need to confront them, but Leslie tells me to be very sure I'm ready, first. We do some role-playing. What would I say to Frank, what would I say to mom? I know what I would say to my brother. Tanya is a mystery, though. I don't know how much she knows. Maybe Frank ruined her too. She hasn't told me. Leslie tells me I better talk to Tanya before I make any moves.

December 20: Another problem. Billy Corgan has found me. He is a misfit, he has no other friends, and he doesn't seem to be involved in any sensible social activities. I was shocked and dismayed to see him at the door, but for old time's sake, I let him in. It was nearly Christmas after all. He's so pessimistic about everything. Complains constantly. People are no good, picking on him all the time. Everyone is against him, and I am the only person who cares for him. If only I felt strong enough to tell him the truth. I don't want his smothering any more.

He's started to call me at home far too much. I never gave him my work number, but he must have followed me and found out where I worked. I've told him not to call me there, but he doesn't listen. I don't know what to do about him. I've told him to 'get a life' as they say, but he insists on being involved in almost every facet of mine. He's like a third leg and he's driving me crazy. I'm prepared to spend a wee bit of time with him, just to ease him into city life, but that's all!

January, 1994. A New Year. Time to deal with Billy, Frank, Wanda, Tanya and Luke. I'm ready. Billy is becoming such a nuisance. I never wanted to be hard on him. It's just that my need of him is over. I need to know who I am now. Leslie asks if I am ready to confront my family. Who knows? I think I need to speak. To say something to everyone I once loved. Just what that speech will be about is a mystery at the moment. It'll come.

January 7: I've been able to put up with Billy before, even though he was bothersome. I've asked him to give me some breathing room. I'm going to ask TJ about securing a Restraining Order against Billy. At least then, he can't contact me, or come near me. He keeps pleading his love for me, and I am afraid he'll do something awful to himself if I decide to get mean, but what else can I do? He is more domineering and arrogant all the time, demanding to know where I'm going, criticizing my activities, following, trailing, harassing.

January 10: The last straw. Billy told me to quit my job. If I don't, he'll put a stop to it. Told me I was too involved with that… lawyer. I don't know what Billy will do, but TJ deserves to know.

January 11: So I told him. Apologized for burdening him with problems. He's been so helpful to my recovery. While I was at it, I decided to take a chance and explain what I wanted to do with my parents and Luke, namely to sue them for damages for sexual assault. He was surprised. He looked at me differently after that. I hope I haven't spoiled the relationship by all that self-disclosure, but it seems to be the only thing I can do at the moment. I talked about a Restraining Order to get rid of Billy. TJ said of course, that could happen, but sometimes Restraining Orders don't work. The creeps involved often become more belligerent. One has to be careful. Any breach has to be reported immediately.

January 14: I feel sort of foolish, and I told TJ. He said I should always come to him with all my problems, office or personal. He says he will always be there for me, anytime, anyplace, anywhere. Sure. Others have told me the same thing, but this time? Maybe he's for real. After all, he put together the lawsuit, the Restraining Order. I owe him something. I have a feeling I know what it's going to be.

January 30: No moves yet from the boss. I haven't discouraged him, though. I don't mind being in the office. Days, nights, weekends. I guess I've thrown myself into my job. TJ's so nice to me. I'm involved with most of TJ's business. I like the responsibility. He's now given me the Lazy Valley file. It's truly awesome, but I'm learning to handle it. I have a good comfort level with the job now. If I can do this much, how much more would be involved with going to Law School?

Sometimes I check my answers to questions against how TJ responds. My advice is quite similar. Of course, I don't know as much as he does, but I get along okay. I can expand on it. Maybe if I save my money, I can cram in some legal courses, maybe take the LSAT entrance exam next year...

On top of that, I think TJ is putting the make on me. I got the paycheque today, with a big raise. My pay stub had the following note on it: 'Ali, you are doing a fabulous job, and you know how much my practice and myself rely on you. The increase in your salary is a token of my esteem and gratitude for your services and excellent assistance. I look forward to a

long and continued relationship. Would you honour
me with your company at the Country Club tonight?'

Ali had stapled the note to that page of her diary. I
could have gone on, but my eyes would look bleary
enough in the morning. I tucked the diary away,
turned off the lights, and tried desperately to settle
into a dormant state that did not involve Ali.

Chapter Twenty-three

Suzie James was a busy woman indeed.

If you had asked TJ what his wife did in her spare time, he would have said that she didn't really have any. He often said that Suzie was engaged usefully in the community in that elusive 'spare time'. Their two kids had hockey commitments, softball, ballet, music lessons. Suzie had parent-teacher interests, she volunteered at fund-raising bingos, casinos, and generally raised consciousness about her husband's positive citizenship. It was something she felt she had to do in order to launch his political career. James told everyone what a magnificent woman she was, how she never wanted to bother him, realizing how important he was: a veritable gift to society. He spared no breath telling everyone that his smallest whim was her first and utmost concern, that there was nothing she would not do for him to perform every endeavour to her utmost ability.

Yes, she was a driven woman indeed. She thought of herself as everyone else's saviour. If someone needed her, she just slept less. She wanted the world to know that they could count on her.

That's the story everyone heard from TJ.

The truth was that he really had no idea what Suzie did between 7 a.m. and 7 p.m. He didn't really care as long as he could comfortably create a picture of her to his colleagues. Didn't matter much if the portrait didn't fit the likeness.

Suzie might have told you almost the same story if you'd asked, which you probably wouldn't have. No one ever thought to question the generally accepted notion that Suzie was a fine upstanding citizen. She pulled off the routine so well that everyone assumed... no one really knew. She left out a few realities, of course, just so the portrait would look nice. Looking nice was a priority in southwest Calgary; an essential facade to impress the community.

Suzie had noticed that her husband was dreadfully burdened with some pervasive work problem. He looked haggard and harassed, obviously under some unusual pressure which she could neither resolve nor ease. She believed that it paid to keep him relaxed and entrenched in the routine she had fixed for him.

The origin of his concern was unknown to her. She had quizzed him now and then, hoping he would let something slip. Her own involvements went so much more smoothly if she could uncover his. If she could free his time in some way, the rest of her life managed to tick along quite nicely.

And she met Walter as often as she could, while the kids were in school.

Suzie had trained as a dramatic arts teacher in university. She'd thought, at first, that acting would be her raison d'étre. The realities of her life shifted perceptibly when she was on stage. She could be anything she wanted to be: poor, ugly, intelligent, foolish, and most especially in the recent past, anything but a lawyer's wife. Her world was a stage, but the backdrop was ragged if you looked closely. There was a swimming pool in the backyard, a successful husband, two cute kids, and patches on every emotional hole.

She didn't know how long the stitching would hold together, but when she had met Walter, she had ceased to care when it would unravel.

Walter McDonald was a local actor who owned and operated Borealis Productions, a Murder Mystery production company. Suzie and her husband, in one of their rare moments together, had attended a performance at the Deane House, a wonderful little historic site beside Fort Calgary. The leading actor had intrigued her with his audience involvement. She had never seen a murder mystery performed; the genre had remained unexplored in her university career. Audience interaction had been a new concept for her. She had fallen for Walter good and hard, and the attraction had been mutual.

Suzie took the time and trouble to trace him through Borealis Productions the next day. She remembered dialing the number and wondered whatever on earth she would ask him. Could she see him again? Learn more about murder mysteries? Maybe join the Company? Would he go to bed with her?

Walter McDonald had expressed undisguised pleasure that she had looked him up. He was naturally warm, always willing to discuss his artistry with the uninitiated, and Suzie was vitally interested in his art.

The questions were asked. Could she see him? Her days were such that she had lots of spare time to learn about alternative drama. Within a few weeks, she had joined the troupe. Within a few months, she hadn't needed to ask him if he would go to bed with her.

How to explain to her husband where she was at night, while she acted with the troupe, was another matter altogether. Borealis had weekend engagements, so usually the children could be with either of their grandparents overnight. She never had to explain to her husband, because he never asked. Often she spent the night with Walter. Her husband believed she had had a pleasant weekend with the kids. TJ never inquired, because TJ didn't care.

Suzie's relationship with Walter was more than sexual, although that part was the blast of her life. Walter encouraged her interest, facilitated her talents, and wrote her into roles that challenged her abilities.

He understood. When her parenting responsibilities and duties called, he rehearsed around her. She worked hard at her job, and felt that Walter respected her talents.

Suzie explained to him long ago that she was in a dead marriage, but her children were everything to her. She requested of Walter that a stage name be advertised for her in the Company's roster, and hoped that she would never encounter any of her husband's colleagues. If that were to happen, she would deal with the problem as events transpired. So far, so good. No one knew, no one suffered.

The game became complex sometimes, though. She had to be thinking ahead. Concentrating. Chess.

She judged that her husband was fiercely preoccupied. His schedule was hectic and he was run off his feet by all observations. In addition he was into austerity these days, telling her that money was tight, trim household expenses, personal entertainment, lunch with the girls, things like that. She hadn't been to lunch with the girls in months, and she had grown her hair longer so as to avoid the foolishness of wasted time at the hair dresser. She had practised frugality for the better part of a year, and the Old Boy himself hadn't even noticed. Besides, if he was so busy, where was the money? If he was doing well, his natural tendency to spend money would take over. Heaven knows she had witnessed that trait more times than she cared to remember. TJ might not have been the most generous person around, but if he had a dollar, he liked to spend it and to flaunt his wealth with others so that they would see how successful and prosperous he was.

Suzie was puzzled, but it wasn't worth the aggravation to ask him questions. Nagging was not her style anyway, and she frankly didn't care enough to pick too closely at him. She hung out in the background, doing what she could to alleviate any unnecessary pressure that was levelled at him. The less he was aggravated, the more freedom she had.

One of Suzie's rules had always been to keep away from her husband's legal or office affairs. There was the matter of confidentiality, of course. She didn't need the hassle or implication that any of her husband's friends or associates might think she knew their business. She wasn't naturally meddlesome or intrusive, and her life was big enough. TJ's business was TJ's concern.

Sometimes he shared some particular case or insight with her, without mentioning specifics or names. She didn't mind listening; the cases were intriguing. Occasionally she even offered some unusual insight, and she knew he would act on it.

Lately, the eggshells had been getting higher and deeper, though. She was tired of walking on them. The crunching was becoming annoying.

The departure of Mrs. Smidge had been a case in point. Suzie had always liked the lady. TJ seemed to have counted on his ex-senior accountant, always remarking on what terrific work she did. Suzie had been quite shocked that he had let Mrs. Smidge go. What was even more peculiar was that he never mentioned why he had done so.

She had to ask. Casually, of course. Did he want to share anything with her?

His response had been to shoot into a dreadful rage. Frothing, actually. Accusing her of getting involved and worrying about things that were none of her concern. And why was this, that, or the other thing not attended to? Why couldn't she mind the business he left her with during the day?

Well, she had done nothing to bring on that temper tantrum. Nothing but inquire about someone who had been in his employ for a long time. She realized then, quite consciously, something she had known for a long time, that no one really mattered to TJ but himself. Certainly he did not care about her, not even his children. Right? She might have pursued the matter if she had cared, but it wasn't worth it. Mrs. Smidge was gone and after all, TJ had informed her that he had not left the old lady destitute. Suzie would have cared about that.

Instead, she noticed a new face at the office. A young beauty by the name of Ali York. Aha, a new conquest, she thought.

Ali seemed like a sweet young woman, although Suzie found her strangely nettling. Ali was just a little too sweet, perhaps. There was something annoying about her, almost like too much salt in the stew. You couldn't see it, just taste it. Ali was always polite and considerate of Suzie, but something irritated Suzie anyway. Maybe it was a territory-thing.

Suzie was a little surprised at the twinge of jealousy she felt. What was that all about? It wasn't as though she was in love with the man any longer. Suzie wasn't sure that she ever had been. So it must have been a territory-thing. Who had the man? Who had access to money, prestige, even the occasional bit of sex with a good-looking, successful man?

Suzie sniggered to herself. She should at least have some control over who entered the harem. She even felt a little sorry for poor young Ali. TJ was no prize after all - in or out of bed.

Maybe it was the idea of aging, of not being as desirable as you used to be. Hey, of just being usurped! TJ had not played ball so close to Suzie's kitchen window before. It was territory, after all. She had always played everything carefully so he would return to her and the kids. She'd thought about leaving a few times, but the idea of liquidating her life and potentially harming her children as a result of her pride... well, it just didn't seem right. Not yet.

Besides, he had always been discreet before. Suzie felt that as long as her husband tried to keep the trysts from her and from filtering down to her children, he could dance to any tune he pleased. That was her justification for continuing, and she stuck to it. That line of reasoning didn't seem quite so sensible any more, though. Not with Walter in her life.

If she weren't real careful, the guilt would set in. Did men ever bother to feel guilty? Of course not.

Men never did. Suzie had never met a man with antennae, real or imaginary.

She was quite sure that Ali and her husband were an item. Not just a one-night stand, but a convenient relationship. Suzie would have been hard-pressed to put on such a command performance herself as those two seemed capable of.

That Ali. What a gorgeous young woman, after all. Long brunette hair, soft brown doe eyes, a petite hour-glass figure, and legs that went aaalll the way up. Completely in control of her life, in love with a man she could see every day and seemingly happy in her work. And Suzie?

She admired herself in her bedroom mirror. Playfully, she donned one of her husband's golf shirts, then a baseball cap he wore occasionally. She was an actress, after all. Was there any part she could, or would not play? She thought she was capable of almost any role. Suzie the artist couldn't help but admire the statuesque beauty of Ali York. Suzie the lioness growled at the threat to her cubs, and prepared for the hunt. Suzie the philosopher could understand the sexual attraction to Ali York, but most of all, Suzie the actress could make all the world believe in illusions.

Chapter Twenty-four

I had been avoiding Ali's diary, trusting instead to forensic science. I couldn't manage the pain of the diary right now. The body on the floor was part of the job. The woman in the text deserved empathy. But if she had chosen to tell her own story, who was I to decide that some forensic specialist could do a better job?

I was sitting on my deck again, rubbing softly the paisley cloth of Ali's diary. It was like a tape. If I opened it, the buttons would be pressed. I would hear her voice.

I flipped through some entries from the late '70's and '80's. I heard her talk about lack of friendships. I was curious about her survival instinct. What did she do as a teenager, when her female sexuality had been affected by the peer group?

March 15, 1983: No one would ever want someone like me. I feel dirty inside, like I can't scrub off the filth.

April, 1985: Men are such simple creatures. So easy to manipulate. I feel so powerful when I can turn them on. Then I get rid of them, before they can hurt me.

1985 was a bad year for Ali. She would have been in her early twenties. Horny, free, beautiful, and so very dysfunctional. She got around that year.

July, 1985: I have power. I can have my pick of men. Billy Corgan, watch out. You have competition.

An entry early in 1986:

I wrap myself in my cocoon quilt and write private letters to Miss Diary. I feel like if I can disappear under my quilt, no one can hurt me. If I avoid a fight, maybe people will like me better. Every fight is like taking on Frank. I can't win. Best to just hide.

Ali left the diary for a long time before she resumed writing again. The entry I read next was dated about two years ago.

October, 1992:

Moving from Red Deer to Calgary is a big deal for me. I finished the Legal Aide Program, and received a certificate at the college, and where do I go from there? Life in the big city. Besides, it gets me away from family and now, Billy. Sure, I'm dazzled by Calgary. I don't have much money to start off, but I found a nice little apartment on 13th Avenue. The people at the St. Louis coffee shop down the way tell me to watch myself. It's a rough neighbourhood. Really? I say. Couldn't be rougher than Frank York's happy little home. Some people might think it's dreary and dilapidated, but the apartment is mine. I have a sunny south window, and I have put my bottles on the ledge. When the sun comes through, they're the best little suncatchers. I have my own space. Luke isn't here, and Billy won't find me easily.

This place is easy on my head. I am relaxed enough to work on the baggage. All I need to find is a good therapist. A lady who will understand my problem. Some one I can trust with all my secrets.

I heard that you could get treatment in Calgary for my problem. Every now and then I have those ugly dreams, and all I can see is Luke, and Frank.

November 3, 1992

I found her. Leslie Reynolds. She is a beautiful lady that I feel sort of attracted to. She listens. She said the word: incest. I watched her face when I told her my problem. It didn't crack or move. Her mouth didn't make a sound. I waited. She waited. No one's ever waited for me before. Go on, she said, and suddenly I didn't know how. Go on to what? I didn't know it was possible. Leslie says it is. I trust her.

November 7, 1992

I am looking for a job, of course. About time, but I just enjoy the peace and tranquillity so much. I am not sure what kind of office I would prefer. Small fish in a large pond or large fish in a small pond. Benefits and remunerations are better in larger firms, of course. But if I am to make myself indispensable, it had better be in a small firm. A sole practitioner would be great. Women lawyers, no thanks. Got to find a man. They are far easier to manipulate. Other women hate that. I need a man who's not too old, handsome, charming, maybe someone who stimulates me intellectually. Nothing wrong with fantasizing.

November 10, 1992

I found a job. A hot shot lawyer named Theodore

James. He could hardly keep from grabbing me. I felt the old power come back, and I knew the job would be no problem at all. He's an older man, sort of fatherly. So I know what to do with him. Most of the people who interviewed me blabbed about what a positive learning experience I would get from their office. I am surprised to note how many types of lawyers there are. I looked in a lot of places. Some guys were egotistical. They seemed impressed with their firm and position. As though it made the man. Gag me.

December 6, 1992

Leslie listened today. I told her I'd found a job in a lawyer's office. I need to succeed. Told Leslie that I was a perfectionist. I just want everything to be okay. My big fear is that I might be mediocre, that I won't please my boss. Leslie says it's normal for me to feel so driven, as though I always have to please someone. Lots of incest victims are like that, but she asks me questions like, what did you do for yourself today? Well, the answer is: nothing. Except that I like to watch my glass bottles catch the light. Sometimes I sit for a long time doing this, and I forget how long is time… and I don't even care.

December 17, 1992

TJ bought me lunch today. I was a little afraid at first, it's so soon. He's married, too. But you hear about these marriages of convenience. Suzie seems nice, but we don't hear from her much. I am spending a lot of time in the office. I want to make sure everything is perfect. What if Mr. James should find out that I'm not perfect? What if he finds out I'm contaminated?

December 20, 1992

I don't know what set it off. Chestnuts roasting by an open fire, maybe. Jack Frost nipping at my nose. Rudolph the red-nosed reindeer. No good memories. Leslie heard me while I moaned and held her hand. The past is unbearable for me. I can only use the language possible for the little girl who was violated. Moans. Not too loud, or others will hear. Deep guttural sobs and breath so painful... my chest crushing with the weight of him. Who? Daddy. And Luke watching from a corner. No words. I cannot speak. You can speak. You can speak. You can speak... scream. Make the voice loud enough to hear... whose voice? Leslesleslie, no mine. My own voice. I hear myself cry out. I hear myself shout NO! I hear my own pain... it comes from inside me.me.me.

Christmas

I bought a little wreath to hang on my door. My bottles glimmer in the low light, and giant fluffs of snow glide softly down behind them, past the window I can open or close if I want. I am content, but am I happy? I don't think so. Billy hasn't found me yet. Neither has Luke. The world is better today.

A New Year, a New Life

I still get depressed. I have been to the doctor to see about antidepressants. Leslie says that is a good thing. She says that depressed women are strong and valid. And pills are tools, not crutches.

January 10, 1993

I have always been intrigued by the law. I watch those lawyer shows on T.V. just to imagine how I could nail Frank. I know I could never really be a lawyer. Frank and Luke always said I was too stupid. I was lucky they had a legal aide program in Red Deer. I have a plan. If I can make myself indispensable, how could Mr. James get rid of me? My body isn't bad, either. That ought to help. The work is never boring.

January 27, 1993

I am not naive, you know. I have a body that most men just want to keep around them all day long. But geez, I'm smart too. I wish people would give me credit for that. TJ does, but I know he really wants to get me naked. He's not lazy, but he would rather not deal with the little stuff. I can hope to control a lot of the operations if I play the game right. If necessary, I might have to bed him down.

February 4, 1993

If I didn't have to work for a living, I would like to write a bestseller about lawyers. Foibles, characters. Most are good-looking, it seems. Some are flashy dressers. Some are studious, overly serious. But one thing is very clear. Law is business. The better they are at manipulating the law, the more money they make. I need to be a part of that power.

I shook myself back to reality. Ali, Ali. How limited your scope of things. Blessed with a beautiful face, a lovely body, a mind to work it all out. You fell into the biggest trap in the world. Solidarity with patriarchy. And like most of us, you couldn't disentangle yourself.

I thought for a moment. When I see other women step into the leg-hold, I stand by and 'tsk, tsk' a whole lot. What part do I play in bailing them out? Or, an even bigger question: Was I unaware of my own trap? The trap might surround me even as I bemoaned the fate of others. If so, could I ever get out?

No wonder I hated to read that diary.

Chapter Twenty-five

I was tired again, and hoping I could avoid Richard for a few days, but he would know. He always does. Maybe the clue is my excessive snoring when he comes home after his shift.

I drove to work in a droopy frame of mind.

Sheedy and McInnis were waiting for me at the station with big grins on their faces. I didn't know if it was from bar-hopping or some new discovery.

"You two look just sweet in those cowboy hats," I observed

"C'mon, Holt," sneered McInnis. "It's Stampede. Get with the program."

"These shit-kickers are great!" Sheedy hiked up half a blue-jeaned leg and showed me his prize cowboy boots.

"Keep your eyes on the ladies, Sheedy. If you go around admiring your feet like that, you might miss something." warned McInnis.

I sneered at them both. "I refuse to dress like a moron. Jeans is as far as I go."

"Well, Sergeant Speirs will like your butt better than your detective work these days, Holt." McInnis took the liberty of circling me to examine the goods.

I whacked him with the back of a file folder, knocking off his very silly cowboy hat.

"What about my detective work?"

He grinned at me. "I didn't phone you back last night because I thought it might be too late, but the prints on the business card match the coffee mug. Just as you thought."

"Yes!" I fisted my hand, pumping my arm up and down. "I knew it. But that's all we have, guys. Only the coffee mug. I can't wait to see TJ's face when I toss that one at him." I smirked.

"Are we going to pick him up", queried Sheedy breathlessly. "Can we, Sam? Can we, can we? I can't wait to tell my mom I handcuffed the Cowboy Cutter."

"Not yet, Sheedy. You know better than that. The evidence is circumstantial so far. If we pick him up, there'll be twenty-seven lawyers waiting to get him out. We have to wait for the right moment. Besides, I want to check out Billy Corgan."

* * *

In the end, I was ready to send back my order. I paid Corgan a visit that night at home, thinking maybe he would get out of line if I had to pick him up at his work. Corgan was about the queerest bird I'd ever met. He held me at the door, aloof and completely unintimidated. He had the strangest eyes. If he had undressed me with them, I would have known what to do. But it was more like he was assessing how I would taste stuffed with sage or an apple in my mouth. If he had dragged out a knife and fork, I would have run for my life. Instead, I decided to play a hunch.

"You were Ali York's boyfriend, were you not, Mr. Corgan?"

His gawking eyes relaxed just a bit. He stood up straight, puffing out his chest.

Bingo, Sam.

"Yeah, I was. Please come in, Ms. Holt. I'd like to tell you about me and Ali."

"I'd be delighted, Mr. Corgan."

I surveyed his apartment. There were several pictures on display of Ali in her healthier days. He watched me taking it all in. I sensed that I would be unable to fool him by being polite. It was probable that few people had ever been polite to him. He would be suspicious of that tack. Besides, I was prepared to dislike him intensely. As it turned out, disliking him wasn't hard to do.

"You cared deeply about her, didn't you, Mr. Corgan?"

"I loved her."

That was it. The emotion was hidden, inaccessible to me, but it was there. The air was palpable with threat of some sort. To me? Maybe. I was beginning to get the heebee jeebees. It was the… unnaturalness of his exchange. He spoke at last, relieving some of the emotional fog between us.

"For as long as I can remember, the only girl that I've ever been interested in was Ali. She was the only one who was ever nice to me back home. She sympathized with me, and defended me from the creeps in school." A ripping vehemence emanated from his voice, then softened.

"I had a crush on her right from the first time I ever saw her pretty little face. I guess you'd call that infatuation, right?" He waited expectantly.

"Yes, I know what you mean." I nodded emphatically. Now I had him.

"But it deepened. I loved her so much. I respected her. I would have crawled a mile on broken glass for her. Ali never knew how much I loved her. She never believed me, because she didn't know what love was all about. That... family she came from. They were disgusting. All of them. I made everybody know that if they ever hurt Ali, they would have to deal with me," he snarled viciously.

I wondered if he knew of the incest. I wasn't about to tell him.

"You must have been... unhappy, when Ali decided to move to Calgary to find a job."

"Oh, sure, but she always talked about moving. She finished her paralegal training at Red Deer College, and I always hoped she'd change her mind and stay there. I guess I couldn't blame her. I really, really wanted what was best for her. I knew she'd never survive in a big city without me, so I made plans to follow her. I never told her, of course. I wanted to surprise her."

"I just wanted to show her, to prove to her somehow, just how much I loved her. I even helped her pack, tried not to get in her way..." his voice trailed off somewhere.

'That's not the way I heard it', I wanted to tell him. I felt that this nut case would tolerate no contradictions to the fairy tale. And a fairy tale it was indeed.

"I let her move. Then I moved after her. I watched her for a few weeks. I slept in some hovel downtown until she found a place. Then, I decided on a basement suite a block away from her apartment, just so's I'd be close if she needed me, y'know. A little furnished place. Perfect and cozy for two, if she wanted to be close." He smiled hopefully then.

I smiled back to indicate that I was reading the fairy tale just as he wanted it to be read. And his diction changed. From proper to poor-boy. What new mask was he wearing?

"I didn't want to waste too much money. I wanted to show Ali that I could take care of her when we got married."

Lucky I'd read Ali's diary. I was able to carefully avoid asking the question if Ali had talked about marriage. She'd had no intention of marrying anything or anybody. In Corgan's case, it would have been a Thing, for sure.

"I had a lot to do. I needed to find a job. Got one with Finewood's Wholesalers out in Forest Lawn. I'm pretty capable, you know. Most folks wouldn't think so, but I am."

I accepted his version of reality. Finewood might tell another story.

"Mr. Finewood is okay, y'know. He needed someone to assist him in unloading the inventory, shelving, displaying. I hoped to be a salesman someday. I might still. But what's the use now?"

The question wasn't meant for me. Billy gave me a sick-calf-in-a-hailstorm look. I couldn't handle the pitiful types and Billy Corgan was indeed quite pitiful.

His look changed while he stared through me.

"Mr. Finewood is a widower with no children. It's a private business. I knew that I was into a great chance. If I followed orders the way he liked, did whatever he wanted, well, I knew that my future would be made. I'd be able to take care of Ali, and then she could get away from that lawyer-guy."

I took a chance, mentally bracing myself for god-knows-what. I took out my notepad, although I really didn't need it. Maybe I thought it was armour or something.

"Our records show that you received a Restraining Order from Ali some months ago, Mr. Corgan. Would you care to comment on that?"

"I couldn't believe it!" he roared, "I just knew it was that lawyer-guy. Ali would never have done that to me. She would never hurt me. I knew she would want to hear from me, to know that I was close by. She'd never use it against me. It was just a piece of paper that her fancy-pants lawyer made up so that he could have her all to himself!"

He shook his head hypnotically. "I called her at the office, and at home. She wasn't mean or nothin'. I just knew it wasn't her that sent that piece of paper. I just thought I'd visit her at home y'know. I would'na visited her at the office, because that lawyer-guy would've used the law against me. He did in the long run anyway."

"What happened, Mr. Corgan?" By now, I was some curious.

"Some o' your cop-guys came to the store. Fred came to get me from the back. He was nervous. Said there was two cops at the front that wanted to speak to me. 'Course I came up there. They said I was 'in breach of a Restraining Order'. Fred couldn't believe it. Kept askin' me if I was in some trouble with the law. I didn't want to answer, so I just said nothin'. I got my pride, lady." He glowered at me.

"Go on, Mr. Corgan." I wanted him to know I was only listening.

"I stuck out my chest, lifted my chin, an' said 'Take me away, you guys.' Fred kept mumblin' at my back 'til I wanted to punch 'im. Those two cops hand-cuffed me and took me to the Cop Shop. Some guy… said he was Deputy Counsel acting for Legal Aid. Told me I would be brought before the Judge to tell 'im why I shouldn't be jailed for contempt and breach of a Restraining Order. Hah! As though some fancy-pants judge really wanted to know. That smarty young lawyer told me that I better say somethin' like how I didn't know exactly what the Order was about, and that I didn't know that I couldn't talk to Ali. 'Nobody tells me what to say!', I thought. But I decided to do what I was told anyway. Fooled 'em all. The fancy-pants judge looked really mean, so I told him it wouldn't happen again, so sorry.

Can't remember what all he said to me, but I heard 'im mention somethin' about how he'd let me go this time, being as how I hadn't been violent, that Ali and me weren't married, and 'said applicant' Ms. York was employed by her solicitor. He just warned me that if I breached the 'said Order' again, he would incarcerate me for 30 days and fine my butt off."

Corgan was mimicking the judge at this point, making his body move in exaggerated, choppy gestures. I began to wonder if he knew I was still there. This was no guy who liked to engage in communication with other people. His world included himself alone, and of course until her demise, Ali York.

"I can behave myself when I want to. Yes I can. I thanked the judge and apologized. Yes I did. Poor Ali. She was influenced by that lawyer-guy. What could she do? She was under his spell. She couldn't help it if he controlled her so well."

He started rocking back and forth, and all sorts of expressions claimed his face as I watched him.

"Where were you on the night of Ali's murder, Billy?"

He stared at his floor. "I was with Fred Finewood. We had dinner together." Then he raised his eyes to me suddenly. They narrowed dangerously, in a challenge to me to call him a liar.

Instead, I surprised him. "Did you know Maureen Rogers, Mr. Corgan?"

He leaned forward violently, and with the thrust of his body, each time he exclaimed: "Nope, Nope, Nope."

Enough was enough. Billy Corgan was losing it, and I neither could, nor wanted to help him. I got up and made my way to the door, conscious of the fact that he probably wouldn't follow me. I thought he had no more to say.

"I promised I'd get 'im, promised I would."

My hand halted on the door knob, ready to hear him, but he kept rocking, and finally turned his back on me. I couldn't escape the feeling that his next movements might be unpredictable, perhaps directed malevolently towards me. So I left quickly, pretending to close the door. I heard Billy whisper softly to himself:

"I promised to follow that James everywhere, and find as much dirt on him as I could. Everyone has a few skeletons in their closet. Ali and James, what if... if... they were lovers? I'll make 'im pay for turning her against me. There'll be a day of reckoning, Mr. high-and-mighty James. Yes there will".

"What a kook." I shivered.

* * *

I wasted no time getting Sheedy and McInnis to check Corgan's alibi with Fred Finewood. When they returned, I grilled them:

"What was your interview like with the old guy?"

"Oh, he's an old salt-of-the-earth type, Sam," reported McInnis. I asked him if he knew of Corgan's whereabouts on the night of the murder. He said he couldn't remember, at first. Then he changed his story. He didn't have much to say, really. Told us he was upset about Billy Corgan the day the boys hauled him away. Kept telling us he didn't want no trouble, Billy was a fine boy really, just had some bad breaks."

"That's when he changed his story," revealed Sheedy.

"He wanted us to know that he and Corgan had dinner together the night that Ali York was killed. He seemed kind of hesitant, sketchy about his recollections, you know. He's getting on in years, claimed it was becoming harder for him to remember details-like." interpreted Sheedy.

I wasn't satisfied, and told them so. "Well, from what I got out of Corgan, I'm surprised that anyone would have dinner with this guy. Even his own mother. Did you think Mr. Finewood might have any reason to lie, especially since he rather abruptly changed his story?"

McInnis shrugged. "Why tell that account if it wasn't correct? What would he get from relating an alibi for Corgan?"

"Just smells funny, that's all."

Sheedy mulled things over. "Why would Mr.

Finewood lie? I'd go along with Corgan's alibi. He's probably not the actual murderer of the York girl, unless the timing of events is out, maybe he's Houdini, maybe he pulled off the crime in between or after the dinner with Finewood."

"Yeah, maybe." I muttered weakly. "I guess I still have to talk to TJ."

"Sounds like fun, Sam. Wish you luck!" They both disappeared before I could bemoan my fate any further.

There was that coffee mug thing. Maybe he'd dropped off a file or something. Somehow, TJ didn't seem like the culprit. It was possible that Ali had brought the mug home with the prints on it, but that scenario didn't seem too likely, either. Only one thing to do. Pay my favourite lawyer a little visit.

Chapter Twenty-six

Another Monday morning, twelve days after Ali's death. Stampede was finally over. From my experience as a native Calgarian, I wondered sometimes if Stampede was ever really over. I always looked forward to the day when I could walk the streets again without encountering strange droppings that defiled my shoes. I developed new strategies every year to avoid the tortures of participating in carnival idiocies, although I liked wearing my jeans.

I always had to swallow hard before I met with condescending people like TJ. Favourite lawyer or not, he was a prime murder suspect, and I would enjoy reminding him of that reality. For some odd reason, I felt the need to check my appearance in the rearview mirror.

A mental check-list: thirty-seven. Seen better days, babe. Instead of zits, you've got facial hair. A few map lines around the eyes. Silvery grey glimmered here and there in the chestnut mop I still retained. School reunions seemed to wreak more havoc on the men than the women. At least I would never be bald.

Breasts no longer firm as melons. Brain power better than it's ever been, though. A sad commentary on a woman's life that just as she begins to age and gain some intelligence, her stock value on the general market begins to decline.

'Get a grip, Sam.' I said it out loud. 'You can still fuck, fight, hold the light, and drag out the dead.' A passerby on the street looked at me strangely. It wasn't every day of the week that middle-aged women sat in their cars talking to themselves. Maybe I had a future as a baglady.

I sighed and pulled myself out of the car. Marching into the ivory tower, I congratulated myself at making the rank of Detective before the age of forty. Even if I did end up as a baglady, street life was less dull than ending up as someone's secretary, forever condemned to a half-life in the ivory tower.

The elevator opened quietly just outside the law office.

Rene the Receptionist looked up and greeted me warmly. After checking the appointment book, she smilingly stated, "Mr. James will be pleased to see you, Ms. Holt."

No shit, Sherlock, I said to myself. I think not. She smiled and offered me a chair while I waited for her to announce my presence to his Oneness. I sat down to eyeball some golf magazines.

He did eventually emerge from the sanctum.

"Ms. Holt. How can I help you?"

"You can start by inviting me into your office, Mr. James. We have business to discuss."

He flushed, but said nothing. "Of course, please come in." He let me lead the way. Could it be that he admired my thirty-seven year old backside? That notion wasn't inconceivable.

He closed the door behind us.

I started right in on him.

"Mr. James, do you have anything further that you would like to share with me now, with respect to your relationship with Ms. York?"

"Ms. Holt, I thought I made it quite clear to you that my relationship with Ms. York was strictly business. I had no social activities whatsoever with her."

"I'm not interested in who or what you screw or why, Mr. James. I am, however, interested in knowing why my detectives found a coffee mug with your prints on it at Ms. York's apartment."

He recoiled slightly at my offensive manner. I had learned long ago that men responded well to hearing their own language from the lips of a female. At least at the outset. In the long run, they'd get you for it. It is unlawful, ideologically, for a woman to speak man-talk.

I had no reason to believe that TJ would be an exception to this rule.

He cleared his throat slightly, resuming his seat at the throne. "Well, my fingerprints. How did you acquire them, Ms. Holt?" The man never stopped thinking.

I chose not to answer him. He could try and figure it out.

I examined his bookshelves. Lawyer-stuff. Greek mythology. Pretty picture books. I watched him from my peripheral vision. Don't make eye contact. Let him look for me. I continued to examine his superficial book collection and then addressed him.

"As you might have guessed, Mr. James, my call is for a specific reason. It would be remiss of me not to inform you that I have added you to my list of suspects in this murder investigation. What I don't

understand is why you would want to kill your secretary and her friend, Maureen Rogers."

"You mean to tell me that I am suspected of two
murders!? I... I am outraged! I didn't even know Ms.
Rogers. I, I... knew she was Ali's friend from school.
They had lunch sometimes... I never knew her or
talked to her. I wouldn't know her if I saw her on the
street..."

"Where were you on the night of Ms. York's
murder?"

"I was at my office working."

"Any witnesses, clients, office staff?"

"I, I was working alone, as I do frequently. I
spoke to my wife and a couple of clients, several
times. I'm sure my alibi can be corroborated."

"Excuse me, Mr. James", I turned to face him
now. "But no alibi exists. Telephone calls do not a
story constitute. And you have not yet explained to
my satisfaction how a coffee mug with your finger
prints on it came to be found in Ms. York's apartment."

"I have no idea, I tell you! But I am sure there
must be a plausible explanation."

"In addition to that item, we have a witness who
claims that they saw a man who looked like you in a
late model car, the same model and colour as yours,
leaving the York girl's apartment complex on the
night of the shooting."

I followed his face closely. He looked genuinely
perplexed.

"I have no explanation for that, Ms. Holt. Your
witness must be unreliable."

"Well, let's look at what we have here, Mr.
James", I spoke quite coldly. "One: There is a witness

that puts you at your secretary's apartment on the night of her murder. Two: A car similar to yours has been identified as driving away from the complex on the same night. Three: the mug with your finger-prints. Four: no alibi." I shrugged, pulling up my hands in display. "What's a poor detective to do but believe the worst of you?"

"Those factors themselves are a weak link to my guilt, Detective."

"Quite true, Mr. James." I paused for a moment to take an uninvited seat.

"Except for the Motel Registration Clerk who is willing to swear that you and your former secretary checked into a nearby hotel under the name of Mr. and Mrs. J. Jones sometime prior to the murder. I am sure that it's only a matter of time before the hand-writing is identified as yours. That I.D. will establish clearly that you and Ms. York had a liaison of some sort while she was engaged in your employ. Of course, screwing your secretary is no crime in itself, but you have repeatedly claimed that you were not involved in a clandestine relationship with Ms. York. Purely business, employee/employer stuff. You have not been open and candid with me. It seems to me that you hold some cards under the table, Mr. James. Cheating in the old west was grounds for a shootout. Stampede was last week, but I can still exact old west rules for old west behaviour. Your lack of candour and honesty would appear to leave the Department with no choice. We might be obliged to act accordingly, unless you can provide me with some compelling reasons why I shouldn't arrest you right now."

He examined me quite seriously. There was a hint of nervousness in his eyes, I could see it. His smile, when it came, seemed rather weak. There was a possibility, of course, that he wanted to maintain a certain casual image, and that I really had him quite panic-stricken.

"This is insane, Ms. Holt. There are people out there with axes, child molesters, don't tell me you want to book me?"

"I am seriously thinking of doing just that, counsellor, for the murder of Ali York. I'm sure I don't have to tell you that it would be extremely prudent for you to retain the services of an attorney in order that he might advise you as necessary. Some police officers might arrest you here and now on the basis of unsubstantiated evidence. I wouldn't do that, you see. I realize the implications of a charge being levied prematurely, and the damage that might well be unnecessarily wreaked on a career."

"I appreciate your concern, Ms. Holt. But you needn't worry about my welfare. I can take care of myself."

I leaned forward just a bit, folding my hands in front of him. He didn't miss the opportunity to check out the size of my bosom. I spoke fiercely, "Get your ducks in order, Mr. James. The law is hot on your tail. If you have something to hide..", I shook my head at him, "your day of reckoning is just about here. Do you have your own counsel?"

"Yes, of course... I" I watched him think frantically for a few seconds. "Ian Marty. He's excellent, but I tell you I won't be requiring his services..."

Ian Marty. Good gawd, what direction would my life take next?

TJ didn't notice my momentary start. He stared at the paper on his desk, then looked at me, despondently.

"Detective Holt, would you be so good as to give me prior notice if you expect to charge me? If the worst happens, I would wish to contact Marty. I need him there with me if I'm charged."

"I'm not at liberty to make a promise like that", I shot back at him. "Of course, I'll do my best to make sure that you are kept up to date on all developments, as well as the position of the police, and of course, whether or not you will be charged."

I rose, and offered my hand. He stared at it, as though it might offer some sort of surprise electric shock. I retracted it. Civilities seemed kind of odd at this point, anyway.

"Goodbye for now, Mr. James. Try not to be too smug. If you're not worried, you should be." I left him with his hands folded, staring abjectly at my skirt. It was hard to judge just what he might be thinking, but I believed I had him quite concerned, despite his affected nonchalance.

Smoking with indignation, I marched out of his office and strode quickly to my car.

The man was truly a jerk. I was so exasperated with him. Why?

I stole a glance at my reflection in the rearview mirror again, noting the warning: "Caution, objects in the mirror are closer than they appear." Reflections rarely conveyed positive images.

Chapter Twenty-seven

It wasn't the first time that TJ had been shocked momentarily out of his sensibilities. He was beginning to feel schizophrenic, as though his brain was leaving his body everytime something like this happened. Another frontal attack. How in the name of blue chips did Sam Holt get off storming into his office and accusing him of double murder?

He felt his heart rapping on his chest, shouting to leave. But he wouldn't let it. Not yet. He had immediate need of all his reserves. He had been through so much. He would not break. He would not lose his composure. He had managed, he thought, to give the impression to Sam Holt that he was quite unconcerned about the imminent charges.

His guts still felt as though they were liquifying. His composure was slipping. The sweat pouring from his body was an underground stream from which his heart would eventually emerge palpitating, battling for life.

He thought he should tell Suzie. She would know what to do. She always did. She would mop his fevered brow and set him down in front of his hearth to enjoy an evening fire.

TJ felt his body begin to rumble, like the tremors of a volcano. Uncontrollable tremors. Shock waves. He picked up the phone, just barely able to control his ragged breathing.

Suzie knew immediately that something terrible had happened. Her voice became panicky. "Tell me, TJ! Is it one of the kids?"

"No, no, they're fine." He was sadly disappointed at her sigh of relief. "It's me."

"You?? What's the matter? Did you lose big on the stockmarket or something?" She really couldn't fathom his pain at all.

What had he done to deserve this?

"I… I might be charged with murder." A simple statement. He waited patiently for her to scream, to become hysterical, anything. Anything but laugh.

Which is exactly what she did. "You're kidding me. You? Murder? You phoned me to tell me that??" Suzie did not even ask whom he had been accused of murdering, but she must have had an idea.

"Be calm, Suzie. Everything is under control. Put on a good face for the kids, our family, and friends."

"You're really serious, aren't you?"

He decided to chance her good will. "Suzie, I need you now."

"When have you ever _not_ needed me?" she remarked, rather viciously.

"I… I have always needed you." He groped - for what? He couldn't say. There was no response from her. He gave up at last. "I'll be in contact with you soon, luv. I have to call Marty now."

He really couldn't be sure whether Suzie cared or not.

TJ hung up the phone, then reached for a telephone book to find Marty's number. He must have searched for fifteen minutes before he snapped out of his catatonic state.

Marty. Marty would help. Of course he would.

TJ managed, somehow, to punch the number, and get past the secretary without crumbling. It had been so long since he and Marty had golfed together. Oh, what he would give to bring back those easy days.

Marty greeted him heartily, but realized immediately that TJ was in no frame of mind for a sporting conversation.

"Talk to no one, do you hear? Say nothing and get over here as quickly as possible. I'll clear my appointment book. Under no circumstances are you to talk, or say anything to anyone, however harmless it might seem. This is a messy pile of garbage, TJ. I don't need to remind you how grave the situation is. And bear in mind, you're presumed guilty until proven otherwise."

* * *

"Don't tell me if you did it." Marty waved his hands, like wings, in front of TJ. "I prefer not to know. I want to believe the best of you."

Ian Marty had been practising criminal law for over twenty-five years. His skill and courtroom ability were nothing short of legend. He was a brutal cross-examiner, and he had one great characteristic that most criminal lawyers don't possess: a superb brain. Marty would have been equally comfortable with constitutional or criminal law. It was the good fortune of the legal profession that he had chosen to hang his coat in criminal law. His comments, courtroom openings and closings, and general witticisms were quoted widely. He had carved a name for himself, indeed, in the minds of the Old Boys.

Marty was always crazy-busy, but he made himself available to other lawyers. He felt that it was his duty to assist when another lawyer got into a crackly situation. If advice and counsel were necessary, Marty was right on the job.

TJ was an ardent fan. Rah, rah, Marty. TJ had referred a few clients in Marty's direction over the years, never dreaming that he himself would need Marty one day. Apart from the odd golf game as a foursome, he and Marty hadn't seen that much of each other over the years. TJ felt a bond, though, a closeness and admiration for a first-class agent of the law.

Marty would never have admitted to TJ that the admiration was mutual. You didn't, among men. Legal men. TJ was spunky and enthusiastic. The freshness of his appeal rubbed off infectiously. Marty always marvelled at the way TJ had built up a practice and yet still found time to engage in outside charitable concerns. If Marty had his druthers, he would have wished this pain on lots of other lawyers who didn't work as hard as TJ. Didn't seem right or fair, somehow. But life wasn't fair. As far as Marty was inclined to believe, TJ was as straight as a grizzly's dick.

TJ, on the other hand, was relying on Marty's brilliant abilities as a strategist and technician. Marty had an astounding knowledge of the nuances of law, rules of evidence, and an uncanny ability to grasp all technicalities and fine points of the issues. So TJ was quite relieved when the crusty Ian Marty assured him that he would get right on the job.

"Now then. Tell me exactly what is going on. Tell me what they have on you. Tell me why they might be charging you. As you're talking, remember that I'm your lawyer. Don't hold anything back that might surface later on. I might be able to diffuse a bomb now, but a later revelation makes us both look like idiots, and I don't like to look like an idiot with shrapnel in my face. The worst possible scenario is when a person doesn't tell me about some critical piece of information, or leaves out a whole bunch of details. Contrary to popular belief, what I don't know will hurt both of us. If the Crown adduces that evidence at a later date without my former knowledge, and especially if I have been working at cross-purposes, that kind of non-disclosure is often fatal. So let's make it simple. Tell me everything I need to hear.

Remember that something might appear quite critical, or even unimportant to you, but I may believe the exact reverse. You are not objective. When a person is under the type of pressure and scrutiny that you are, they are not likely to think or act rationally. Your judgment and perceptions are skewed. So, TJ. I'm the lawyer. You're the client. Go slowly and carefully. Whatever you tell me should be consistent. I'm going to turn on my recorder, and you can have your transcribed conversation later.

TJ had to pee. The amount of coffee he had been drinking was making him feel disjointed. The relief time would help him formulate, in his own mind, what approach or tack he should take. One thing for sure, he would be telling Marty sweet diddly-squat about the Lazy Valley Project. If the matter ever came up, he would simply say that a hundred items crossed his desk every day, and he simply could not cover them all. Marty had as much said that he didn't want to hear what he shouldn't, and there was no point in telling or disclosing everything. All that wasted disclosure would do no good, and would certainly not be of any advantage to him. He would relay only the details and facts that would help to dissipate the cloud of suspicion, or imminent charges.

TJ straightened his shoulders, admiring himself in the mirror. Why, even Marty's presence would intimidate Holt and the entire police force. They might even rethink their position about prematurely laying charges that would irreparably harm his illustrious career. Marty would be sure to tell them that if they proceeded with charging his client, they had better be damn certain that they could make the charges stick. If they couldn't, Marty would proceed against the Police Force and the municipality and the Officers involved, to seek substantial damages, general and punitive, for malicious and false prosecution. He would make it abundantly clear that laying an indictment against his client was insupportable when the Police knew, or ought to have known, that his client was innocent.

They wouldn't be able to make the charges stick. The undisputed consequence of their premature and irresponsible action would be devastating and catastrophic. His practice and livelihood would be forever prejudiced, and possibly even destroyed. Who would have the audacity to argue against such legal rituals? Sic 'em Marty.

TJ returned to Marty's office, sat down quite gingerly, and opened blithely with the comment: "How much time have you got, counsellor?"

In anticipation, Marty leaned back as TJ leaned forward to start his infamous story. After he had warmed up, TJ became even more verbose and longwinded. Marty interrupted him on numerous instances. After what seemed like days, TJ heaved his final sentence and sat back, quite spent.

"Are you sure, now, that you're telling me everything?" queried Marty. TJ confirmed that he was holding nothing back.

"Well then, counsellor, if you have told me everything, and I remind you that you better have, I will review what the Police have on you. So why am I left with this feeling that you are withholding something from me? Again, I repeat that you cannot expect a full or proper defense unless I am apprised of all the information that is available to you." Marty let a few seconds lapse, then moved on. "Alright, notwithstanding all this other mumbo jumbo, on the basis of what you have said and what we can assemble, let's look at the evidence that the Police have to link you with the York murder.

First, they have a mug. Not great, but it is possible that the mug was taken by the York woman from the office to her apartment. Maybe she didn't wash it, although that's implausible. It might well be that the mug was planted in her apartment by someone else who wanted to put you at the scene of the crime. It's quite damaging evidence, but not necessarily fatal in itself. It's not likely to either get you charged or convicted. A nagging issue, though. How did the mug get in her apartment? The implication is that you drank from it and left it there on the night of the murder, possibly, or some other time. You state that you were never at her residence.

"So," continued Marty, "the mug is not helpful, but it can be of some value to the Police. It's not the end of the world. There are a zillion ways that the mug could have been transported there. We will just have to make light of it. Pass it off. Take the position that the mug's presence is no big deal and hardly definitive."

Second, the Police allegedly have a witness who saw you at the place of the crime, near the time of the murder. If the witness' evidence was so incriminating, I bet you we wouldn't be talking right now. You would have been charged a long time ago. The witness is probably some old coot who thinks of themself as a neighbourhood blockwatch captain or something. Maybe they saw someone who looked like you. I'll bet the witness hasn't been able to pass an eye test in years. We could probably prove an advanced case of cataracts, lack of lighting, distance constraints, or age. We won't be too concerned about the witness.

Third, the apparently same witness, or another one, we're not sure yet, allegedly saw a vehicle matching your car's description leaving the apartment complex premises. This sighting would likely have been subsequent to the murder. If that's a big deal, or worth anything, I'll let you win the next golf game."

TJ laughed, and some of the tension slipped away.

"So, it's difficult to guesstimate how many similar vehicles there might be in our fair city. It is safe to say that there are probably a thousand or more similar cars with the same colouring. Big deal. Their third piece of evidence stinks.

Now for the finale. Fourth, the Police allegedly have you and the York woman checking in and out of a local motel. Inside, you both have some fun for a few hours. The Police cannot prove that the liaison in question between you and your former secretary was long-standing in nature, or that another similar rendezvous had occurred. They can, however, show that you were at the love nest, being the motel, and that you were there for a considerable time period. Of course, the rendezvous was not business-related. The conclusion is inescapable that you and Ms. York were enjoying some pleasurable time off."

Marty winked at TJ.

TJ merely looked stunned. "But, I...

Marty shrugged and went on.

"In itself, the tryst is no big deal. You have stated, however, quite unwaveringly, that your relationship with Ms. York was entirely business. You never once engaged in social activities or otherwise with her, never went to her apartment, and so forth.

So you lied. And the Police know you lied. They can prove it, too. If you lied about your relationship with York, then it follows that you might have lied about other things; to wit, that you had never been at her apartment. If you're lying, then ergo, you might well have, for whatever reasons, done the poor woman in. Why would you have done that? I can't surmise any reason. If you did it, why would you have also meted out the same fate to the poor Rogers woman. This is all quite confusing and farfetched, perhaps. The liaison is the most damaging evidence that the Police have in their favour.

It's easy to justify why you didn't tell the Police about your amorous connection with Ms. York. Clearly, you wouldn't want your wife or colleagues and friends, even office staff, to know of the relationship between the two of you. Granted you did take her to dinner at public places but that could be construed as business related. I find that understandable.

There are two murders involved, however, and you have an obligation to tell the truth. You could have told the truth, admitted your relationship with York and requested the Police to keep it quiet. But you chose to lie, and in doing so, you have established yourself as a prime suspect. You indicated dishonesty, or the ability and willingness to lie, and you have therefore opened a panorama of possible events that were shielded from the Police previously.

As a result of your relationship with the York woman, whether a single occasion or numerous liaisons, the Police have now ascribed to you a motive for the murder, one that they didn't have previously. Maybe Ms. York was blackmailing you. Perhaps she knew something that you didn't want her to know. Maybe she threatened to go to your wife to spill the beans. Maybe she said or did something that you found unforgivable.

Yes, TJ, the fourth piece of evidence is hard to deal with. When coupled with the others, the Police may well believe that they are in a position to charge you for the York murder. If I'm not much mistaken, the public is clamouring for results from the Police. The 'Cowboy Cutter' compromised the gaiety of Stampede Week, and the tourism industry has been jeopardized. Your indictment, whether fair or even reasonable, would quell the cry for justice. You are a highly profiled, successful lawyer with a wife and children. The public would be happy to make an example of you, to defeat your success, one perceived to have developed at their expense. This is Calgary, you know. Alberta. The red-necked quarter will happily tell you that we don't need judges or lawyers here. We shoot our own snakes.

I think we have problems. Without making a big deal of it, I'll go talk to Detective Holt. I'd like to know what's going on in her mind, put her off your trail, and warn her of the dire repercussions that might ensue against her Department if you are wrongly charged and your reputation sullied. The consequences might be a multi-million dollar lawsuit against the Police, herself, and anyone else that we might include. I will, of course, try to couch that threat so that it doesn't look like one, but rest assured, she'll get the thrust, shall we say, of our position."

Marty leaned back comfortably, clasping his hands behind his head and smiling.

Samantha Holt. This would be an amusing exchange.

* * *

TJ had to acknowledge that life had been somewhat fortunate to him lately, despite these problems. He was generally quite pleased with developments in the Lazy Valley Project. He had managed to fool them all. Reclining in his chair, he ruminated and reflected on his own brilliance.

But the charges. The 'evidence' that the police department had against him was meagre indeed, but if they chose to make his life difficult, the harm to his reputation would be irreparable. It didn't matter a snuff if the charges were later disproven or not. He was irritatingly worried about it all. That Sam Holt! Marty would take care of things, though. He decided to put police investigations right out of his mind for the time being.

The Project had been entirely sold out, all borrowed trust funds had been repaid, all improperly secured monies replaced or repaid, and all unlawful actions which had been taken were reversed, corrected, or resolved as though the original illegalities had not taken place. The Group of Seven Corporation was disbanded and fully repaid from the Project. The upshot was that he was now in receipt of considerable funds, since all debts were discharged and funds repaid. He was in marvellous financial shape. Odd, but it had taken a mortgage default to get him to this stage. If he had known then what he knew now... well, wasn't that always the way. He would never have taken those chances. He simply would have had the mortgage company walk away from the mortgage loan.

His heart still thumped audibly, it seemed, when he reflected on the fact that it hadn't been all that bad. Pressure was good for the soul. He had relied on his ingenuity, skill, and brilliance. He now had some financial independence. He could be a lot choosier over the work that he would take in. He wouldn't work as hard as he used to.

What to do with his spare time? Not spend it with Suzie or the kids. Surely not. Play a little golf. Climb some mountains.

He had replaced Ali with another Red Deer graduate, and although she wasn't as clever as Ali, he was pleased with her progress. He had put her right on the books, after he had safely doctored them himself. The next auditor wouldn't suspect a thing.

He leaned back, a god in his own mind. Dealing with mortals had amused him; what silly beings they could be sometimes. He closed his eyes, replaying the game and the images again. Before the mental film rolled, he couldn't help but notice Detective Sam Holt, right there in the periphery of the frame.

Chapter Twenty-eight

I had no idea why that TJ exasperated me so.

Well, no, that's not quite true. I did know. I hated to be patronized.

I wanted to slap him and shout 'wake up, TJ', but I really didn't like him that much. Some gods had to topple before they became aware of their own clay feet.

Ian Marty was a surprise. Of course I had always admired Marty. He was intelligent, honest (professionally, at least), and it was no wonder at all that TJ had retained his services. There was a strong possibility that TJ might not be charged, but it had been a smart move to retain Marty just to snoop around, and maybe attend to some damage control if that action became necessary. By hiring Marty, TJ was removing himself effectively from the picture. He was allowing someone else to do what he was not able to do with any sort of objectivity. TJ knew enough to realize that a lawyer who is his own client is truly a fool. Perhaps Marty could also be useful to me.

I was driving a little too fast, and slowed down as I waved to a patrolman I passed. He shook his finger at me.

Sure, Sam. Get a ticket for speeding. Traffic cops would love to nail you.

Sheedy and McInnis were waiting for me at the station. They were always waiting for me. Didn't these guys know about the concept of self-starting?

"The Sergeant's waiting for you, Sam", whispered McInnis. It must be bad. McInnis never whispered. "It's not going to be pretty."

"Well, then, good thing I am."

I breezed past him, heading straight for Sergeant Speir's door. I thought that any quick action on my part would surprise the sarge. Avoiding him would be a mistake.

"Holt!", he was shouting already. "Where have you been? There's a murder investigation…, no, two murder investigations, carrying on around you, in spite of you. What idiot dubbed you the detective-in-charge?"

"I believe it was you, sir."

"Don't get cute with me. Sheedy and McInnis have been hanging around here all day making telephone calls. Sheedy brought in two loaves of banana bread yesterday. Do I pay him to do detective work or bake bread? And another thing. I'm tired of hearing about the 'Cowboy Cutter' everytime I open the newspaper. Do I need this crap?"

"Well, sir, I…"

"And another thing. Frank York called me yesterday to complain about your obnoxious behaviour when you paid him a visit - in Red Deer? He sure can harangue and malign. Weren't you taught to respect suspects or informants, whoever they might be?"

I raised my eyebrows, and shot home my advantage.

"Oh, sarge, you didn't really want to say that."

He cleared his throat, and looked momentarily nonplussed at his own folly. "Well, no... I... um... you know what I mean!" he stated, a little less vehemently, then changed his tack.

"Suppose you tell me how you're handling this investigation, so that the next time Frank York phones with the threat of a lawsuit, I can tell him to piss off." With that, Speirs sat down. I knew the worst was over.

"Frank York is a prime suspect, sarge." I followed Speir's lead, helping myself to the chair across from him. "Ali York was an incest victim. Daddy is in denial. Seems that her brother, Luke, was also involved. You know the old adage, chief. 'Incest, the game the whole family can play' It's in poor taste, but the phrase says it all. We've checked out his alibi, and he seems clean."

"What about this Billy Corgan character?"

"He's a character, alright. We note from his extensive file that he was in trouble quite a bit, petty crimes and stuff like that. He was also deeply involved with Ali York. Even though he has an alibi, I wouldn't rule him out as a suspect. Then there's the lawyer..."

Speirs slapped his hand over his eyes. "Please don't tell me there's a lawyer involved. Please don't."

"I have to, sir. Sorry. He's not even a nice lawyer."

"I wouldn't recognize a nice one if he kissed me, Holt. What about this guy?"

"Circumstantial evidence, really, but it's all we've got. We found a coffee mug in York's apartment with prints all over it. The prints match those of Mr. James, our lawyer. He's been tentatively identified as matching the description of a man who, the neighbours claim, visited York. There's good reason to believe that he was also involved with York in a clandestine relationship. I'm reading Ali York's diary, and his name comes up often. I use the diary to..."

"Holt, tell me something. If you want to uncover the truth about a happening, what do you do? Dig in archives, find pictures, talk to witnesses? Or do you read diaries that have only marginal relevance to events at hand?"

He waited.

I waited. To see if he showed any other signs of slipping off the edge.

"Where is this line of inquiry taking us, sir?"

"I mean, how can you waste your time on a diary? We need facts to take to court. Linearity. Pieces of paper. Evidence. Do I have to draw you a diagram?"

"No sir, of course not. But I would disagree with you on that point. What you really need is the voice of a dead woman. Ali gives us that voice. I wouldn't want to listen to anyone else. They're lying, she's not."

"What am I going to do with you, Holt? They told me you were the best. I heard you could survive in the bush, find your way around. What did you bring on that survival weekend you're so famous for? Anthony Henday's diary?"

"I didn't need a voice to tell me how to survive, chief." I smiled at him placidly. "I listened to the wind." I watched him watch me for a few long, long, seconds.

He growled at last. "Get out of here and get on with it. And Holt..."

"Yes sir?"

"Tell Sheedy I'd like another piece of that banana bread, wouldja?"

* * *

Marty wasted no time visiting me. "Good morning, Samantha", he jockeyed. "I see you are up to your usual shenanigans, trying to prove that old adage 'the Mounties always get their man.' In your case, it's the wrong man, but you persevere foolishly."

"Marty, where have you been? I haven't heard from you in months. You've been uncharacteristically elusive." I batted my eyelashes mockingly.

His expression darkened somewhat. My, oh my, that man was truly fine, still.

"Let's not be testy, Sam. This is business. And remember, you haven't even charged my man yet. Judging by some terribly scanty evidence that you have, I would dare say that no charges should be laid. No need to remind you, I'm sure, of the dangers fraught with the actions of hasty detectives who lay charges on the basis of unsubstantiated evidence. You don't even have enough to bring the proceedings to trial. Is there a place where we can talk just a tad more privately?"

"Indeed there is, counsellor. Follow me."

"My pleasure, Samantha." He always called me Samantha. He was the only person I knew who still called me Samantha.

We sat down in an interrogation room and he got right to business.

"So, my dear. Let's look at what you have, which, with respect, is not very much. You have a mug, which really doesn't amount to a pile of prairie oysters. The mug might have travelled to York's apartment in any number of ways. You also have a car, which resembles that of my client's in colour and make. Maybe. You have someone who claims that they saw someone who looks like my client - maybe - at or near the scene of the crime. Lastly, you know and have firm evidence that my client had a little roll in the hay on at least one occasion with the late Ali York. The only thing of any consequence is the latter evidence, and the only reasons that it's of any consequence is that my client was not entirely candid with you.

Of course you understand why he wouldn't be candid. He would want his romance private and secret, so that his wife and family wouldn't be compromised in any way. The romance and its non-disclosure, or even a little white lie, is far from what you could call conclusive evidence. I would respectfully suggest that you don't have much in the way of such evidence to link my client with the York murder. Furthermore, even if there is some evidence, albeit minimal, and even if you would be inclined to lay a charge just to get some of the heat off your back, I would remind you of the dangers inherent in such a tactic. Irreparable harm might ensue to my client's good name, reputation and practice. I have no hesitation at all in warning you that such dastardly action and conduct on the part of the Police would lay them open to an ugly civil suit. Watch me nail you all for malicious prosecution, harassment and every other name which I can come up with. There has to be a sense of fair play and decency here. You don't have to take rash action simply because something must be done to put the Department in a good light.

"Are you done yet, counsellor?"

"Not quite. Look", Marty drawled, "we both know that the way is not clear to charge my client. If you should, by some chance, get there, you will let me know if new evidence comes to light, so that I can accompany him to the Police Station. At least offer him that dignity. We don't need to grandstand with the press. Imagine. A big deal where television cameras would be on scene to show a mortified individual being handcuffed and lead from his comfortable and well-located residence to the Police Headquarters."

"Really, Marty, you sound almost as though you're pleading. And yes, as a matter of fact, I would love to watch that very thing on T.V."

"It sells newspapers, Samantha. Unless you own stock in one, I would appreciate your sensitivity on this issue. I want your word on that. I also need any more evidence that comes to light."

I nodded absently, and Marty seemed satisfied, but I wanted him to consider something: "We both know, Marty, that neither one of us will be able to control what someone might do."

I realized that Marty's remarks in no way indicated what he believed about TJ's innocence. Marty was only doing his job. Covering the contingencies was the act of a first-class lawyer. Preventing TJ from being charged was Marty's immediate responsibility. If the worst happened, I knew that Marty would work fervently to have the charges tossed, and do his utmost to ensure that the charge did not result in a committal for trial. A preliminary inquiry would be utilized to demonstrate that the Crown had no case, and that the case was not worthy of trial proceedings. Failing that scenario, Marty would defend TJ as best he could. Jury and trial proceedings were often a crap shoot at best. Innocent people sometimes got convicted. Guilty people sometimes got acquitted. The notion of justice was all about perceiving justice to be done. It was a glorified belief only in aphorism, not in practical application.

So I worried. Marty stared at me, waiting… then got up to leave. "Business done, Samantha. Are you free for dinner?

I ignored him momentarily.

"You know, Marty, I like to follow my wee inner voice. The more I hear and see, although none of it makes any kind of sense, I get the strong inkling that your man is up to his yin-yang in something quite disgusting. I can't imagine why he might have murdered the York woman, or Rogers. But the wind will turn soon, I can assure you. Right now, you're just being paid to nose about, but get lots of rest, would you? It won't be long before you earn your grit, pal."

He winked at me.

"And Marty?"

"Yes, luv?"

"Business is business. Love is bullshit."

For once, the legal voice had no response.

* * *

I curled up in a local park to read Ali's diary. Her life had become complex by the early spring of this year. A lot of hostile players wanted to shoot her down.

February 16, 1994: We've initiated the lawsuit against Frank, Wanda, and Luke. All of them have been served with initiating pleadings. I'm beginning to sound like TJ, I know, but that's not all bad. Separate

counsel has been retained by them, I'm told. Lawyers for all of them are threatening to issue counterclaim documentation against me for malicious prosecution, abusive process, and so on, ad yuk. TJ tells
me that the threats and rumblings are just that. Nothing to get worried about. I don't need to be concerned
about possible counterclaim proceedings. No point
in advancing that line of attack. The defendants 'possibly risk cost exposure and/or needless antagonism
in the initiation of unmeritorious and vengeful proceedings.' Those were his very words. They sound
like a disease or something. So I guess I'm not too
popular. Wouldn't be the first time. One thing puz-
zles me, though. I talked to Tanya the other day. She
was so <u>angry</u> with me. She threatened me. Said she's
never going to speak to me again if I proceed with
the lawsuit. Well, that's her loss. She'll come back,
in time. She just kept repeating: 'I'll never forgive
you. Never, ever, for what you are doing to our
brother and parents. You're ruining our family's
good name, disgracing our parents, and subjecting
both of us to ridicule. The rest of our lives will be a
shambles. It's a death sentence.'

Well, what could I say? I'm on a roll, now. Besides,
Dad didn't just fool around with me, I'm sure of it.
When Tanya comes out of denial, maybe she'll help
me.

Mom phoned me too, weeping and carrying on. I've
seen her do that before. It doesn't do anything to
gain my sympathy. She could have stopped it. Now
I can't stop this. She says that she is not worried for
herself, but Frank is suicidal. So what? She says he
goes from rage to fits of depression. Am I supposed
to comfort him? She said that I was ruining Luke's

life and his marriage. Really? Doooo tell. To make a long story short, there was a lot of weeping and wailing going on. My life with them is over. At least the one that had been. If Tanya can get her act together, maybe we can make a different kind of life between the two of us. Maybe. But I doubt it.

February 23: Frank has joined some sort of support group. He phoned me to tell me that I am being manipulated by my therapist, that if we can all just come around as a family, we can beat this thing. I would say he has a vested interest in creating some stupid block to counter my claim, but he said I have some kind of 'Syndrome'. I have to ask Leslie about it. I hung up on him, anyway. I didn't dream his abuse. All I have to do is recall…, and I can run to the bathroom, ready to puke. Sometimes I think if I can puke enough, I can get rid of the memories. False? Not on your life.

February 25: You know what I really can't stand, most of all? Mom knew of the assaults. She did nothing about it. Just stood by and let it happen. Where was her power? She never helped me escape. Maybe she didn't know how.

February 28: Leslie told me all about the False Memory 'Syndrome'. She said that some people had organized to challenge accusations of incest. The name sounds real 'scientific', and that sways the discussion for some. Even some law schools were listening carefully. She warned me that this support group maintained that therapists like herself were incompetent. I laughed. Well, what else can you do? 'Leslie,' I said, 'I didn't fantasize anything about Frank or Luke. I suppressed it for years and years. If

I hadn't met you, I'd still be doing that. The incest was ruining my life. You have to make a move in one direction or the other. It's not just that I want to get Frank, or Luke. I want the world to know about incest.'

'I know, I know.' she said. 'It's your voice we need to hear. Not mine, or Frank's, just yours.'

It's the first time anyone has said that to me. No coercion. No suggestions. Just use your own voice.

March 2: I have to balance my life a bit more. My old school chum, Maureen Rogers, looked me up the other day. I was so glad she did, and I realized that I've been much too busy at the office. She asked me about Billy Corgan, because she knew him from Red Deer. 'How is that little slime bucket, anyway?' I told her the 'slime-bucket' was alive and well, and I had met worse. She claims I haven't, and that I could do much better. I kept quiet. So many words could drop like tiny bombs to wreck a good moment between us. I decided to tell her only about TJ and my job. 'I'm so busy at the office, my boss really likes me, I have a lot of responsibilities, I got two raises already.' She says she's not surprised, I was always so smart. I tell her it'll be great having her around. She was always so good at accounting, and if she's game, I might ask her about some of the things in TJ's books where I can't understand the entries.

March 10: I often feel that when I'm talking to clients or witnessing documents, that I am the lawyer. They all treat me with respect, asking the same questions, I think, that they would ask of TJ. Fulfilling and challenging. That's my job. Besides that, he actually trusts me. The job is a great escape from my other problems. I don't know if I'd be able to cope if it wasn't for him. The only time he ever chided me was when I asked him to explain some details. He said 'Don't be so concerned about everything. You'll get the hang of it eventually.' It was a reprimand, but he did it so nicely that my feelings weren't too hurt. He's patient and gentle. Not at all like my father.

March 13: The auditors came today. I was so nervous. They took two days to look over the books. TJ didn't seem rattled, but I think he should have been. After they were gone, we went out for some dinner. He makes me feel special. I must confess that I'm warming to him, something I never thought I'd do with any man. He actually encouraged me to think about going to law school. Said he would sponsor me, provide me with a set of articles and an office after I graduated. I was so excited. I'm going to think about it, really.

March 21: Something is wrong. I don't know everything about the law, but I really think I should know what's going on with the ledgers. I'm confused by some entries, but I don't really want to talk to TJ about it. He has such confidence in me. Why are the entries there? He keeps babbling about his baby - The Lazy Valley Project. Why are funds transferred from one source to the other? I don't get it. There's no tracing some of these entries. I can't account for several of them, or the lack of funds where the notations should be obvious. I spend lots of time trying to figure it out, but I'm getting nowhere. I think I'd better ask him at the risk of jeopardizing his faith in me.

March 30: TJ keeps talking about calling in the C.A.'s to help me out with the entries. I don't want to bother him, so I keep trying to grapple with this mess. I just get more frustrated, though. I've decided to call Maureen to discuss some of these entries. Maybe she's seen the same kind of thing where she works.

April 1: April Fool's. I have no other explanation for what's going wrong with the books. I itemized the problems for Maureen. She says either I'm absolutely off track, or there's something wrong with the books. How could there be? Old Mrs. Smidge got her walking papers last year, shortly after I arrived, but some of these entries have been made afterward. As far as I know, I'm the only one doing the job. Some of the trust accounts look like they've been readjusted. My stomach is just churning. Maureen says that if the entries are incorrect or improperly entered, it is urgent that the errors and inconsistencies be corrected immediately. Good gawd! What next? She scared me silly, but assured me that TJ would be grateful in the end if I corrected everything immediately. So I worked at the office until 9 o'clock, then decided to call it a day.

I phoned TJ's house when I got home. Impulsive of me, I know. He has a life. His wife made that abundantly clear, too. Suzie doesn't like me. I don't know why. He came to the phone and I blurted out the problems to him. Told him I couldn't seem to fix them, and we wouldn't want any more trouble with the Law Society. He was real quiet, then told me that I had acted admirably. Both my friend and I were correct, he said. Promised to get his accountants on the job pronto. Who was my friend? I told him. Ah, of course, he was deeply grateful for all this extra assistance.

So why do I not feel relieved?

So. The books had been out of order. The cards had been stacking against TJ. What did he have to hide? Where would I start? I hardly knew.

Time to get back to the office. If the chief wanted me visible, I'd be visible. The phones rang while I tried desperately to catch up on paperwork. The calls were all queries about the 'Cowboy Cutter'. Phone calls to police offices were always taped. You never know what could be picked up. Sheedy was sharing his banana bread recipe with some of the guys when he picked up yet another phone call.

"Sam, it's for you."

I grabbed it from him. "Sam Holt here."

"Ms. Holt. I'm so glad I could get through to you. I've been trying all afternoon. This is Tanya York."

'Whoa', I thought to myself. The plot thickens. I tried not to let too many seconds elapse between my shock and my voice.

"Ms. York. What a surprise."

"Yes, of course it must be. I... I wanted to know if you were any closer to nabbing my sister's killer. We are all so agitated and concerned but don't want to pester you."

Tanya's sorrow leaked through the phone to me. "I can certainly understand your interest, Tanya, and your call is not a bother at all. I'm happy to talk with you. My very sincerest condolences."

I heard her voice break, shattering into heavy breath. "Ms. Holt, I need to talk to you about Ali... about who might have killed her. I can't keep this all to myself anymore. Can I... could I... come to see you right away? I'd like to come this afternoon, before… before something happens."

"Of course, Tanya. I'll be here all afternoon. Would it help if a police cruiser came to pick you up?"

"No, no. I'll be there shortly. I don't want to make it obvious."

"Who are you afraid of, Tanya?"

"My brother, my father. You talked to them both. I can't hide or run anymore. I need to see you."

"I'll be waiting, Tanya." I had chosen to call her by her first name. It was a good way to introduce trust.

I waited for her until 4:30, despairing of her appearance. At 4:34, she slid through the door, looking rather furtive, and apologizing for her delay.

"Not to worry, Tanya. I thought you might have encountered some problems." I was more than a little curious, now.

"Can we go someplace private, Ms. Holt?"

"Why of course. You won't mind the interrogation rooms, will you?"

She shook her head. I decided not to offer her any coffee. She would have spilled it all over herself because she was shaking. That, I didn't need.

We took a place in a quiet little interrogation room, and I waited patiently while she wept. The sniffles became sobs. I touched her, recognizing a primal moment that had to be acknowledged. There was no set time for grief. It would come and go.

The sobs eventually subsided, but not before going from tidal waves to ripples.

"My sister and I are incest victims, Ms. Holt." She watched my reaction, trying to determine the degree of my horror.

"That is no secret any more, Tanya", I responded. It was enough. No secret. "Life is too short to guard a secret so religiously. Sooner or later it has to come out."

She heard me through her stupor and shock. "Yes, yes, it does. I want to tell you about my father." I waited, hoping she wouldn't bring up details about the incest. I was going to refer her to Leslie Reynolds if she did that.

"My father threatened me when Ali activated her lawsuit." Now it was my turn to be surprised.

"Why you?"

"He always expected me to help him with Ali." Her face was craggy with hate.

"He phoned me one night. He was devastated when served with the papers. He said he was sure that when the 'lies' came out, it would certainly destroy him, his career, and all that he worked for. I was secretly hoping it would. He ordered me to try to persuade Ali to change her mind," Tanya fluttered two fingers in the air in a quote imitation, "to cease her foolish conduct." He talked endlessly about ruination, his, mom's, Luke's... and mine. I thought about that for awhile. I decided that my life had already been ruined quite enough, so I chose to be Ali's enemy, but that's not all. He told me to tell Ali that no one would believe her story. Everyone would think it was concocted. He even joined a support group. Imagine that." Tanya sniffled a bit, and I waited for her to go on.

"He couldn't stand the fact that something was completely out of his control. Mom was bawling and shrieking, I could hear her in the background. He told her to shut up, he didn't need another snivelling woman bugging him. He yelled at everyone at once, shouting that there was no way on God's green earth that any woman, least of all his daughter, would fuck up his life. Those were his very words. I was always scared of him. He reminded me that he had always had his way with women. That included Mom, Ali, and of course, me. He threatened me then, saying: 'If you can't handle your baby sister, and I have a feeling you won't be able to, I'll have to deal with it myself. And it won't be pretty.' I asked him what he meant by that. He said maybe he could get Luke to do the dirty work. That way he could keep his hands clean. You have to understand my father, Ms. Holt. He would have no second thoughts about harming Ali. He had spent her lifetime and mine doing just that."

I didn't pretend to understand the man. How did one understand sociopathic scum? I nodded anyway.

"So are you saying that you suspect your father of murder?"

"Yes, either him or Luke."

There. It was out.

"I want to help, Ms. Holt. I have so much guilt. I turned my father's threat into my own, directed it at Ali. If it's possible, I want to make amends. I want Ali to know…"

Her voice trailed off. I decided to nurture her a bit.

"Will you be okay, Tanya? Are you okay to be alone tonight?" I honestly didn't know what I would do if she said no. Take her out for Chinese food? Invite her to my place?

It was the gesture, of course. She nodded. "I'll… be… okay now."

"Tanya, your sister, as you know, was deeply troubled and was seeing a therapist by the name of Leslie Reynolds. I can give you her number. She can help."

She glanced at me then, gratefully. There must be something about incest victims not wanting to make eye contact. They are too afraid of someone 'knowing' their secret, as though the truth could be read in their eyes. My knowledge of her truth allowed her to look at me comfortably.

"Thanks, Ms. Holt. I'm going home now. I want to sleep. I think I'll be able to, now." I gave her a hug, and felt a great sigh of her relief against my body. She would be okay. It would take time for her to heal, but no one had murdered her spirit.

* * *

Richard had prepared a lovely little chicken caesar salad. He ordered me to sit down and take my shoes off.

"Y'know, Richard, it's only a shame that we don't have a dog to bring me the paper, and oh, you forgot my pipe. I'll retire in the drawing room after dinner to imbibe my favourite Port."

"Don't get cocky. I only do this because I love you. It's your pheromones."

"My pharoah-who?"

"Your pheromones. A pheromone is a chemical exchanged between members of the same species that affects behaviour. They're sex attractants, alarm substances, territorial markers, slug-tracks, you might say. The female secretes them, the male comes looking for the juicy little rascals."

"God, I love the influence I have on you. Where did you get that nonsense?"

"Don't flatter yourself. I can resist temptation, but you must drive the boys in the shop quite crazy. And I got it in Genetics 101, first year Nursing School."

"I never thought of it." Did I really drive them nuts? What malarkey.

"Got any women at the Police Station?", he inquired.

"A few. Some clerks, patrols, dispatchers," I counted mentally.

"Bet they all menstruate when you do."

"Oh cut it out. Okay, okay. What do you want me to do for you?"

"We're going to a murder mystery at the Deane House this Saturday night."

"Why??? Richard, I live murder mysteries. Do I need that crap?"

"It's not crap", he sniffed. "Besides, the script is Mark's opus performance. You'll enjoy it."

Resigned to my fate, I asked Richard about the Deane House.

"Great little place to eat," he announced. "Quaint. No smoking. I've heard that it's haunted. There were apparently a few violent deaths that occurred in it. It was built for an R.C.M.P. superintendent by the name of Richard Deane. People have allegedly spotted lots of ghosts inside. There's a man sitting in the study, another guy floats down the stairs regularly, and a beautiful woman in white stares out of a mirror in the attic. Mark tells me that no one in their right mind goes into the attic alone. It's cold, even in July."

"Sounds like a great time, Richard. Just the nerve medicine I need." He frowned at me. I wondered sometimes how he endured my sarcasm.

I sat up long after Richard had gone to bed, thinking about the case. I couldn't stop pondering about TJ. All roads lead to him as the prime murder suspect. He had no alibi, the presence of the mug put him at the murder scene, and there was an I.D. of him and his vehicle. Then there was the Rogers connection. If Ali's suspicions of the unthinkable - embezzlement, were true, then TJ would be displeased, to say the least, that she and Maureen had stumbled on the evidence.

My own feelings baffled me. I just wasn't sure. But the more I looked at the evidence, the more I tried to convince myself. I just had to keep raking through the sand, that's all.

After Tanya's disclosure, I checked with Sheedy about the York's alibis. They came out clean, in a manner of speaking. Luke had brought in the softball parent's list, I had made a few phone calls, and discovered that his alibi checked out as well. The murderer, I believed, had to have some connection with Maureen Rogers and a motive that included killing Maureen. The anger connections of Ali's family didn't extend to Rogers.

So, how would I put pressure on TJ? Seems that only lawyers can do dirty work effectively on other lawyers. Of course I had Marty in mind.

When I first began to connect this story, I told myself to leave as much of my sordid past and any self-disclosure out of the picture. I reckoned that the story was really about TJ and Ali, with maybe a sprinkling of other people filtered in. Now I realize that my own story was linked intricately with that of Ali and TJ.

Marty was my lawyer, alright. Marty and I had

had an affair a few years back, and he had been unhappy with the closure. He was fun, we had some laughs, the sex was great. He was also married at the time, or separated/initiating a divorce, depending on which story you wanted to believe. The truth didn't matter much to me. I knew the affair would have an inevitable end, preferably before Mrs. Marty caught on. Besides, it's a truism that the Mrs. Martys of this world have their own lives, and don't always really care what their Mr. is up to. At least that's my opinion. Looking back, though, I'm not proud of my unfortunate relationship with yet another legal-eagle. I broke it off with him when the terms began to take on the usual overtones of male/female power differential. I had a career, Marty had another life. He was distressed when I said goodbye. A good diversion is hard to find, but I knew he'd be successful eventually.

Marty had phoned me off and on over the years, half-heartedly trying to light an old flame that I thought had burned down a long time ago. Men are such peculiar characters. The best of them honestly believe that women have no other life that doesn't include them. Marty was no exception. Maybe he really did carry a torch, but I couldn't afford to pursue him. Besides, his marital status had not changed, that much I knew.

I decided to phone him about his client: Theodore James.

His secretary put me right through. Marty's voice greeted me cheerfully.

"Samantha, my love. It's about time that the phone call was yours."

"Marty. Good to hear your voice." It was, in fact. It was softer than I heard it the other day. A great bedroom voice.

Stop it right there, Sam.

The pause had been too long, and he was smart enough to pick up on it.

"You free tonight?"

"Even if I were, you're working for TJ. We don't need conflict of interest. I need your help."

"Hey, you know I've always said to you 'anytime you need anything, Samantha-honey, just call.'"

"Yeah, yeah, Marty, I know. So I'm calling in a favour."

"Anything, luv. Tell me what it's about."

"There is another piece of evidence that you need to hear about."

His turn to pause. "I was afraid of that."

"I need you to ask TJ about the Lazy Valley Project."

"What about it? Why would I do that?"

"I need to know everything, and I mean everything, pertaining to TJ's involvement with the 'Lazy Valley Project'. Furthermore, not only do we require, right now, a full and exhaustive outline pertaining to the Project, but we also need TJ's authorization to audit his books. Naturally, we'll be looking for activity of the monies involved with the Lazy Valley Project. Matters are still preliminary and only tentative, so no one else needs to know of the audit. Your client won't need to be concerned about the Law Society being advised of the audit investigation. If everything turns out okay, it will be just our little secret between the three of us. If he grants consent and he turns up clean, no charges laid. On the other hand, whether or not he grants consent, and especially if there are problems arising from all of this, we're going to lay charges against your client. One of those charges will be for the murder of Ms. Ali York."

"Whoa, woman, slow down."

"Save your breath, Marty. Feel free to tell him I sent you."

"Samantha, you're muscling me. I don't like it."

"Tell me, Marty, how's married life. Still sweet and secure?"

He laughed then. An unmirthful guffaw full of bitterness.

"Okay, you win." His voice softened into the seductive sound I loved. "I miss you Sam. I like the mental gymnastics. Like to get together and practice sometime?"

"Sure, Marty. I'll buy you dinner if we pull this one off."

"You really are a bitch, Holt."

"But you love it, Marty."

I hung up.

* * *

"Okay, TJ," drawled Marty, after he had recounted the gist of the Holt conversation and the warning. "Tell me simply about the Lazy Valley Project, what Holt is alluding to, and why. If it's all so important, why didn't you tell me about it before?"

TJ whacked the ball into the fairway. He had been irritated by the circumstances of this week. First, Holt had come to waste his time and badger him, then Marty had phoned and insisted on golfing with him this morning. To top it off, Greg the golf pro hadn't been there to chat this morning. And now Lazy Valley again. Where would it all end? He wished the world would leave him alone to get on with business as usual.

Marty droned on.

"I can only assume that the particulars pertaining to the Project are not pretty, otherwise you wouldn't have conveniently forgotten to brief me about it. I want you to know that Holt may not realize that I am in the dark over the Project and its implications…"

Marty's turn to drive. The ball flew nicely down the fairway.

Marty smoothly continued, "I was noncommittal of course. I think Holt was positive that I knew nothing about the Project. Otherwise, I should have at least tried to do something to dilute the strength of her ugly allegations." Marty peered at TJ, trying to guess at the accused's reaction to the conversation.

"The other thing to bear in mind is that Holt wouldn't be too smug about the information, in any event. It's not her nature to be like that. She might be a tad embarrassed that she only uncovered it lately. I'm assuming that's the case, otherwise matters would have developed a lot more quickly."

TJ said nothing in his own defense. Marty continued.

"You might wonder why I am being so calm and nice to you when I should be reaming your ass out. From the look on your face, I'd say you don't need any more enemies. A few more friends might even things out." Marty waited again. TJ was ashen. Marty went on, if for no other reason than to relieve the growing tension.

"I must confess that I'm getting old and soppy in my dotage. If I were you, I would only hope and pray that the soppiness is a temporary aberration. I will have to conduct your defence quite differently. If

I'm as weak in my defence as I am now, counsellor, and as weak in character as you have been, never mind your lying, you are up to your pintail in piranhas, pal. Do you want another lawyer?" Marty would have added more, just for the sake of being verbose. He really didn't know what else to do.

TJ slumped down, then, right on the green. The guy cried. Actually wept. Marty felt like a terrible villain at that point, but he knew what he was doing, and it worked. He was totally confident that he would get the truth from his client after that.

TJ realized, at last, that he was in terrible trouble. His only hope would have to be in Marty. The troubles were irreversible. He would need far more than a great lawyer to rescue him from this one.

Perhaps it had been a mistake to play God, after all.

'The play's the thing…'

I have heard that guilty creatures sitting at a play
Have by the very cunning of the scene
Been struck so to the soul that presently
They have proclaimed their malfactions;
For murder, though it have no tongue, will speak
With most malicious organ. I'll have these players
Play something like the murder of my father
Before mine uncle. I'll observe his looks
I'll tend him to the quick. If but a blench,
I know my course. The spirit that I have seen
May be the devil, and the devil hath power
T'assume a pleasing shape; yea, and perhaps,
Out of my weakness and my melancholy —
As he is very potent with such spirits —
Abuses me to damn me. I'll have grounds
More relative than this. The play's the thing
Wherein I'll catch the conscience of the King.

(Hamlet 2.2: 590-605)

Chapter Twenty-nine

The Deane House is a pretty place. You can sit and have tea and goodies on a Saturday. Pick a cosy spot by the window and let the Elbow river swirl hypnotically beside you. Across the river is the archaeological site of Fort Calgary. The geese and ducks jockey for territory on the river banks. It's a place to sit all afternoon if you can. Joggers take over the bicycle paths, and the geese yield a bit of space as the athletes fly by. That is Saturday.

On Friday night, the Deane House is a site of murder. On this particular Friday night, Borealis Productions presents a cast of social has-beens, all potential murderers. Richard seats me elegantly at the best table in the house. The program is displayed right beside my cutlery. I pick it up to search eagerly for Mark's name and role in the play. I never expect to find: Suzie James. Only she's not Suzie James. She's Susan Harper. Her cute, dainty little image smiles exquisitely at me from the glossy paper.

Susan Harper plays Victoria Snodgrass, a wealthy heiress who has been jilted by her lover. Victoria has an axe to grind and a pistol to point. Five other people are portrayed as potential murderers. Mark plays the victim, George Snodgrass, who is a modern British remittance man estranged from his smouldering wife, Victoria.

I slap my hand over my eyes, emitting a low moan. Richard glowers at me, but I don't have to explain my guttural rudeness.

"What's the matter with you?" There is worry in Richard's voice, and a more-than-subtle annoyance.

"Take a look at Victoria Snodgrass," I whisper.

Richard gives me a quizzical look, examines 'Susan Harper,' then looks back at me.

"Yup, she looks like the killer, alright. Guess we don't have to participate in this play. Thanks to the brilliant lady detective, we have yet solved another murder without even scratching our nail polish."

"Oh, stop. I mean Susan Harper isn't really Susan Harper!"

"Thank you for sharing that with me. Now would you like to tell me what planet you're living on?"

I sigh deeply. "Oh, Richard, I'm not sure myself anymore. Susan Harper has an assumed name."

"No law against that."

"No, but it's peculiar, don't you think?"

"Depends on who you think you really are."

He is right, of course. Suzie James had a double life. There is a long pause as I stare, quite catatonically, at an old vase in front of me.

Richard breaks my reverie.

"So, who is she?"

Remembering my professional ethics, I abruptly reply, "I quess I thought she was someone else."

He glowers at me again, but says nothing.

The lights dim.

ACTION.

Chapter Thirty

We poked around the Deane House, joining in the festivities of the Murder Mystery and looking for clues as to whodunit. Richard was right into it. He checked under bedspreads, in drawers, kitchen cupboards. I half expected him to come back to me proclaiming that he had found Colonel Mustard in the library with a candlestick.

As for me, I just watched Suzie. By now, she was aware that I was present. It occurred to me that she had many faces. One for Ali's funeral, one at least for the murder mystery, and goodness knows how many others. One more face, no doubt, for the man who was her lover: the director and owner of Borealis Productions. How did I know that secret? Richard told me as we ate dinner. Mark had revealed that secret to Richard. The two lovers had seemed inconsequential until now.

The plot thickened.

I waited for Mrs. James to finish her act, at which time I requested her presence at my table. After commending her on the fine performance, Richard, feeling a nudge from me under the table, tactfully excused himself.

Suzie and I eyeballed each other and she took the initiative. "I understand you have my husband by the short and curlies, Detective Holt."

I raised my eyebrow at her choice of expressive English. "You might put it like that, Suzie. I'm far more interested in your perceptions regarding his behaviour in the recent past, however."

She smiled condescendingly. "I have been extremely concerned about him."

What mask was this?

"He has been tired, cranky and irritable for some time. His old business friends and associates have stopped calling him at home. We often had to take the receiver off to get some peace and quiet. When I asked him about it, he shrugged, gave me some curt response about being quite happy, and he couldn't care less. Well, where was I to take that? They were his friends, not mine."

"May I offer you a glass of wine, Suzie?"

"That would be nice, thanks. It's been an exhausting week."

"Yes, I imagine you juggle quite a bit in this line of work. What interested you about murder mysteries?"

"I was a drama major at university. I like clues, Detective Holt. Setting them up. Wondering if people can find them. Sometimes you even have to act." She smiled again. I was being baited. For what?

"On the continuing topic of my beloved husband, Detective Holt. Lest we forget why we're enjoying this wine together?"

She cocked her head at me quizzically. Was she really anxious to tell me all about hubby?

She sighed. "He was always complaining about money. He used to be quite flippant about how we spent it. Quite a generous fellow, actually. Gave it away to all kinds of charities. When anyone commented on it, he always responded that it was important to help those who needed help, a social obligation to put back into the system what you took out of it. Unless you get into trouble yourself, of course. His concern about money was quite sudden. I believe my husband is an astute businessman as well as a busy, successful lawyer. Why money would become a prevailing concern, I simply cannot fathom."

"Do you think he might have had some sort of business reversal?"

She shrugged. "I have no plausible explanation, Detective. He spends excessive amounts of time at the office. I assumed, at first, that he was busier than a fiend. Of course, it didn't take long to realize that his beautiful secretary was also a draw."

She swallowed her wine in a great gulp, and stared straight ahead.

"Would you like another, Suzie?"

"Don't mind if I do."

I beckoned the waiter, and bought her another drink. It would be her last on my tab. I pursued my questioning.

"If he spent so much time at the office, don't you think he might have been making money hand over fist?"

"Seems logical. But I reckon there was some sort of problem. Something that Ms. York couldn't quite solve, you know." She met my eyes. "I just stay alert, Detective. I have two children whom I need to protect. If their father is in some sort of trouble, I have to know about it. If he chooses not to tell me his woes, I start sniffing around."

And what did you scent, Miss Suzie? I didn't voice my question. She was on a roll.

"He has seemed less anxious in the recent past, Ms. Holt. Until quite recently, when he told me of your squeeze, he had not looked so drained and haggard. I suspect his pressures have been relieved somewhat, despite Ms. York's unfortunate demise."

She didn't seem sorry at all.

"As a lawyer's wife, you become aware of bad files, the ones that drive him crazy. They always work their course, but until that happens, the lawyer acts as though the world is coming to an end. Problems often loom larger than they really are, but things get resolved."

"What about Ms. York's assistance to your husband. Do you think she helped matters?"

"Hmmph. No doubt she did, Detective. She was a self-important young woman. I guess that's how you have to be these days. My husband remarked often that Ms. York was completely indispensable. I caught the inference.

Anyone could see that Ali York was lovely. I thought she was marvellously attentive to my husband's concerns. Men appreciate that sort of worship thing. I'm no longer young, Ms. Holt. You begin to feel vulnerable in middle-age. Younger women appear to have so much more power."

"Tell me about it, Suzie. But do they really? What is power, anyway?"

She ignored me. "I was quite prepared to let my husband enjoy his little fling as long as my family and lifestyle did not suffer from it. At least his bad temper wasn't brought home as often. I won't tolerate that sort of childish behaviour in my home. Whatever her role, Ms. York took the pressure off me. If anyone is going to disrupt my life, it will be me."

She examined me seriously. "I will protect my children at all costs."

She paused for a moment, considering her conclusion.

"Please don't mistake me, Ms. Holt. I like everyone, really. I get along with people regardless of who they are, or their station in life. I felt an uncharacteristic dislike of Ms. York, however. I admit it. Perhaps it was jealousy, although none of us like to admit to emotions like that. She spent an inordinate amount of time with my husband. Ali York was striking, beautiful, smart and exuberant. Obviously quite in love with life. She reminded me of what I might have been. Her relationship with my husband was only secondary. There. At last I've spoken it. We women compete too much for the attention of men, for the privilege they give us in that attachment."

She sighed unhappily. "If I knew how to disentangle myself from that privilege without hurting my children, I would just simply do it."

"Are you thinking about disentangling yourself, Suzie?"

She looked at me quizzically, then another mask appeared on her face, and she remained mute until I asked another question.

"Your marriage is hurtful, Suzie?"

"Marriage isn't just about putting up with someone's foibles, Ms. Holt. My husband was emotionally, mentally, and financially abusive to me. Until quite recently," she looked absently around for her lover, "I had made light of those occurrences. I didn't want anyone to know. I had sensed for some time that my husband was flawed, somehow. I just put it down to the 'no one is perfect' routine. But it's more than that. I believe he could be dangerous, Ms. Holt. In the right circumstances, I could be genuinely afraid of him."

Walter McDonald sauntered confidently over to our table.

"Ready to go, Susan?"

She glowed. Yes she did. A woman in love. And she would undoubtedly repeat all her mistakes with this man. What about her children then?

Suzie introduced me to McDonald. I voiced all the right niceties, made all the right faces. He was truly lovely. Just as lovely in his male-way as Ali had been in her feminine way, and probably no one would murder him, excepting perhaps some jilted husband.

Oh, the world was a complex place, where murder can be placed in the genre of fiction and entertainment. A place where art can reflect life, despite what the critics tell you.

And who was I to judge Suzie James, or even Susan Harper?

Chapter Thirty-one

"Alright, nice and slow," Marty prodded TJ, "start at the beginning and tell me everything and all there is to know, so that I won't have any further surprises. I don't want to be caught off guard again. Don't colour anything, don't try to make anything more pleasant than it really is. Don't spare any morsel of information, and let me be the judge of what's relevant. I'm in no rush, we've got the whole day in front of us, and I don't have to remind you that what we're talking about will impact on your future like nothing else ever has. We must be as thorough and careful as possible."

Marty was purposely longwinded and gentle. He had never seen a man cry like this before. He sensed that TJ would truly unburden himself, and that nothing would be held back. Marty would get the facts this time. He had some inclination of what was about to unfold.

He shuddered to himself. This one didn't bode well.

"I'm not sure how this all started," began TJ. A standard disclaimer, but more would ooze out.

Marty listened. He had heard some great stories in his time, for sure. It took TJ several hours to relate and recount the sequence of events leading up to the present. Marty hadn't yawned once. The sordid series of events culminated in the ultimate private confession. It was engrossing. Truth was indeed stranger than fiction. TJ's position was far worse than Marty had imagined.

If all this information came out, and it surely would, Marty knew that there was no doubt whatsoever that TJ would be disbarred as a result of the embezzlement and defalcations. Repayment of all stolen funds was certainly commendable, however that did not erase the thefts at first instance. Further, TJ's motives for the thefts were hardly pure. They were selfish; designed to better his personal position. There was little doubt that he was in an intolerable position of conflict throughout the proceedings, regardless of the surprising eventual findings of the Law Society. TJ would not only be disbarred, but he would certainly also be jailed, and the incarceration would run into the next century for sure.

He helped TJ off the course, assisted him into his car and told him that he would contact him later. Marty needed to think.

'What a mess,' Marty mused, 'this is one of the times when the job is unbearable.' There was certainly no satisfactory or acceptable way to deal with the speculations. Except for the problem of two murders, the thefts might have remained uncovered. But for the ongoing murder investigations, Marty would have no difficulty in simply burying the information respecting the embezzlements. A solicitor-client privilege would be in force, and Marty would be under no obligation whatsoever to turn his client in, or to disclose any information however serious or injurious. The solicitor-client privilege was paramount, overruling all other obligations.

Marty muttered to himself.

'If Holt is contacted and advised that the books are not available for auditing or inspection for purposes of confidentiality or whatever, then it's for sure, given the knowledge of the police respecting the Lazy Valley Project, non-access will result in charges being laid... well, TJ's going to be charged with, at the very least, the murder of Ali York. As if that wouldn't be enough, the records will be secured or subpoenaed in one way or another, then the police and the Law Society will have access, and both will demand their piece of skin.'

Marty had some thinking to do, for sure. If Holt was given access, or limited rights of inspection to the books without anyone knowing about it, namely the Law Society, what then?

Holt and her henchmen would have nothing to do with the excuse of providing no access to the books, regardless of its validity. It would stop the examination of the records for the time being, but TJ would be charged, and Marty would gain nothing.

If the books were scrutinized, however, Holt would discover the embezzlements, defalcations and thefts. Even though the funds had all been repaid, and Holt had stated that the sole purpose of the record examination and expedition would be confined solely to the murder proceedings, the police would, in all likelihood, have little choice but to charge TJ for the embezzlements. Then the Law Society would be notified accordingly. Well, one couldn't expect Samantha Holt to give a rat's ass about a gentleman's agreement. In any case, a possible motive for the crimes was as clear as winter ice. TJ had conducted some tricky manoeuvring with the accounting records and Ali had discovered them, resulting in her early demise. Likely Holt was making the same connection, but Marty couldn't be sure of that.

Marty was developing a throbbing headache. Three extra-strength painkillers were in order. He gulped them down, swallowing hard. One thing was abundantly clear. There was no solution. TJ was doomed.

When the pain in his head had subsided a bit, Marty tried to further analyze the situation. He knew precisely what he would do. He had played some rotten hands before and had managed to make the best of bad situations.

He knew exactly how to treat TJ. He had to make sure that TJ would obey him blindly and not do or say anything unless expressly instructed to do so. Given TJ's state of mind, that trick wouldn't be hard to pull off. Marty wanted TJ to be scared silly, but not so fearful that he would lose hope. It was a tough balancing act, and he didn't like to play with his client's mind, but where was the choice?

When he had reflected on his position, Marty called TJ to outline the plan.

"Look, ol' buddy, the situation is pretty near hopeless. We are screwed if we allow access to the records, and we are damned if we don't. Regardless, disbarment and incarceration for a long, long time appear to be inevitable. Our options are certainly few and quite limited. If we had an alibi that would show that you couldn't have been involved with the murders, we might be able to avoid the audit and any charges. We don't have an alibi, so I want you to understand fully, the grave implications of your situation. There are some consequences and awesome repercussions to all of this. You must lay yourself entirely in my hands as a sacrificial lamb. No moves can be made unless I make them first. Whatever you do, don't lose hope even though the situation may appear hopeless. If an alibi came forth, that would certainly be a break. In the interim, leave the police to me."

* * *

I hadn't seen this much of Marty in months. I couldn't decide whether business really was business. It might be up to me to decide.

"Marty, what a pleasant surprise. Who visits me more than you do?"

"Samantha, my love. You and your henchmen are shoving against an open door. My client has no objection to opening all his books for your examination, audit, or whatever. Before he does that, however, he has to get the required consent from the Law Society. He has to get a court order directing the inspection. If he allows the police access, unlimited or otherwise, to his books, he runs the risk of sanction. He would be accused of conduct unbecoming a solicitor. I have discussed your request at considerable length with my client. We believe that the Law Society would not likely find out about the audit, but permission must nevertheless be acquired. However, accidents or disclosures do sometimes happen in a variety of ways. There is no guarantee that we wouldn't comply with your request and get hammered by the Law Society. Regardless of your findings, in our favour or otherwise, that scenario would happen.

Also, if the Police were to secure a Court Order authorizing and directing the audit or record

investigations, we couldn't consent to it without permission from the Law Society. Undoubtedly, the Order
would be discovered and even if TJ came out squeaky
clean, as he has done before in the recent past, and
the record examination discloses nothing of concern,
no doubt TJ would be brought up on the carpet by
the Law Society as a result of the investigation and
Order. There is every reason to believe that he would
be severely reprimanded as a result, whether he is innocent or otherwise, given the recent investigation.
Numerous parties and solicitors are still smarting
from the earlier investigation, and the fact that it resulted in no formal charges being pursued or laid
against my client."

Marty was wonderfully cool. I couldn't help but
admire the guy.

"If you have any solutions to our problem", he
added crisply, "please let me know. It must be clear to
you that we have nothing to hide. We are willing,
even anxious to allow you access, but we are being
squeezed in both directions and running into problems at every corner. Please bear with us,
Samantha-honey. Give me a few more days to see if
some resolution might come about. Something that both
of us can live with. That's not an unreasonable respite."

Samantha-honey, my butt.

"Look counsellor," I spat at him impatiently, "in
case you don't read lips let me tell you, point blank,
that I don't buy a word of what you are saying. Do I
look stupid to you, is that it?"

He smiled. Or rather, leered. He knew it would
make me furious.

I forged on, furious with him. "For me to accept
what you're saying, I'd have to be more than stupid.

You're playing games. That tack, coupled with what I've uncovered respecting the Lazy Valley Project, not to mention all the other items pointing to your client's involvement, make me wonder why TJ wasn't charged a long time ago. But I'll let you play your game or earn your money, if that's what you're doing. You have ten days to allow us access to the records we need. If you don't, for whatever explanation you give, let me assure you that Theodore H. James will be charged with the murder of Ali York.

I realize that you have a job to do, so I will give you my word that you will be notified of our prior intention to charge your client. I'll give you the opportunity to escort Mr. James to the Police Station, so that he need not be handcuffed. We don't need to embarrass him. It goes without saying, counsellor, that if the York murderer is found prior to the ten day period, and if that party happens not to be your client, then we can cancel the 'look at the books plan.' I hope you like my wording, and maybe we can both direct our attentions to other, more interesting diversions."

I watched him mull things over in his cagey mind, looking for all the world as though he were the person who stood accused. He looked old and tired then, and I felt sorry for him. Our jobs didn't allow us to be friends, and certainly not lovers right now. Perhaps we would never be close again. I regretted that, but I wasn't sure why.

Marty reached for some pills, flicked them out of the package, and popped them absently into his mouth. I spoke to break the discomfort.

"Don't be too hard on yourself, Marty. Life is too short."

He spoke, finally.

"I was wondering when you'd shut up so I could ask you for coffee, at least."

"Sounds like a good plan, Marty. For old time's sake."

* * *

"No way!" I yelled.

Sergeant Speirs was trying to tell me that there had been a big break in the York and Rogers murders.

"What? Who?" I felt ridiculous.

"Sheedy and McInnis are recording the confession even as we speak. She's been warned, we've read her rights, and she's waived her right to counsel. She's anxious to talk."

"She? There was no female suspect."

"Guess you were wrong, Sam. Come with me."

I entered a side anteroom with Speirs. It faced, through a one-way mirror, into the interrogation room. We could hear every word.

When I saw who they had, I sat down, hard.

"It's just a matter of time before the actual confession occurs, Sam. I wanted you to see and hear it for yourself."

There were others in the room, waiting for the confession to occur. There was no doubt in their minds that the killer was right before them.

The sarge could have knocked me over with a feather. I had worked so hard, imagined a lot of different possibilities, but never in my craziest dreams had the face of Wanda York appeared. This situation was incomprehensible.

Wanda was clearly overwrought; sobbing and uncontrollably weeping, her body convulsing into spasms everytime she tried to speak. The kleenex someone had given her was twisted into a lump. I felt that I just had to say something.

"How do you figure, sarge, that you're going to get a confession out of Mrs. York? She's in no shape to be questioned. Sheedy and McInnis are hovering over her. She's clearly intimidated, as well as emotionally unbalanced at this point."

I wanted to knock on the window, to remind McInnis that this was a sensitive woman he was interrogating; one who had suffered unimaginable hurts. Just because I could muscle Luke York around was no reason for McInnis to think that he could apply the same pressures to mother-York. Sheedy looked uncomfortable. McInnis was pressing her, insistingly and demandingly. The lady just couldn't deliver, although perhaps they were making some progress, because her spasms and shock quivers seemed to be settling down. She was doing her best to regain her composure. Sheedy left the room and returned presently, carrying a mug of something.

"Here's your cup of herbal tea, Mrs. York."

Bless old Sheedy. His gentleness was having the desired effect. She gulped loudly, and presently her sobbing ceased.

Wanda York began to talk. She was slow and plodding, but she had her emotions under control, speaking at last in a regulated fashion. McInnis occasionally interrupted her, trying to get her to speak about the York and Rogers murders. Both Sheedy and McInnis were cautious at first, but I watched their frustration grow as she steadfastly avoided speaking about those horrors.

She chose, instead, to talk about her personal horror: the early life of her family. She rambled on about how she had met Frank York, her early wedded life, the arrival of Luke, Tanya and Ali. I watched her clench her jaw as she spoke of the earliest difficulties in her marriage. I wondered if Sheedy and McInnis perceived Wanda's growing anger as she spoke. It was well-channelled, and wrought perfectly in the context of this situation, but I thought it unlikely that it would ever result in a confession to murder.

It seemed like their 'confessor' had a great deal to relate before she would get to any conversation that resembled what they wanted. I expected a confession alright, but one that no one within hearing distance of Wanda would anticipate. Sheedy and McInnis gave up trying to manipulate her. She had, in fact, lived with the best of manipulators.

Gradually, their patience paid off. Wanda York's story began to move toward the time period shortly prior to the murder of her daughter. I saw Sheedy and McInnis shift in their seats, hardly able to contain their excitement over the next words to come out of Wanda's mouth.

The words never came. I knew what she had come to confess: her complicity in the incest of her daughters and the abuse of her son. Or was I merely second-guessing the reason for her distress?

The poor lady was growing increasingly tired. Her show of emotions had spent her energy. She continued to breathe deeply, but her breathing became labored as Sheedy brought her another cup of herbal tea. She halted a few times, staring into space. I knew it wouldn't be long before she'd have to take a bathroom break as well, but Sheedy was propping her up. She couldn't go on. She was running out of steam, and they simply could not keep what little remained of her engine.

"Sergeant" I pleaded, "she needs a break, and you're not getting what you want from her."

He nodded reluctantly, and signalled for a clerk to interrupt Sheedy and McInnis.

Great. Just blooming terrific. Wanda York fainted before they could lead her to the bathroom for a break. We called in the police doctor, who chastised everyone soundly, ordering that there would be no further questioning today. The doctor said that Wanda's blood pressure was wild, clearly indicating an imminent stroke or cardiac arrest. We dispatched her to the local hospital for observation, and it wasn't long before the York clan was ready to crawl through the telephone wires to throttle me personally.

Sergeant Speirs got a call from the York family lawyer, who cited previous abuse, of the department (me), towards Luke York. Big deal, but Speirs didn't need to hear about it. The Chief of Police was pulled from home, and arrived amidst a medley of accusations and insinuations. How did Wanda York come to be at the Station? For what purpose? What did the police do to trigger the heart attack or stroke? York's lawyer was yapping on, making threatening and menacing statements about launching an action for harassment or malicious prosecution. Demands were flying all over the place for explanations, disclosures, damages, and so forth. I got really tired of it all, but I felt compelled to stay and support the guys. It was Sheedy and McInnis' first rodeo, and neither one of them had expected to be catapulted off the bull quite as quickly and violently as this.

I had no idea what to make of Wanda York's arrival on the scene, and with her untimely exit, I had no idea where to go next. Maybe she had some purpose in coming to the station, but I believed that her purpose had been much like Tanya's. To confess. What? Mother-guilt? What business what that of ours? If Wanda truly felt as though she needed to make things right, our interrogation room was the wrong place for her.

It remained only to be seen if she recovered, but in any case, Wanda York was a poor source of information, it seemed to me. I had been around far too long to take seriously what promised to be only a superficial offer of news. Wanda York's appearance was sensationalized within the Department, but I believed it had no particular relevance to the case. I would have to proceed carefully, though. Sensations governed everyone's thinking in a crisis. We would all just have to wait and see.

* * *

"Suzie," TJ uttered her name quite softly and tentatively, "we must sit down and talk. All hell is shortly going to break loose, and you had better be prepared for the worst. I need your help. If you want to keep me around, you are going to have to help me dig this ditch. It's a long story, and I won't bore you with the details. What I will tell you is that, well… I have done some things I'm not proud of, and that I would never repeat if I could have another chance. I am innocent of what the Police think I've done. I need your trust and belief in me, and your aid in getting the Police off my back.

Unless a miracle happens, I'll probably be disbarred and charged with embezzlement and misappropriation of trust funds. A prison term is likely, almost a certainty. I repaid all the borrowed funds, and no one has been hurt by my errors and misjudgment. But it's worse than that. Somehow, through a web of circumstantial evidence, tenuous assumptions and speculations, the Police believe that I am involved in the murders of my secretary, Ali York, and that other woman, Maureen Rogers. Naturally, I could never do such a thing, even if I had reason or cause, and I didn't even know the Rogers girl. You know me well enough to confirm that. I wouldn't have hurt Ali for anything. You know how important she was to me as a secretary and right-hand assistant. The accusation makes no sense at all. The Police have no other suspects, however, and they're under public pressure to nab the 'Cowboy Cutter.'"

"It would just make everybody so happy if a high profile lawyer like myself could be hurt and publicly embarrassed. Never mind the consequences of falsely laid charges and the irreversible damage to my reputation."

He stopped to gauge his wife's reaction. She looked absolutely dumbfounded. He assumed it was because of the charges. He forged on, trusting that Suzie would help out.

"You know, Suzie, I told Holt that I was at my office working on the night of the murder, but I believe I was actually at home that night, putzing at this and that. You were out for part of the evening, remember, but I don't recall where you were, or what you were doing. I don't even remember asking you where you were going or where you had been. You left and returned so quickly, it seemed. Can you recall that, Suzie? Because if you can, you can probably provide me with a desperately needed alibi. I've been reluctant to bring you into this sordid business, but I have no choice, and I need your help."

Suzie wasn't sure if she would be sick from the shock, or ill from her husband's whining. Disaster. And everything about her life had been going so well.

"TJ, you must be mistaken. I am sure I must have been at home. Where could I have possibly gone? Even if I had, which is unlikely, why wouldn't I have told you, even let you know when I would be home?"

"Don't you remember, Suzie? You had my car that evening, you called me from the cellular phone saying that the tire was low, running as though it were flat, and what should you do? I told you to drive on it, if you could, and that I'd have the garage take care of it the next morning."

Suzie nodded slowly. "Yes, of course I remember, but it was awhile ago. The details are fuzzy. I'm afraid I'm having trouble concentrating, anyway. If you want me to say that I was out, well... I probably went to the store for groceries. Maybe I stopped for a coffee somewhere, who knows?"

TJ was profoundly grateful for his wife's support and facade of strength. He wasn't certain what he was going to do with the new found alibi. Maybe he wouldn't need to use it. He wasn't stupid enough to believe that the alibi was significant, inasmuch as he had informed Holt previously that he was at his office, not at home. Besides, an alibi provided by his wife might not hold much weight. The assumption would be that she was lying, only doing what any good wife would do to save her husband from an ig- nominious fate. He reasoned that some alibi was better than none. He wasn't crazy about the idea, but he knew he'd have to rely on an alibi from Suzie. He mentally prepared how he would have to school his wife so that she would have the alibi down cold. It would have to sound as believable as possible.

He called Marty later to let him know that he had an alibi. TJ believed that it couldn't hurt him, although he figured its worth was minimal. Funny that the alibi was entirely true, but he knew that everyone would discard it as a fabrication. One thing confused T.J., though: why had Suzie forgotten something that was so clear in his mind?

Chapter Thirty-two

Marty smiled smugly to himself. A week ago, it had appeared that things couldn't get much worse, and that his client would be charged for the murder of his secretary, Ali York. Disbarment would also occur, no doubt, but that was the lesser of the two consequences, then incarceration. He hadn't known what his next move would be, so he just stalled and temporized, hoping against all the odds that some solution or defence might turn up. Wait long enough, and all the hands get turned over.

First, his client had found an alibi. It sounded fabricated and was fraught with problems, of course; like that of a supporting and sympathetic wife who was likely to lie, and the whole scenario indicated once again that his client had lied about his whereabouts at the time of the murder. Still, it was an alibi. He could work with it.

Secondly, the entry of Wanda York onto the scene had been an unexpected surprise. He was uncertain what her involvement or attendance at the Police Station had indicated, but it was certainly easy to assume that it had something to do with her daughter's death. Maybe it was an indication that she or someone she knew was a prime player. The inescapable conclusion followed that perhaps his client was in the clear. So, with all this new ammunition, Marty felt certain that he could refuse Holt access to TJ's records. Holt would not be able to charge TJ, given the alibi and the timely appearance of Mrs. Wanda York.

He snatched up the phone to call Samantha Holt. The thought of yet another encounter with this fine policewoman tickled him immensely. Marty liked to be the initiator. It was an easier role to play than trying to ward off blows.

"Samantha-honey. How goes the battle?"

Her voice was impatient. "We're winning, Marty. Need you ask?"

"I just thought you might be feeling some pressure as a result of Mrs. York's visit the other day, not to mention my client's alibi. By the way, would you like to see me tomorrow? At my office, of course?"

"I'd be delighted, Marty. And please, don't worry about my pressures. They are few and light compared to yours."

He chuckled mirthlessly. The woman was so good at jousting. Marty was dying to ask Holt if she was still planning on charging TJ, if access to financial records were denied. A lot of questions moved around in his mind. What was Holt's opinion respecting the alibi and insinuation of Wanda York into the fracas? He was too cagey for that, however, and it was not in his personal best interests to piss off the great detective herself.

* * *

She walked towards him, her long shapely legs heralding her presence. He wanted just to look at her then, forget the fact that they had this ugly case to deal with. He wanted... oh, he wanted. To be a man for a change, not a lawyer. One couldn't always be both. He sighed. Maybe when it was all over, he could talk to her like they had in the past.

"Hello, Detective Holt", opened Marty. "How are you feeling today?"

"Terrific, Marty. Was there ever any doubt?"

She smiled at him then, and his heart turned over. Keep it legal, Marty, he reminded himself.

"Before we go on and say anything further, I want to commend and compliment you on the consideration that you have extended toward me and my client. It was almost, shall we say, gentlemanly of you. You might already have wrongly charged TJ for the murders. You've given me every opportunity, fairly, to prove that he was not involved in any way with the crime. I believe that there is no plausible or valid reason to charge him."

"I wish I shared your confidence, Marty."

He led her gently into his office. As they both took seats, he continued:

"With the introduction of Mrs. James' alibi, and the evidence which Mrs. York is bound to give in due course when her health improves, it is clear that my client could not possibly have committed the murder. You'd best keep your investigation open, Samantha, and look for the right party. Also, I am conjecturing that you will no longer require access to my client's financial records for audit purposes. It won't be necessary to overcome the confidentiality hurdle associated with that granted access."

Marty tried to make Sam Holt feel as though he was sharing quite generously with her. He was quite pleased with the job that he had done, and hoped that Holt had bought all of it. If Samantha had cause to believe even a part of it, or to have any doubts at all, he was hopeful that his client would not be charged, even if access to financial records was refused.

Marty had made the decision long ago that he would not give access to the police at all, with respect to the records. He would not be willing to part with anything, or any information that might result in his client being in worse shape than was already the case. Of course the police would eventually gain access to the records, but that was a problem for the future. He would deal with that situation when it came up again. His strategy was clear. Buy time, then buy a little more time, and something miraculous would happen to keep his client from disbarment and criminal proceedings. He had to make sure that his client was given every possible chance.

"Are you finished, counsellor?"

My, my, she was curt. The circumstances didn't warrant such abrupt dialogue.

"I'll tell you this, counsellor, I'm sure not impressed with the alibi, especially since it's from his wife. Somehow, I just don't trust her recollection of events. Would she not do anything to save her husband? For the alibi to work, your client would have had to be at home, not at the office. You'll recall that he made that statement to us earlier. So, for me to believe that the alibi is sound, and the wife is telling the truth, you will have to overcome one teeny little point"… she squeezed her thumb and forefingers together, and the sarcasm in her voice was unmistakable, "that is, your client's chronic proclivity for lying. A jury will assume that Mrs. James would do anything to save her husband's ass. I have trouble with that one myself, but then I'm not the jury. Nope, I don't buy the alibi. It doesn't even rate as good fiction, counsellor."

Marty frowned at her cynicism. She went on, unstoppable in her conviction.

"Secondly, counsellor, I wouldn't be telling the truth if I didn't tell you that Mrs. Wanda York's surprising appearance didn't cause me to change my position and attack. I wondered why she had entered the whole gambit, what she might have to relate, and why she hadn't come forward earlier, especially if she had anything of worth to advance. Maybe she does, maybe she doesn't. Maybe she was confused and sticking up for someone who didn't warrant defending. As you are undoubtedly aware, Ali York was suing her family for all sorts of ugly things. I suspect that Wanda's alleged 'confession' had more to do with that complexity. But all that is purely speculative. I'm assuming that she had nothing positive to add to the solution of the murder proceedings. I have no choice but to make that conclusion final, because Mrs. York died twenty minutes ago in the hospital. Of a heart attack."

Marty was stunned. Tremendous bad luck. Or perhaps good luck, if the elderly lady were to have testified or made some sort of problematic statement that was of no assistance to TJ's defence. Marty's shock must have registered on Sam Holt, for she spat out suddenly:

"Let me save you some time, counsellor. We don't attach any substance at all to the alibi provided by Mrs. James. Also, while we would have liked to have heard what Mrs. York had to say, we have no difficulty in assuming that she had little or nothing of value to offer. Thus, and finally, without me backing down, you understand, if we are not afforded access to your client's books within twenty-four hours from now, Theodore James will be charged with the murder of Ali York. Wanda York's 'confession' would have been a type of evidence, but in my mind, and trust me, the view is shared by my commanding officer, TJ is the guilty party. He will be charged accordingly. If I thought there was any way that we wouldn't be able to get a conviction, I wouldn't bother charging him. The truth of the matter is that, on the basis of the facts in hand, your client will undoubtedly not only be disbarred, but also go to jail for a long time, for the murder of his secretary. Lord only knows what else might come up.

So, my friend, the ball is in your court. If you are not going to grant us access to the financial records, I'll expect to see you and your client at the police station sometime tomorrow afternoon. If that doesn't happen, you have my word that we'll come looking for him. It will be far less traumatic for him to voluntarily submit to the charges. As to whether bail should be granted or not, I want you to know in advance that we'll be opposing that formality. I will insist on TJ surrendering his passport, at the very least, and remaining in custody pending further proceedings. The possibility of his flight from this jurisdiction would appear to pose a real concern."

* * *

TJ heard Marty's voice on the phone, and felt instant panic. Marty's announcement was resigned, and all TJ could do was say 'when'?

"Meet me at my office early this afternoon. We'll go to the courthouse afterward, where I understand that you will be formally charged with the murder of Ali York."

DENOUEMENT

denouement: the solution or unravelling of a plot in a play, or a story. Outcome. End.

From the French: unravelling a knot.

Chapter Thirty-three

Theodore James was charged, surprisingly, not only for the murder of Ali York, but also of Maureen Rogers. Shortly after that formality, his books were audited again by the Law Society and the police. The thefts were soon discovered, and disbarment proceedings activated. Before TJ even had a chance to utter any remorse, if in fact that had been his leaning, numerous additional charges of theft and embezzlement were added to the roll. It seemed inarguable that TJ would be imprisoned for a considerable time period, even if he were not found guilty of the murders. A lengthy jail term was likely even on the basis of the systematic thefts. The sole mitigating factor associated with the embezzlements was the repayment of all funds that were stolen. No parties had suffered as a result of the unlawful conduct of Theodore H. James.

Suzie James was surprisingly supportive. TJ couldn't believe that she was so nice to him, even though he had clearly stolen money from clients, had allegedly murdered his former secretary and maybe another woman, and had bedded his secretary. Even he realized that he had never earned that sort of loyalty from his wife, and couldn't imagine whatever motivated her to stand by him. He determined that if he were ever able, he would repay her and do everything he could to reciprocate that same loyalty and support. However, he might never get the chance.

He spent a lot of enforced time now, wrestling with possibilities of what he was to do and how he should handle matters. He decided that he had never given up before, and now was no time to start. He was accustomed to adversity; he would meet it head on. Marty advised him to consider plea bargaining, or he would be dead in the courtroom. TJ put on a false show of bravado and shrugged off the suggestion, asserting that there was no way he was going to toss in his chips. He refused to accept the murder charges without putting up a good, hard battle.

So he tried to stay upbeat. His future appeared bleak, to say the least. Even when he tried to play out the best possible outcome of the proceedings, he still had to fight depression. It just wasn't fair, all this abuse heaped upon him. He had, after all, made a great recovery from the Lazy Valley fiasco. No one had been hurt, and scads of people had benefited from his courage and conviction in completing the Project. If he'd been a contender in the Olympics, he'd have a medal by now, and T.V. commercial offers.

As for the players in the Project, numerous parties and trades, otherwise unpaid, received full payment for services rendered. The fact that he had assumed control and stewardship of the Project had ensured its successful consummation. He still believed that he had been brilliant and daring.

'All for naught', he brooded. He would have been better off simply sitting still like a frog on a log, like most other people.

'Hang in there', he comforted himself. 'It can't get much worse.' He had taken to talking to himself of late. 'It can get tough, too. You'll be hindered and hampered by lack of money. Not to mention embarrassment. All your friends, if you've got any left, will desert you. The only people you can count on are your wife and kids.'

He forced himself to smile. 'Remember that you're a lawyer and trained to deal with situations such as these. It's up to you to help Marty work hard, and to provide the best defense, so that the least harsh consequences might transpire. You must not be convicted of the York or Rogers murders. You must devote all your working fibre to guaranteeing that you won't be found guilty of murder. Theft, you might live with. Maybe that will be softened by the payment in full of all monies taken. Throw in a few character witnesses, heads of philanthropic organizations and so forth, all attesting to your good name. Evidence would have to be led as to what would have happened to the Lazy Valley Project but for your intervention. Remind everyone of the sterling results achieved as a result of your determination, acumen and brilliance.'

The murder charges were based solely on circumstantial evidence. They would undoubtedly be thrown out. The thefts could not be defeated. The best he could hope for was disbarment and a minimal prison term. It was just possible that he would be out for good behaviour in less than one year. After that, he might still have some money left over from what he had made on the Lazy Valley Project. He could write a book that elaborated upon his exploits. Of course it would be a best seller. That in itself would make him a wealthy man. There. Make something possible and positive from adversity. Onward and upward.

* * *

TJ hadn't done trial work for a considerable time period. Hadn't even been associated with it. He was working like a madman, and couldn't believe how much work was involved in the preparation. The preliminary inquiry had been nothing but a mere formality. The pre-determined notion existed that he should stand trial for the murders of both his former secretary, Ali York, and the other murdered woman, Maureen Rogers. It had been pre-arranged that the charges would not be dealt with respecting the theft and embezzlement proceedings, until the final disposition of the murder charges had been determined. If found innocent, James would plead guilty to the theft or embezzlement charges, provided that some form of plea bargaining and sentence arrangements might be made before disposition as to sentence was carried out.

On the other hand, if he were found guilty of either or both of the murders and sentenced accordingly, it wouldn't matter much what the Crown intended to do respecting the theft charges. He could only go to jail for a certain period of time. After that, nothing mattered much. In either scenario, disbarment was almost a foregone conclusion. Even if he were acquitted of the murder charges, it was highly unlikely that he would ever be able to have his license reinstated as a practising solicitor. No one would be that forgiving.

Marty had done considerable homework in that area. The general consensus stacked against TJ. The thefts and embezzlements would stick, even if he didn't admit to them. His license would be revoked, in all likelihood cancelled, for the duration of his lifetime. TJ attempted to concentrate on the murder proceedings. If he could beat them, and he was confident about that, then and only then, would he allow his mind to deal with the theft and embezzlement proceedings.

Miraculously, and as further evidence of his brilliant, scheming ways, the Crown had shown how Mr. James had overcome the Lazy Valley mess.

Ali York, the deceased former secretary of Mr. James, had been his accountant as well as his secretary. She had been exceedingly clever, and knew of all the ongoings. Ms. York had been aware, in all probability, of the theft by her boss of trust funds diverted for the Lazy Valley Project purposes. York must have discussed these financial discrepancies with her friend, Maureen Rogers. This woman had been an accounting peer in another office. Even though Rogers may not have known about the particulars, Mr. James would have wanted to deal similarly with Ms. Rogers.

"Ms. York must have discussed the accounting improprieties at the James law office," hammered away the Crown Prosecutor, "York was a friend of Rogers', she may have been uncomfortable with the accounting ledgers. She may have believed that she was overlooking something, and requested Rogers' advice or assistance. It is quite likely that York, for purposes of confidentiality, did not disclose too many particulars to Rogers. You might ask, how did Mr. James know that Rogers learned something from York, so that he knew he also had to deal with Rogers? The answer to that question is quite simple: clearly, James and York were lovers, as evidenced by the motel records.

York was undoubtedly infatuated with her boss, and would have done anything for him. She respected him highly, we understand, and would only have believed the best of him. When her queries concerning accounting matters were rebuffed, ignored, or simply overlooked, she must have sought assistance from Rogers. She would then have told Mr. James of her request for assistance so that he would be pleased with her, and so that she could demonstrate her expertise to him. She was doing her job, was not bothering him or encroaching upon his valuable time. It would probably not have occurred to York in a million years that her respected and respectable boss would help himself to trust funds, at random and dishonestly. York needed to seek assurance elsewhere that she was simply overlooking something.

"So here we are" the Crown Prosecutor continued, "the Lazy Valley Project is finished. Everyone is paid, and all trust monies are returned. Undoubtedly, a substantial profit is left over for our Mr. James. Yes, and almost unbelievably, even though thorough investigative proceedings are launched, for some inexplicable and unfathomable reason, Mr. James is somehow wholly exonerated by the Law Society. Unbelievably, he is in the clear, and his only obstacle to a full and unblemished recovery is his secretary, Ali York. Perhaps also her associate and accounting colleague, Maureen Rogers, is an obstacle. It is true that Rogers might well have had only an inkling of wrongdoing at the James Law Office. In itself, that would have been sufficient for Mr. James to conclude that he had no alternative but to get rid of her. As far

as concerns York, given her adulation and unrestrained admiration for him, as well as her
unquestionable affection, you might well say that
there is no way she would have related any wrongdoing to the Police, the Law Society, or anyone else. No
one could be certain of that, however, least of all
James. Further, the accused did not want to be obli-
gated to anyone, least of all an employee in his office,
and his temporary mistress. He might well have
wanted to terminate the relationship, and/or the employment. Who knows what the spurned Ms. York
might have done at that time. No, it was clear to our
Mr. James that he had no alternative but to kill, in a
cold-blooded and heartless fashion, his devoted secretary, Ali York. It is equally clear that he had no choice
but to also kill Maureen Rogers, just in case she knew
something. What she knew, or might piece together,
might prove his undoing. If he killed Ali York, he
would have to kill Rogers, because when the latter
saw what had happened to her friend, if she hadn't
already put two and two together, surely the murder
of her friend would have caused her to take decisive
steps without delay.

"Now," the Prosecutor went on, "if you haven't
got enough proof that the man you're looking at,
Theodore H. James, is the murderer of Ali York and
Maureen Rogers, then let me bring to your attention
certain other salient and not easily dismissable facts.
There is the mug found at the York residence with the
accused's prints all over it. There is the sexual liaison
with his secretary, which he could not afford to leave
outstanding, for the reasons we have just noted. There
is also the fact that there was no forcible entry to the
York residence, and no sexual assault. Of course, York

would have allowed her lover, Mr. James, unrestrained access to her apartment. He may even have had his own key. With a large looming exclamation mark, he hasn't seen fit to take the stand in order to deny any of what the Crown has said and proved beyond a reasonable doubt.

It is quite clear why he hasn't done so. He has nothing to say that would not incriminate him further.

Oh yes," the Prosecutor exclaimed, "I did forget to mention that the accused has a rock solid and tight alibi. But I have to explain the creation of that alibi. Apparently, the accused has always maintained that he was at his office on the night of the murder, however, he remembered some time afterward that he had been at home with his wife. He now remembers, and his dutiful and loving wife supports his new story. 'Yes', states Mrs. James, 'my husband was with me at our home on the night of the murder. Yes, I am positive that was the case, and no, I am not mistaken.'

Well, you might say, the believable accused says he was his home, and the equally believable accused's wife says that he was with her on the night of the murders. Therefore, you had better look for another responsible party. Clearly, the accused would not like to perjure himself. Why would he do that when he is only charged with murder - embezzlement charges to follow. What, pray tell, would prompt a dutiful and loving wife to commit perjury? If you think, surely nothing, then you must acquit the accused. Spare us and the Court. James is lying, as he has lied in the past to us about his being at home or even at the office, because we know where he was. He was out murdering his secretary and later the equally unfortunate Ms. Rogers.

As far as Mrs. James is concerned, she is probably so bamboozled and perplexed, so stunned, that perjury is the furthest thing from her mind. She is a devoted mother and wife, and believes, as a good and true-hearted woman, that she has no alternative but to rally to the defence and assistance of her husband. He tells her that he is being framed, and that he needs her to vouch for him and substantiate his alibi.

What would you do? What other choice would a loving wife have but to provide her husband with a much-needed alibi. 'Maybe', she reasons, 'if I give him the alibi that will be enough to allow him to go free.' Further, she also reasons that she loves him and knows him. There is no way in her heart or mind that she could ever believe that he would murder anyone. He must be right. Someone must be framing him, and Mrs. James must rise to his defence. She needs a husband. Her children need a father. She wants her life and lifestyle to continue as before. She has no choice, incontrovertibly. There exists no other alternative in her mind but to rise to her husband's defence.

The defence also states that the Crown has not shown a murder weapon. The defence has not proven the accused to be at the scene of either of the murders. The mug could have been placed at the York residence in numerous ways. The defence also says that the Crown has identified the vehicle as belonging to the accused. So what? There are a thousand similar cars. The accused was not identified as the driver of the vehicle. Yes, the defence has some points, but so does every defence, and clearly, with what we have before us, beyond a reasonable doubt, the accused is the murderer of both Ali York and Maureen Rogers.

Chapter Thirty-four

The press were like frothing dogs, all leaping on a dry bone to tear off what was edible. The same ugly bunch that had erroneously named the elusive killer "The Cowboy Cutter" behaved as though they had been penned up for years, while a cruel keeper had fed them raw meat from time to time. They preyed on TJ and his family and everything about him, as though he were the worst rogue that had ever walked the earth.

Beating the murder charges seemed somewhat iffy, given what was happening in Court. Everything was cascading in resplendent fashion over TJ. The ugly press that he was receiving would ensure that he would be disbarred for the embezzlement and theft charges. He felt sure that he would also be incarcerated until rot set in. The public and press were roaring for blood. One didn't have to be Sherlock Holmes to know that TJ wasn't floating well in this hostile ocean of animosity.

Marty tried to support him: "Realistically, and legally speaking, there shouldn't be a snowball's chance in a heat wave that you get convicted for the York, and certainly not the Rogers murder. However, things don't always go the way they should. The circumstantial evidence against you is undergoing some interesting framing. That evidence is assuming a higher level of belief and credibility than I thought possible. Your own defence is being discarded as insupportable, uncorroborated and the ranting of a dishonest lawyer."

"What's the public saying, Marty?"

"Well, generally, Joe Q. Public thinks you've betrayed your professional trust. I hear the word 'sociopath' a lot these days. You're branded as merciless, brilliant, arrogant, and spoiled. Always had your way, and probably still would if your legal friends came to the rescue. Problem is, TJ, when 'disbarment' is heard, legal colleagues disappear as fast as rats jumping a sinking ship."

"Marty, try to make sure that no one hurts Suzie or the kids, would you?"

"You can count on me for that one, TJ."

TJ reflected on his treatment of Suzie during their marriage. His remorse on this one was genuine. He had subjected her to public and private humiliation. Suzie had remained steadfast, stalwart and loyal. She had exhibited grace under pressure, and before everyone, she was the only positive press that he received. One reporter had been heard to comment that the accused couldn't be quite as bad as portrayed if his wife was so gracious. Others thought she was crazy. Marty, for one, was incredulous at Suzie James' composure and presence.

The dramatic arts community was quiet on the topic of Suzie James these days. No one would have thought to ask them anyway.

The truth was that Suzie James was acting. She practised in the mirror every day. How to appear unrattled. Grace. Composure. Keep it together. Protect the children. Looking Good. Looking Innocent. Walter McDonald had suggested that she lay low for awhile. Let the press have their glorious moment in the sun, and she could come back to work for him when all this garbage had been shovelled into the right pit.

She had agreed, of course. Suzie had also decided something else. Susan Harper was a good name to keep.

Marty talked to her about the future. Said he'd made a promise to TJ to take care of her.

"Thanks, Marty, but no thanks. I've been taking care of myself for a long time. My parents are still around, thank God. I've got a terrific support system."

"TJ wasn't good to you, Suzie." He didn't mention the abuse and the embarrassment in court. He didn't need to. Her face was a mask, and Marty was secretly afraid of its power to disguise.

"Marty, my name is Susan, now."

Marty nodded. She could be anyone she wanted to be.

TJ was dangerously lacking in friends. No one called on him to offer advice, assistance or encouragement. His wife's family was conspicuously absent. So was his mother. Suzie came by with the kids as often as she could, but as the weeks progressed, the children had to be forced to visit their father. Eventually, even Suzie's visits became infrequent. He may as well have been some extra-terrestrial being for all the humanity he was receiving.

The court case dragged on for what seemed like thirty years. Marty made much over the unsolicited attendance of Mrs. Wanda York at the Police Station to confer a confession. He was somewhat successful in delivery that Mrs. York's likely reason for being there was to provide some sort of explanation, or confession to the murders. Why else would she have come? How could that have anything to do with his client? The judge, the jury and even the public were not buying it. Perhaps if he had a chance to highlight it, much could have been made of the elderly lady's appearance at the Station. So much of what he tried to introduce was rejected and thrown out because it was hearsay evidence. Sure, she might have been trying to say something that would exonerate James, but so what? It was clear to everyone that what had actually transpired was far short of what was necessary to inculpate her and her family, thereby exculpating TJ. The jury was left to surmise why and how Wanda York came to be at the Police Station. Several plausible explanations came to mind, the most obvious one being that someone from the Police had called her and asked her to come to the Station, for whatever reason. That reason would remain a mystery.

TJ eventually ran out of money, spending the hard-earned profits of his nefarious activities. Marty advised him of the financial shortfall. TJ went to his old standby: Suzie. This time she raised some money. Not much, but enough to keep Marty on to finish the job.

Marty, for his part, was brilliant. His skill in presenting evidence and cross-examination was electric. He dealt with evidence in a light that was favourable to TJ. Marty's brilliance entailed convincing the judge that a particularly incriminating piece of evidence, Ali York's diary, could not be utilized in the defence due to the hearsay nature of its contents.

Marty even impressed his client, lifting him out of the doldrums just a tad. Regardless of the outcome,

TJ couldn't complain about the counsel. No one could say that Marty hadn't done his job. He wasn't popular for it, either.

Finally, all evidence was in. The Crown had presented its case, with the defence doing its best to rebuff it. Marty had been pilloried in the press almost as harshly as TJ.

Marty's summation was brilliant. He stressed that his client could not be convicted unless the jury was certain beyond any reasonable doubt that Mr. James had killed both women. If they held any doubt at all, just one, they had a clear and unequivocal obligation to acquit Mr. James on both charges. Marty reminded the jury that they did not have to like his client, or his client's profession. They didn't have to like anything or any part of his conduct. They had a duty to remain fair and impartial, and to be separated from any distaste or dislike that they might feel.

"In other words, ladies and gentlemen of the jury, you may despise my client, but still, if you are not certain beyond any shadow of doubt that he killed these women, ruthlessly and in cold blood, you must acquit him, even if the thought of letting him out on the street turns your stomach."

He had named the monster: Theodore James was disliked, even hated by most people, if you trusted the scuttlebutt. Marty didn't believe for one second that the jury was exempt from this rhetoric. He stressed that the Crown's case was circumstantial at best, and that the evidence linking his client to the murders was almost negligible. Marty sketched the other possible responsible parties that might have murdered the girls. The best bet was Wanda York herself. Why otherwise would she be at the Police Station but for the purposes of making a confession or providing some evidence? Had this come out, his client might surely have been vindicated.

Guilty, guilty, guilty. Thus cried the public. Thus demanded the press. The more analytical approach of the lawyers and anyone else who took the time to be objective, indicated that Mr. James was not guilty. There was no proof beyond a reasonable doubt that he was.

Chapter Thirty-five

TJ accepted the fate which the jury handed him – conviction in the murder of Ali York. He had fought such a valiant battle, but in the end he had succumbed to an ignoble defeat. He who had risen to such mighty heights fell with a terrible thump. He had been acquitted of the murder of Maureen Rogers, and while sentence was pending, freed on bail with his passport surrendered. During this waiting time, he was charged with fraud, embezzlement and a slough of other charges related to trust irregularities and defalcations. In post-trial discussion, Marty had advised him to plead guilty to the charges. Marty also believed that it was possible to strike a deal with the Crown, whereby TJ would only have to stand accused for some of the thefts. Others would be dropped. He hoped that the Crown would concede to a sentence that ran concurrently for the murders and the trust fund thefts. TJ sat and listened in shock, as Marty informed him that he would be eligible for parole in fifteen years. There would be no confinement in a high security penitentiary but in one more lenient, where he might be able to make some practical use of the lengthy incarceration period.

TJ listened to Marty but was immersed in his own thoughts. He, Theodore H. James, was not going to prison. How could he cope with the riffraff that dwelt within the prison walls? He had tried all his life to rise above scum and mediocrity. How could he live amongst such inferior beings? He dug out the unregistered gun which he had hidden amongst his personal papers at home. Methodically, he made his way to his office building. He, who had reached such glorious heights, could handle no more. Cowardice had set in. He searched unhurriedly for just the right washroom, then sat down in a toilet cubicle. Breathing heavily for a few seconds, he drew the gun to the front of his palette. It seemed so easy to squeeze the trigger.

He woke up, if you could call it that, in the Macleod Auxiliary wing. He was blind, confined to a bed, and could no longer speak. Strangely though, his mind was sharper, more attuned to sensation. In time, he developed some new abilities, which none of his caregivers noticed. One was his enhanced sensations: his sense of smell and hearing. He was generally pleased with his rebirth.

He heard the doctors say that it was a miracle he had survived. The bullet had exited his head, wreaking sufficient damage to confine him, with luck, to a wheelchair for the rest of his natural life. He had enough use of his hands so that in time, he could write on a magic pad via special computer. He began to believe that perhaps his life would not be completely useless. There were some positives. He wasn't in prison.

Suzie visited when she could. Everyone admired her loyalty. Given her husband's past exploits, philandering and the like, no one would have blamed her had she not visited at all. Many expected divorce, but the new Susan realized there was nothing to be gained from that. She was at peace with herself. She had made the choices necessary to her well-being and that of her children. In addition, her exemplary behaviour had ensured that no one, absolutely no one would cast aspersions on her behaviour, whatever it might be. After all, what was a woman to do?

Suzie forced her children to visit their father, and TJ was pleased with how they had turned out, in spite of him.

TJ thought that maybe he could write a book about it all. Suzie might benefit from it. Marty could help him find a publisher. It was a goal. One needed goals. He could see himself on some talk show, a visual horror to everyone. The book would sell lots of copies. He might even write a few bestsellers. The thought of success under such perverse circumstances made him quite giddy. His head hurt whenever he got too excited.

He relaxed in his chair and waited for dinner. The three best things in his life awaited him. His dinner, his bed, and sleeping. He loved what remained of his daily constitution that had been unaffected by the shooting. His sexual libido seemed unaffected by the mutilation. Leave him alone for a few hours, and he was entirely capable of enjoying his own company.

His fantasies were fabulous.

* * *

TJ was lying in bed after dinner preparing for sleep, waiting to be tucked in by that soft nurse for whom he cherished the warmest fantasies. He was becoming accustomed to the various noises made by his unfortunate room-mates. One of the elderly men had Alzheimer's and was constantly babbling some nonsense. The other was a young stroke victim who could manage no more than a few grunts when excited. The other room-mate was simply old, crying and whining constantly. TJ considered himself far better off than any of them. Strange that he had contemplated ending his life when his second coming was providing him with such joy.

It was past visiting hours. Because of the time, and the fact that he wasn't used to getting visitors, TJ was surprised to hear a friendly voice speak to him. It was low and soothing, and he didn't recognize it. He could not attach a face to it.

"Hello, counsellor. I am so very sorry to interrupt you or encroach on your time just before you go to bed, but I've got a few things to say to you. It won't take long. All I need is your undivided attention.

It's certainly rude to forget old friends, especially when they have meant so much to each other. Ali had forgotten how close we were to one another. I couldn't stand the fact that I was losing her to someone like you, someone almost twice her age. Admit it. You never really cared for her. You were just taking advantage of her innocence and the fact that she would have done anything for you. All you could think about was bedding her, right?"

The voice became more ragged now. TJ still couldn't place it. "I followed her and her stupid friend, Maureen Rogers. She and Maureen babbled about some 'funny' entries in your books. Good ideas sometimes enter my brain when someone else is being crooked. That bimbo Maureen had the nerve to call me a scum bag. She said I was a little weasel who would get what was coming to him, and I was just lucky that a Restraining Order was the only thing coming my way. She should have stayed away from Ali.

I didn't like Ali's friend, and I didn't like the way that Ali was treating me. If I couldn't have Ali, no one else could either. Especially someone as dirty as you."

The voice spat at him. "I murdered them both. It was so easy to plant the mug in her apartment, and it wasn't too difficult to convince her to let me in so that we could discuss stuff. Just like we'd always done. I just wanted to be friends. Of course she believed me. She always believed everyone when they lied. It was difficult to undress her and do nothing more. I just loved her so much. I had to plan things properly. I wanted it to look as though you were the murderer. And then," the voice chuckled now, "getting that fat old Finewood to provide me with an alibi was too easy. He didn't realize how important the alibi was for me, or what charges were lurking in the background. When I told him what might happen to him if he didn't support me in my time of need, why, he was just ever so understanding."

The voice growled. "You took my life away from me, and you even enjoyed it. You thought you were so smart, getting that Mickey Mouse Restraining Order against me so that it was unlawful for me to even be in contact with, or see my lady. You were so happy to hurt me, I just had to hurt you back. I thought my job was done, but I guess not. You're too comfortable here. You're having a fine time, even though your life should be over. Now it will be. Say goodbye, Mr. James."

Billy Corgan, dressed in hospital garb, grabbed a nearby pillow and placed it casually over TJ's face, pressing it with more force than necessary, until he was certain that the crippled lawyer was quite dead. Then he strolled out of the room.

* * *

I reflected on the trial proceedings as I sat waiting in the bush, well camouflaged and downwind. I'd had to relinquish Ali's diary to the Prosecution attorney, and was dismayed to learn that Marty had blocked that testimony. 'Inadmissible in this trial - hearsay evidence'. Marty was nothing if not a clever lawyer, and yet, it had been Ali's diary that had led me in what I thought had been the right direction. In a way, I had expected the inadmissible outcome, given Sergeant Speirs' comments about the diary's uselessness.

I wasn't surprised, really. It was much like my dream-memory of the boys in the neighbourhood carrying the dead deer. They would have more fun playing it their way. In any case, proceedings were in motion and could not have been stopped.

A moment of instinct, call it what you will, prompted me to take photocopies of Ali's words before I gave up the diary. It was one of her final entries that grabbed me:

June, 1994: I don't think that Restraining Order is working against Billy. I feel creepy sometimes, like I'm being stalked and followed. I want to tell TJ, but I feel as though I'm just bothering him. One shouldn't abuse good will. I came home to find my door ajar the other night. Things seem to have been rearranged in my apartment. Maybe I'm losing my marbles. Who knows? TJ is going to teach me how to golf. Maybe a new experience will get my mind away from this creepy feeling. We'll see.

From the periphery of my vision I detected movement. The trophy buck moved gingerly between the poplars, checking the wind for sound or unusual scent. I took careful aim, my sights aligned perfectly to his heart.

I took in a deep breath, then exhaled, allowing my own heart to slow before I fired. Then I heard, in my mind, Ali's last two-dimensional words. The buck dropped on his knees, his severed heart crippling his last breath.

It was November-frigid. Soon, the night would be dark as death. I felt a sudden chill and shivered, but I didn't believe it was the weather. I was struck with the gravity of my own terrible error. As I examined my downed trophy, I berated myself in a sudden realization of my own stupidity in the murder investigations. Dumb. dumb.

I inhaled the cold brisk air. It was finished. Ali's tracks and scent were ever so faint around TJ, but I could smell her essence powerfully around my vision of Billy Corgan.